HEADS
WILL
ROLL

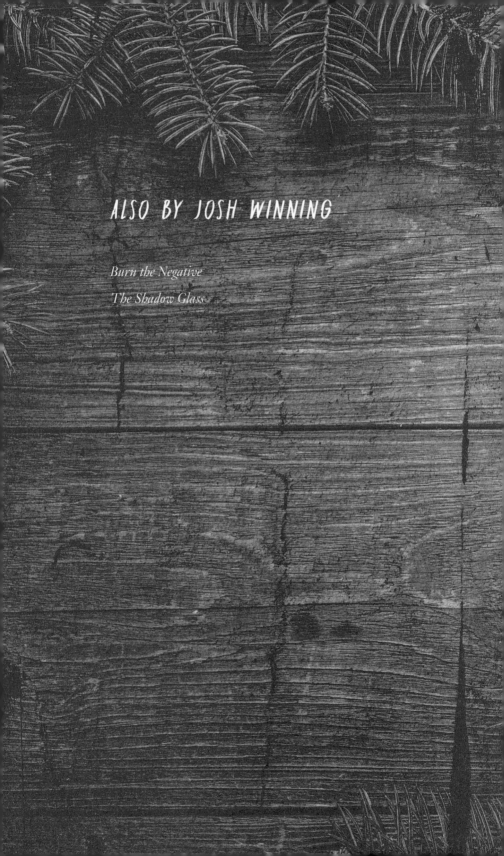

ALSO BY JOSH WINNING

Burn the Negative

The Shadow Glass

HEADS WILL ROLL

JOSH WINNING

G. P. PUTNAM'S SONS
NEW YORK

PUTNAM
— EST. 1838 —

G. P. PUTNAM'S SONS
Publishers Since 1838
An imprint of Penguin Random House LLC
penguinrandomhouse.com

Library of Congress Cataloging-in-Publication Data

Names: Winning, Josh, author.
Title: Heads will roll / Josh Winning.
Description: New York : G. P. Putnam's Sons, 2024
Identifiers: LCCN 2023052043 (print) | LCCN 2023052044 (ebook) | ISBN 9780593544693 (hardcover) | ISBN 9780593544709 (ebook)
Subjects: LCGFT: Gothic fiction. | Thrillers (Fiction) | Novels.
Classification: LCC PR6123.I66347 H43 2024 (print) | LCC PR6123.I66347 (ebook) | DDC 823/.92—dc23/eng/20231107
LC record available at https://lccn.loc.gov/2023052043

LC ebook record available at https://lccn.loc.gov/2023052044

Printed in the United States of America
1st Printing

Book design by Laura Corless and Lorie Pagnozzi

This is a work of fiction. Names, characters, places, and incidents either are the product of the author's imagination or are used fictitiously, and any resemblance to actual persons, living or dead, businesses, companies, events, or locales is entirely coincidental.

YOU ARE WHO YOU ARE.
THE ONLY TRICK IS NOT GETTING CAUGHT.

—GRAHAM, *BUT I'M A CHEERLEADER* (1999)

HEADS
WILL
ROLL

@ThatGurlWillow Oh wow, girl, is this meant to be funny? You better check your sense of humor because this shit doesn't fly.

@ThatGurlWillow Let me tell you what I'm gonna do. I'm gonna go down to my tool shed. I'm gonna sharpen the biggest machete I own. And then I'm gonna slice a bitch up. That bitch? Take a wild fucken guess.

@ThatGurlWillow Canceled!

single bar shows in the corner of my phone screen: just one line out of a possible four. If I were yesterday me, the woman who depended on connectivity to survive, the lack of service would flood my system with panic. It would make me pace back and forth until more bars appeared.

But I'm not yesterday me. I'm *now* me; the one hunched over in the back of a BMW wearing yesterday's clothes, and that single bar makes me damn near giddy with relief.

"Cut me off already," I whisper. "Please just cut me the hell off."

I'm aware that I could stow my phone in my carryall. I could power it off myself without waiting for bad cell coverage to disconnect me from whatever satellite is spinning around Earth firing data at anybody with a SIM card.

But I can't do it.

No matter how much I want to, the command doesn't reach my fingers. The phone has practically grown into my hand, and I need it forcibly removed, like a polished black tumor. Just looking at the screen makes me feel sick and pathetic and lost in a hundred different ways.

I shift my gaze to look out the window.

We drive between pine trees that are so tightly packed, they block out the midday sun. We entered the forest somewhere north of

White Plains twenty minutes ago, driving in a black Beamer that smells like bleached lemongrass, and the road has showed no sign of letting up. It keeps going, like the winding Montana travelogue at the start of *The Shining*, tunneling endlessly into the forest dark of upstate New York.

The gloom is comforting, though. It feels womblike. Protective. Nobody can reach me here. Nobody can take my picture or yell at me in the street or slide into my DMs to tell me real quick just how they're going to take me apart, piece by dripping piece.

I'm breathless with anticipation.

I need this.

I'm so ready to disappear.

Soon, okay? Willow says in my mind. *Soon you'll be free.*

The car hits a bump and I only just keep hold of my phone.

"Sorry, ma'am," says the driver—forties, jowly and bushy browed. "Only one road in and out of this place, and it looks like they haven't resurfaced since the millennium."

"Which millennium?" I ask. My voice is as cracked as the skin around my nostrils, but still he laughs.

Our eyes meet in the rearview mirror and I try not to shrink from his gaze, imagining what he must see. My Lululemon cardigan hangs off me, foraged from the bedroom floor this morning, and my white jeans are stained with the wine that I spilled last night while rushing to switch off the news. My shoulder-length auburn hair is scraped back from my face, tied in a messy bun.

I haven't slept in three weeks.

My eyes hurt.

They beg to close.

"You're on TV, right?" the driver says, and I flinch. Damn. I shouldn't have engaged. I want to revel in the silence as we travel farther from reality's reach. Besides, I'm afraid what I might say. My mouth has never been my friend.

"That show," the driver says. "The one about the girl."

I could pretend I'm getting a call—I've acted with fake phones enough to know I could pull it off—but the lie feels too big. He must have noticed that my cell hasn't made a sound since the airport.

"Willow," I say.

"That's it! *We Love Willow*! My daughter can't get enough of you."

A moth flutters in my chest, beating a fragile kind of hope. I can't help leaning forward in my seat.

"She's a fan?"

"Yeah, she was so into you," the driver says. "She had a poster on her wall. It got ripped or something a couple weeks ago, though. Teenagers, right?"

The moth crumples. I sit back, energy draining from my limbs.

"Right," I murmur. "Teenagers."

We Love Willow wasn't a teen show, but it was popular with the sixteen-to-twenty-four demographic. It hit that sweet spot between youthful optimism and knowing realism. Despite a shaky first year in which we struggled to find our audience, the show's title proved accurate by season three: everybody loved Willow McKenzie, the klutzy midtwenties New Yorker who was perpetually broke, single, and jobless but attacked every challenge with can-do enthusiasm, helped by her childhood imaginary friend, Eliza.

I loved Willow, too. I loved being that version of myself. Upbeat, smiley, and open. Most of all, I loved what she gave me. Not just steady work and financial security for the first time in my life, but a best friend in the shape of my co-star, Jenna. We became inseparable within a couple weeks of filming, real-life roommates by the time season one wrapped. We lived together for two years, until my fiancé, Matt, convinced me to move into his Santa Monica beach house.

In so many ways, Willow made me a better person.

But now she's gone. The show's canceled. All because I can't keep my mouth shut.

I check to see if the driver's still looking at me, and I'm relieved that his focus is back on the road. Still, the fact that he recognized me is unnerving. I should have made more of an effort to change my appearance. Dyed my hair and got a home tan kit. I haven't exactly been thinking clearly, though, and tomorrow never seemed certain. Suddenly I feel as exposed as a raw nerve.

There must be something in my carryall. I root around inside it, dragging out clothes, sandals, and books. I tug out a gray bucket hat that I don't remember packing. It's ugly and shapeless and perfect. I put it on, pulling it over my auburn hair as far down as it'll go. My reading glasses are oversized and ridiculous, an impulse buy that I never wear in public. Also perfect.

Adding these layers makes me feel stronger. Less exposed. If you've got no place to hide, hide in plain sight.

"There's the sign," the driver says, and I look up, just as a wooden placard passes the window, too fast for me to read. "Couple miles left. What is this place, anyway? Some kind of summer camp for adults?"

"Something like that," I say.

He looks at me a moment too long in the mirror.

Even after three weeks, it turns out I still care what people think. Every hate-fueled headline has left a bruise, so many of them that it hurts to breathe sometimes, and a part of me still can't believe that the terrible things people said were about me.

The scariest thing is how quickly it all fell apart.

The day after tweetageddon, Matt flew to New Mexico to shoot location work on his show, *Crime: L.A. Nights*, and he told me I should be gone by the time he got home. I'm still wearing the engagement ring, can't bring myself to take it off. Jenna was there for me for five days, brought me donuts and takeout while I ranted and dry-heaved, and then she ghosted me when it seemed she'd get canceled herself simply for associating with me.

I found myself alone in a house I'd always hated. I never understood why a couple in their twenties needed six bathrooms.

Dark thoughts crept in like rising damp.

Sitting in the back of the BMW, I feel the churn again in the pit of my stomach, and I can't tell if I'm going to throw up or cry.

The tweet was meant to be a joke. I didn't want to offend anybody. I was living in my cozy little Willow bubble, safe in the knowledge that I was loved and understood. That people knew me. They'd get what I was saying.

I couldn't have been more wrong.

I force an inhale and remind myself where I'm headed. Into the calming arms of nature.

As I start to repack my carryall, I notice the tattered color pamphlet sticking out of it. The paper is as thin as silk, but it's all I have. There's no website for Camp Castaway. No Twitter account. No online footprint to speak of. That's sort of their deal.

"This place is so underground, Jason Bourne couldn't find you," my agent said as she handed me the literature two days ago, right after she found me lying facedown in the pool.

I don't remember how I got there. There was a cut on my forehead. I must have fallen and hit my head, then ended up in the water. The empty bottles on the counter were proof enough that I'd been drinking at four in the afternoon. It was sheer luck that my agent had decided to drop by with a care package and found me floating.

Even my lowest moment is a *BoJack Horseman* meme.

When the paramedics were gone, I sat at Matt's breakfast bar with its Victoria Arduino coffee machine and its Vitamix 5200, realizing that nothing in the kitchen was mine—nothing in the whole goddamn house—and clutched hold of the Camp Castaway pamphlet like a lottery ticket before the numbers are called.

The photographs of the forest are soothing. The cute little

rough-hewn cabins look joyful in their simplicity. A woman laughs in a carefree way that makes my body ache. There's a map on the back—a rudimentary sketch of the lake, which is shaped like a kidney, squeezed in the middle. It talks about hiking, yoga, and games. It talks about disconnecting in order to reconnect, and right at the bottom there's the biggie, the single line that sealed the deal: *You will be invited to hand over all electronic devices at check-in for a total digital time-out.*

Sign me up, buttercup.

Because this is the thing. Camp Castaway isn't just a port in a storm—it's a lifeline. A retreat in the truest sense of the word. I'm already jobless after being fired from the show, and now I'm homeless, too, thanks to Matt. After tweetageddon, the studio took back a lot of the money I had left, cited breach of contract, and I used up the last of my rainy-day savings on Camp Castaway. Five thousand big ones for two weeks of isolation.

I reach under the brim of the bucket hat and touch the slow-healing scab on my forehead.

It was an easy decision.

I knew that if I didn't get away, I wouldn't make it through another rainy day.

Ping.

My phone vibrates in my lap, and I jump. I changed my number two days ago and my cell has been pretty much dead ever since. That hasn't stopped me from clinging to it like a junkie, praying somebody will reach out.

Ping. Ping.

I fumble with my phone, heart beating fast. It could be a text from Jenna. It could be Matt. It could be—

A number I don't recognize.

I frown, hunching over my phone, opening WhatsApp.

As I read the messages, I stop breathing. I feel the trees crowding in through the windows. They whisper and press against my face, pushing branches into my mouth, and it's suddenly too quiet in here. Too unbearably quiet, aside from the thud of blood in my temples.

> Nice try, but you'll have to do more than that to get rid of me.

> You're going to beg to die.

> See you soon, Red. 😊

S1E3 "Willow vs. Work"—Willow gets a job at a sushi bar but has to keep her shellfish allergy secret from her new boss, Marie (guest star Lucy Liu). Eliza gets assigned to a kid who refuses to believe in imaginary friends.

II

Hey there, you're early," the man says, smiling as he approaches the car. He has olive skin and is mid-twenties, wearing a light green shirt and cutoff jeans. His black hair is buzzed short, and his dark eyes are sharp but friendly.

I'm not sure how I managed to stand, but somehow, I'm out of my seat. One hand rests on the car door, the other presses my stomach. The scent of pine and dirt fills my nostrils.

"I heard there was an early-bird special," I say. "Don't tell me I'm wrong." The lame attempt at a joke works. The man laughs and shakes my hand, doesn't appear to notice I'm quietly freaking out.

"I'm Tye, camp groundskeeper. Great to meet you."

The human contact is a shock. Nobody's touched me since my agent dragged me out of the pool. Warmth floods my face, but I feel protected by the oversize glasses and the bucket hat. Eat your alien heart out, Clark Kent.

"Bebe apologizes for not being here to greet you herself," Tye says. "She's preparing for the party. But you'll meet her there. You'll meet everybody."

"Can't wait," I say, remembering that Bebe is the "Camp Mom" who's in charge of the place.

As much as I try to focus on Tye, I'm distracted by the knowledge that some threat-happy psycho has my new number. It's not the first death threat I've received. In the days following tweetageddon, my

DMs filled up with graphic rants. My email and old cell number leaked online, and I watched as my safe spaces were swallowed up one by one. The majority of the messages were unrelated to the content of my tweet. People just wanted somebody to hate.

And now one of them has my new number.

I could report it to the police, but I can't risk the chance that they'll tell me to cancel my trip. I can't go back. I can't go home, and not just because there's no home to go back to.

"I'll grab those." Tye takes my suitcase and carryall from the driver.

"It's chill," I say. "I'm used to handling my own baggage—travel and otherwise."

Tye looks at me like I'm a college friend on vacation. "Please, let me. We're going to look after you here."

The kindness in his tone makes me tremble. Either my disguise is working or he's an even better actor than anybody I've ever worked with. There's no hint that he recognizes me from TV or the internet. Maybe even the staff here are off the grid.

I follow Tye to the wooden building nestled amid the trees. It resembles a ski lodge, part timber, part glass, with a peaked roof that points at an immaculate blue sky. As we climb the steps, I hear birds calling to each other, the faraway sound of laughter, and the hire car reversing out of the lot, leaving me behind.

Even here in the small clearing fringed by trees, I'm struck by the sense of space. The *roominess* of the great outdoors. The trees reach up, up, *up* into a limitless sky. I'm so accustomed to the congestion of L.A., the constant battle for air, it's easy to forget that L.A. isn't normal. It's a choice.

I take in my new surroundings and understand that this is it.

Civilization ends here.

I can't wait to get farther into the camp.

To forget and be forgotten.

"Have you been anywhere like this before?" Tye asks.

I flinch, try to focus.

"No. Well, we did summer camp as kids. But nothing this intense."

"Don't worry, Camp Castaway is the *opposite* of intense. You won't want to leave." He's such a picture of vitality that I become painfully aware of how I must look. I tug at my cardigan, feeling hot and awkward.

He opens the door into a small porch. A bank of sage green lockers fills one wall, and through the glass of the next door I see a large foyer where a woman lounges on one of three super-size sofas. We stand in the porch, which seems airless now that the door has closed, and I'm aware of how close we're standing, me and this gorgeous stranger, crammed into the liminal space between outside and inside.

"Have you settled on a name?" Tye asks.

"A name?"

"Sure, a camp name. We don't use our birth names here. It's all part of disconnecting from our lives."

A name. My mind's blank. I stare at the lockers, unable to think of a single name other than my own, and I wish I'd paid more attention to the prep letter sent in the lead-up to my stay.

You had a lot going on, Willow says in my mind, right as I become so aware of Tye's gaze that I feel my mouth opening, blood thumping in my temples as I blurt out, "Willow."

Shit.

Did I say that?

You sure did, Willow says, and I almost laugh. I'm trying to go incognito and the only name I can come up with is my famous-as-hell sitcom character?

I want to take the name back, but Tye's face lights up.

"I like it. I don't think we've ever had a Willow here. One final thing. We'll need you to deposit *that* in a locker."

I look down. I hadn't realized I was holding my phone. It presses into my stomach, warm against me. My gaze goes to the lockers, half a dozen of which are keyless, must already be in use. That means half a dozen campers. Half a dozen people who could hate me on sight.

My gaze goes back to the foyer, seeing the woman on the sofa.

Maybe this was a mistake. Maybe I'm out of my mind. The one drawback of Camp Castaway is that there will be other campers. My breathing shallows as I wonder how many there are, what their deal is, if they've ever watched *We Love Willow*. If they'll make the connection when I introduce myself using my not-at-all-moronic camp name.

"Don't worry," Tye says, "the keys are stored in a secure location. You'll get your phone back on checkout—if you want it, that is."

"There are people who don't take their phones back?" I ask.

"Quite a few, actually. This place is magic like that. Here, you can take any locker you like."

My phone shows the sky.

I didn't think it would be this difficult.

No contact with the outside world for fourteen days.

No email. No social media.

No cataloging every minute of the day.

No strangers judging me.

No guilt.

Nobody threatening to kill me.

Telling me what they're going to do with my torn-out heart.

I open the nearest locker and set my phone inside.

"So long, sucker," I say, trying for bravado, but my voice is uncertain. Strained. I turn the key, which is attached to a polished bronze disk engraved with the number seven.

Tye takes the key and tucks it into his back pocket, and the moment the cool metal leaves my grasp, I feel a lightness in my body that is so powerful, it makes me dizzy. I laugh. Loud, surprised, and relieved. A tingle shivers down the backs of my arms. A huge tumbling avalanche of relief.

My phone and everything terrible about it is gone.

"Holy shit," I say, "that feels good."

Tye chuckles. "We get that a lot."

"Seriously, you could bottle this feeling and make a fortune."

"We're working on it. Here." He opens the door into the wood-paneled foyer, and I walk inside, buoyed by that feeling of lightness. The air is different inside. Fresher. And now that I'm in the foyer, I see that the window is panoramic, filling the entire back wall like a living photograph. The view of the lake is breathtaking. It sparkles in waves, cradled by the forest.

Tye punches numbers into a keypad at the door. The light on top blinks green to white.

"We keep the place locked," he says, noticing me looking. "Not that anybody's ever come out here uninvited. We want our visitors to feel completely at ease."

"Right, summer camp in the middle of nowhere. You must get a lot of Jason jokes."

"Not as many as you might think."

I binge the even-numbered *Friday the 13th* movies every Halloween. They've planted an image of summer camps as seedy hunting grounds where death lurks behind every sleeping bag, but this place couldn't be more different.

Tye leads me across the foyer. "This is the clubhouse. Bebe's office is just over there, and there's a game room through that door. The canteen is on the lower level. We'll pass it on the way to your cabin." He stops at a chalkboard that is filled with activities, written out in so many different colors that they form a rainbow.

"We have classes and workshops every day. Sometimes we go on hikes or hold swimming competitions. There's canoeing, archery, forest bathing, stargazing, sing-alongs . . . you name it, we got it. It's pretty outdoorsy, but there's no pressure to join in with everything. There's no judgment here. The only mandatory activities are stone circle, which is our version of group therapy, and family dinner. We eat together here."

"It sounds great," I say, but the truth is, it sounds better than great. It sounds perfect. For just a moment, I really feel what Camp Castaway is promising. A real-world time-out.

"Hey, Tye," the woman on the sofa says. She has a Jersey accent, looks to be in her fifties. Her bare feet are up on the coffee table, and frizzy brown hair frames her narrow face. She wears an oversize purple blouse and a lot of eyeliner. "Ready for a rematch?"

"Right after I settle in our new resident. Misty, this is Willow. Misty's our reigning mahjong champion. For now."

"You play?" Misty asks me.

I search her expression, but there's no edge to it. No glimmer of recognition.

"I've seen old ladies play in the park," I say, then quickly add, "I mean, not just old ladies. Young ladies, too." I swallow. "I've always wanted to learn."

Misty considers me a moment, her eyes narrowed, and then she shrugs.

"If you gotta learn, learn from the best."

Tye leads me down a wide wooden stairwell and back outside. The fresh air clears my head and I vaguely remember calling Misty old. Great. My first attempt at human interaction in weeks and I'm leading with the insults.

We're on the other side of the clubhouse now. It feels like another world. Trees make shushing sounds as the wind ruffles leaves that are a dozen different shades of green, and birds wheel above us, making distant pleas that echo across the camp.

"We eat most of our meals here," Tye says, gesturing as we pass a collection of picnic benches, and we keep walking, heading onto a boardwalk that winds between the trees. I feel like I've stepped into a fairy tale. Goldilocks meets *The Parent Trap*. I half expect baby Lilo to pop out wearing a fencing outfit. Cabins nestle amid the woodland, set apart from each other, small and cozy-looking. They're not new, but they're not old, either. Pre-loved, I guess.

"We have thirteen," Tye says as we reach the final cabin, and he opens the door. It wasn't locked. "We never fill them all, though. We like to keep the numbers as low as possible, for optimum relaxation."

"Cabin seven," I say, noting the number by the door. Tye looks at me blankly.

"The same as my locker," I add. "Sort of spooky?"

Tye cocks his head as he sets down my bags. "Funny coincidence. Here, I'll give you the tour. This is the living room, and through that door is the bedroom . . ." He faces me and takes a bow. "Here endeth the tour."

I smile, peering around the room. The walls are bare timber, shag rugs covering the floors. The kitchenette has a couple of drinking glasses, some cutlery, and a fruit bowl containing apples, lemons, and limes. The bedroom has a single bed, a nightstand, and a closet.

It takes me a moment to realize what's missing. There's no TV on the wall. No refrigerator under the counter. No digital clocks or air-con unit. There's nothing electrical at all, aside from the lights. It's like we're in the 1920s, if the 1920s looked like Scandi minimalism. The quiet modesty of it, the simplicity, is soothing. Inviting. I want to collapse into the sofa cushions, pull the blanket around me and turn myself into a human burrito. It's a million miles away from Matt's echoey Santa Monica complex.

Then I notice what else is missing.

"Where's the bathroom?" I ask.

"Communal showers are by the lake," Tye says. "Restrooms, too."

I swallow. What if I need to pee in the night? The thought of having to go through the woods in the pitch dark makes me antsy.

Tye must read my expression. "You'll get used to it. Here, check out the veranda."

We step through a sliding door on the far side of the room, emerging onto a small patio with a table and two chairs. The lake isn't far from here. It twinkles between the trees.

I take a breath, filling my lungs with country air, and despite my general state of anxiety, a fraction of the tension I've been carrying for the past weeks shifts.

I'm here.

I made it.

I'm unreachable at last.

III

The *We Love Willow* producers never let me cut my hair. I was forbidden from so much as putting it in clips for the first five episodes of the show.

"Your hair is your brand," one producer told me. "If you change it too soon, the viewers' whole perception of you will be shaken. Besides, why mess with perfection? Your hair is beautiful."

I don't have to tell you the producer was of the male variety.

Standing alone in the cabin bedroom, staring at my shoulder-skimming auburn hair in the mirror, I think about all the ways I've been controlled by other people over the years. The show was a gift—*A hit! People love you! etc.*—and nobody ever let me forget that. If you're tired, you better not complain, because there are five thousand starving actors who'll eat you alive to take your place.

My image was managed to the point of insanity. Sometimes I'd look in the mirror, and I'd only see her. The person I played on TV.

Well, screw them. And screw my hair.

I pinch the razor blade between my thumb and forefinger and bring it up to my face. I don't have scissors. My wash bag contained my regular plastic razor, which I snapped in half to free the thin metal blade, so sharp it nicked me as it came loose.

The driver recognized me in the car, and it was sheer luck that he had no clue about the scandal. I can't risk it again. I don't have long. Tye promised to come back to collect me in a little while for the beach party, and I need to do this before he returns.

I hold the front section of my hair with my left hand and scratch at it with the razor, around my eye line. Long strands come loose, floating to the wood floor. It's so quiet in here without the background hum of electricity that the sound of fraying hair is like teasing wire. I keep sawing, puffing hair out of my face, jaw set in concentration.

My fingers bleed, are sliced to shreds, but finally I'm done.

For the first time since high school, I have bangs.

They're spiky and uneven, make me think about memes celebrating that weird moment in the early aughts when everybody in Hollywood got the "*Scream 3* Courteney Cut."

I tousle the tufts with my fingers. Exactly what I need. The bangs age me. They make my face seem smaller, rounder. They render my cheekbones obsolete. I both hate the way I look, and love it, because I look less like Famous Me, and more like Teen Me. The person who existed before everything went to shit.

It's not enough, though. I need to complete the transformation.

I plait my hair in pigtails. Awful. Perfect.

I pat foundation over my face to flatten my complexion. My freckles are another Willow trademark, but the makeup eradicates them. Dulls my appearance. I look pale, sort of unwell, which suits me fine.

If I can pull this off, maybe I really can start fresh.

Why the hell did I say my name was Willow? I'm practically begging to blow this whole thing up.

I change into the baggy *JADE DANIELS* shirt that I usually sleep in. It's shapeless, swamps me, and when I add my oversize glasses, the make-under is complete.

"She's *not* all that," I say, appraising my new look.

I may be Willow, but I'm not *Willow*.

My wardrobe on the show was high fashion meets clown school. It was all primary colors, loud prints, and pristine white sneakers. So flamboyant that, when I wasn't filming, there were times people didn't recognize me on the street until I'd already walked past them in my black gym gear.

20

Would they recognize me now?

I step back from the mirror, taking it all in, wondering if I can fool half a dozen campers for a full two weeks.

A sound disrupts the silence of the bedroom.

A creak of wood.

I wonder if I made the noise myself when I stepped back from the mirror. But then I hear it again, on the other side of the room, and my gaze travels to the closet.

I swear the sound came from there.

My pulse picks up as I think about the people I saw around Matt's house after tweetageddon. Shadows in the backyard, cameras flashing, the word spray-painted in black on the oak front door—*CANCELED*—accompanied by a cardboard box on the doorstep.

A box full of dead baby rats.

The memory of those poor, dead, pink creatures in the box flushes through me as I walk toward the closet, and the words from the text I received before check-in repeat in my mind.

See you soon, Red. 😃

My hands shake as I tug open the closet doors, dragging them wide to show the interior of the space.

The closet is empty.

The back is solid wood. Hangers rattle on the rail, and I shudder with relief as I realize that must be what I heard. Not somebody crouched in here watching me, but wooden hangers gently knocking against one another in the breeze.

Nobody's watching you, sillyhead, I hear Willow say, in the mischievous way she would speak on the show. *You're not on TV anymore, rememberrrrr?*

She's right. This is going to be fine.

Welcome to Camp Castaway, Willow.

Home sweet middle-of-nowhere home.

When did you first realize you wanted to be an actor?

I was babysitting a kid who lived down the street, and *Fight Me* came on TV. The moment I saw Juniper Brown shooting a drug dealer in the face and then using the smoking gun to spark up a cigarette, I knew I wanted to be just like her.*

Was it tough getting your big break?

It's a jungle out there, I cannot tell a lie. Luckily, my family is really supportive.† They helped keep me sane when things were rough.

What's it like dating another actor?

It makes life *so much* easier, because we just get each other. Matt is such a loving, caring, sweet-natured guy, and he's not at all bothered by my success.‡ [*laughs*] I can't imagine being with anybody else.

What's your favorite movie of all time?

Clueless.§ Alicia Silverstone deserves way more credit for, like, *being* the '90s.

---

* True. I've never had to lie about my love for Juniper Brown.

† Bullshit. What was I supposed to say? "After my grandma kicked my brother out of the house, I couldn't live under the same roof as her, so I got the next bus to L.A. and showed up on the doorstep of our dead parents' friends, who work in Hollywood and helped me get a job as an assistant, and the more I watched actors doing their thing, the more I realized it wasn't that difficult, you just had to pretend, and actors get paid *a lot more* than assistants, so I started going to acting classes and I landed a commercial that went viral because it involved me eating a whole box of Krispy Kremes in a single unbroken take, and that got me an agent, and finally, because I never quit, not ever, I landed my own Netflix show."

‡ Because it meant he could coattail me to get better gigs for himself.

§ As if. I'm an *Evil Dead* fan to the gooey core.

IV

Half a dozen people have already gathered on the beach when I approach with Tye. Sometime after he showed me to my cabin— maybe an hour later, I'm already confused without my phone—a gong sounded, a low chime that filled the forest, and the handsome groundskeeper came to collect me. I feel better now that I've gone "Charlize Theron in *Monster*" on my appearance. Less nervous that I'll be recognized, but still nervous, because no plan is foolproof.

On the beach, I see Mahjong Misty with her wild brown curls, which I notice are gray at the roots. She sits on a log at the campfire, chatting with two men. One looks early twenties and wears a pristine white polo shirt; the other is an Arnold Schwarzenegger clone in designer glasses and a Hawaiian shirt. Another man and a woman sit on the other side of the fire, laughing and punching each other, and a third woman stands at the grill, spatula in hand.

My hearts thuds behind my ribs.

Six strangers.

Six people to deceive.

Six people who could hate me on sight.

As we approach, everybody turns to look at me, the chatter ceasing. Even the woman at the barbecue stops rotating hot dogs. The bonfire spits and cracks in the pit twenty feet from the water's edge.

"Hey, new girl," Misty says, voice scratchy. "Ready to party Castaway style?"

I scan their faces for a scowl. A frown. A snarl.

When nobody says anything, I shrug.

"Just point me to the dance floor," I say. Easy breezy.

"We promise not to make you sing 'Kumbaya,'" says Polo Shirt Guy, flashing a timid smile.

"But fair warning, man, there is the obligatory howling at the moon at midnight," says the shaggy-haired man on the other side of the campfire. His grin makes him look like Animal from the Muppets.

Misty says, "Come on over and join us."

"Play nice, guys," Tye says.

He gives me a reassuring wink and then jogs back up into the woods. I wonder briefly where he's going, then approach the group sitting around the fire. The lake laps drowsily at the shore. Above the trees, the sky bruises violet, the first stars pricking through. Even though the thought of mingling with strangers makes my teeth ache, I tell myself to get it together—I'm Willow now, *Willow 2.0*—and I join Misty and the others.

"Hope you brought an appetite," Misty says. "The grill's locked and loaded."

"Yeah, Dani knows how to sear stuff real good," adds the Muppet guy, shifting round to sit beside me. He wears a military jacket covered in badges and a sloppy grin full of mischief. "So tell us, what are you running from?"

I'm not sure I heard him correctly. "Sorry?"

"Everybody here's trying to put *something* in their rearview mirror!"

"Buck, dial it down," Misty says.

Buck looks annoyed, then laughs again. "Sorry, man, I've been out of the world for two weeks and I forgot about the rules of polite society. Small talk makes me want to tear out my spleen and chew on it."

I can't help smiling. He reminds me of the crew guys who worked behind the scenes on the show: the runners, set builders, and technicians were famous for their bawdy humor and lack of filter. They were fun. Kept your feet on the ground.

As I look around the group, I wonder if Buck is right. Are the other campers running from something, too? I remember that Buck and Misty aren't even their real names—they're the "camp names" they chose when they checked in. Curiosity quivers through me as I wonder who these people really are. What drove them into the wilderness, miles from civilization, to hang with total strangers.

I realize that everybody is looking at me expectantly. They want me to answer Buck's question.

"If you'd seen me run, you'd know I wouldn't get very far," I say. With a smile, I add, "I'm just taking a break."

"Nice!" Buck says. "Like Sheryl Crow says, it'll do you good!"

"That's a *change*," Misty says through gritted teeth.

"I'm Kurt," says the twenty-something Polo Shirt Guy. He sneezes, then gives me another timid smile. "Sorry, allergies."

"Apollo," says the Arnie clone in the black-frame glasses.

"Don't bother with that guy, he's leaving tonight," Buck says.

"You are?" I ask.

Apollo nods. "I'm getting a cab out of here right after dinner."

"He's already dead to us," Buck says.

"Your name is Willow, right?" Misty asks.

I freeze as the name leaves Misty's mouth. It stings my ears. I'd hoped she wouldn't remember what I called myself in the clubhouse, that there'd be a chance to start over.

But the world doesn't end.

Nobody does a double take or points at me and screams, "*It's you!*"

All that happens is that a few of the campers nod their heads, and Apollo says, "Welcome, Willow."

Relief pounds in my chest.

Maybe it's the disguise, or maybe fewer people watched the show than the internet had me believe.

"Yeah, yeah, stop crowding her," Buck says. "How about a drink?" He takes my arm and tugs me away from the fire to a craft table. I catch the scent of cigarette smoke coming off him—his jacket or his hair—and there's the unmistakable undercurrent of marijuana.

"We have prima agua," he says, "plus H2O and then just to shake things up, something delicious called *water*. Or there's green tea if you're feeling wild."

"I'll take water," I say.

"Excellent choice."

As I fill a wooden cup from a ceramic jug, I notice the woman at the barbecue—Dani—watching me. She looks Chinese American, maybe late twenties, and wears a pink denim shirt, khakis and black boots, her hair falling in messy waves to her shoulders. She sees me looking and goes back to the grill.

"The staring stops after a few days," Buck says. "You know, fresh blood draws the pack."

"That's the first time I've been called fresh in a while," I say, wiggling my eyebrows at him. Classic Willow.

Buck hacks a nicotine-tarred laugh. "You're gonna fit right in."

I notice the campers are still chatting among themselves, but their eyes keep drifting to me, and I try to shake off the unease. It's just natural curiosity, nothing sinister.

You're fine. You're Willow now.

On the show, I was able to lose myself in the character. Willow ended up being the best version of me. Always funny, always kind. There were days I wished I were Willow for real. That when the cameras stopped rolling, I would continue to channel her, like the best kind of possession.

Now that I've been fired from the show, I miss her. I miss how she made me feel.

Maybe that's why I said her name when Tye asked me. On some level, I know this is my last opportunity to be her, for just a little while longer.

We get food and gather around the campfire, seven of us sitting on logs. As people laugh and crack jokes, I feel the tension ease in my shoulders.

Buck tells me that he's fixing up an old Harley Hydra-Glide he found in a salvage yard, "and then I'm gonna discover America, Dennis Hopper style." He reveals that he'd never even heard of wellness retreats until he found himself in a car being driven to Camp Castaway. "That was one hell of a comedown, my friend."

A comedown from what, I wonder.

After another sneezing fit, Kurt, the polo shirt guy, says he works in a coffee shop, "which is enough to drive anybody crazy, but it's just until my music career takes off," while Apollo is a sports agent and won't reveal who his clients are, which means they're super A-list.

"And this is Kat, my sister from another blister," Buck says, throwing his arm around a woman with cropped black hair who wears a flannel shirt. The tips of her fingers are stained yellow. Another stoner? No judgment here. I spent most of high school getting baked.

Kat shoves him off. "I'd like to state for the record that we're not related. Thankfully."

"But we're definitely moving in together when we get out of this place," Buck says.

My head is spinning with names, trying to remember who's who out of the six campers I've met, when another woman sits down next to me.

"Sorry I'm late," she says. "You must be the new girl. Buck's not preaching the church of *Easy Rider* to you, is he?"

I almost choke on my burger. The woman is handsome in a stoic kind of way. The firelight flickers across her strong jaw, filling the hollows of her deep-set eyes. She's Black, her hair is in braids, and she wears a multicolored jacket that looks like it's from the seventies.

My throat glues closed. My brain sizzles in my skull. When I was sixteen, my bedroom was plastered with that face. My schoolbooks were tattooed with her movie stickers, and I wore my *Fight Me* T-shirt every weekend. I see her bundling Samuel L. Jackson into the trunk of her car. I see her screaming into the camera as she unloads a magazine into an alien.

Now she's sitting on the same log as me, and I've lost the ability to speak.

Juniper Brown is at Camp Castaway.

Juniper goddamn Brown.

"Juniper," she says, winking. "Good to meet you. Willow, was it?"

My mind hiccups. "Yeah, Willow, hi. I mean Willow is me. Hello."

Smooth, Willow says in my head.

Juniper's using her own name. Not a Camp Castaway moniker. I guess if you're as famous as she is, there's no point pretending to be somebody you're not. I'm famous in a very specific sitcom way, mostly recognized by college kids and teenage girls. Juniper is a living legend. And I guess she's always been a rule breaker.

I watch her push a marshmallow onto a stick and hold it over the campfire. Every part of my body buzzes, feels awake in a way that it hasn't in weeks.

Juniper Brown vanished from Hollywood years ago, hasn't made a movie in a decade, and now she shows up here? Embers drift up from the fire, climbing into the evening sky, and I wonder if this is some kind of Camp Castaway magic. The universe giving me a sign that everything's going to be okay. The hell of the past three weeks is over because, *look*, my very own personal hero is sitting next to me on a log, making a s'more.

Better yet, nobody seems to have any idea who I am, and I'm so comforted by that fact, I could cry.

I want to lean into the anonymity. Cocoon myself in it. Emerge as somebody new.

"Hey, Bebe Banana-hammock made it," Buck says.

I look up to see a woman striding with purpose toward the fire pit. She's tall, her silver hair cropped somewhere between a pixie and a mullet. Lines spider from the corners of her eyes and the sleeves of a cable-knit sweater are pushed up to her elbows.

Hush falls over the fire pit as Bebe, the Camp Mom, reaches us, because she looks incensed. In one hand, she grips the handle of an ax that rests over her shoulder. In the other, she brandishes something black that catches the firelight.

"Anybody care to explain this?" she demands, raising the object for all to see.

V

It takes me a moment to register that Bebe's holding an iPod.

Nobody says a word. All eyes are on the gadget in her hand. A gadget that shouldn't be here, according to the agreement we all signed before setting foot in Camp Castaway. And who uses iPods nowadays, anyway? I haven't seen one in years.

"We have one rule," Bebe says, her voice tight. "One rule over which there will be *no* compromise."

I notice Tye standing back by the edge of the woods, arms crossed, but my gaze is drawn to Bebe. I had pictured the "Camp Mom" as a ganja-smoking hippie brandishing a tray full of home-baked cookies, or a steely businessperson capitalizing on the self-care boom. Not the ax-wielding mama bear who stands before us.

"Camp Castaway is about responsibility," Bebe says. "Responsibility for your own well-being and for the well-being of your fellow campers. And *this* is about as irresponsible as it gets." She waves the iPod. "Anybody want to claim it?"

No answer.

I look around the fire, wondering who snuck in contraband technology. Juniper shows no emotion whatsoever. Misty seems excited by the drama. Apollo looks on edge. Buck can't sit still, constantly shifting his weight on the log, though I get the impression Buck always has ants in his pants.

"Where'd you even find that?" he asks.

Bebe stares at him. He raises his hands.

"Hey, it's not mine. Just thinking out loud."

Bebe lowers the iPod. "A concerned resident reported it to me this afternoon."

Concerned resident?

Somebody snitched on a fellow camper.

I find myself looking at Dani, the girl from the grill. She pokes the fire with a stick, as if unaware that this is happening.

"You went snooping in their cabin?" asks Kurt, the kid with the allergies. He speaks calmly, but his face shows outrage. I remember him mentioning a music career. Is the iPod his?

"Any breach of protocol is taken with the utmost seriousness," Bebe says.

"That thing can't even get on the internet," Buck says. "What's the big deal?"

Bebe's face is a pale mask. "This place demands commitment. It demands that you surrender to the forest. Sever all ties with your life. Anybody breaking the rules is only cheating themself." She looks at each of us in turn.

I'm taken aback by the force in her tone. The belief.

"Last chance to be honest with yourself," Bebe says.

Nobody moves. All eyes are on the iPod. The sound of popping firewood fills the air.

When nobody comes forward, Bebe sets the iPod on an upturned log. She raises the ax and, with practiced precision, brings it down. There's a sound like cracking glass, and a hollow crunch, and the iPod shatters. Black and white fragments flash.

Bebe straightens. She wipes sweat from her brow, leaving the ax buried in the stump. Then she picks up the iPod pieces and tosses them into the fire. We watch the flames smother them. Everybody looks either stunned or deathly serious, like kids caught sneaking beer at a party.

Only Juniper looks faintly bored, and I remember she's seen serious drama in her time. She survived eighties Hollywood.

I rock back on the log as Bebe turns to me. I stare into pale gray eyes.

"We'll talk properly tomorrow," Bebe says, her tone understanding. "First nights are for getting to know your campmates." She turns to the others. "Apollo, your car will be here soon. Are you ready to say your goodbyes?"

He goes around the circle, hugging the campers in turn. They're long hugs. Meaningful. There are tears. When his enormous arms go around me, I feel a weird sense of loss. This person everybody loves is a stranger—somebody I'll never get to know. Or perhaps I'm just mirroring the emotion of the other residents, like I did in acting exercises with my coach.

The second that Bebe and Apollo are gone, people start talking.

"So that's Bebe," says Kat, the stoner in the flannel shirt who is Buck's BFF. "She's kind of a character."

"Kind of a *psycho*," Kurt mutters.

"It was only an iPod, man," Buck says.

Misty shrugs. "Rules are rules. The house always wins."

"Hell of an introduction to Camp Castaway," Kurt says, nodding at me.

"I'm just glad I didn't pack my Kindle," I say.

"Or my vibrator," says Buck. "Man, seeing Bebe with that ax, I'm thinking it's time for some ghost stories. And I have the perfect one to start us off."

A delicious shiver strokes my spine. I realize I'm smiling. Fully, thoughtlessly smiling for the first time in weeks, and it feels amazing.

Ghost stories around the fire? Willow says. *Camp Castaway is already delivering.*

Misty's bracelets jangle as she sits next to Kurt. "Please don't start telling us some trash about a summer camp killer. That hasn't been scary since the eighties."

"It's cooler than that shit," Buck says. "Older, too, I'm guessing." He leans forward and stares at us each in turn. "Ever hear about Knock-Knock Nancy?"

The glint in his eyes causes me to shiver again, and I hug my arms in anticipation.

"Nobody?" Buck looks pleased. "She was a maid or some shit in the late 1800s. Wouldn't say boo to a goose. Super inoffensive, like Hilary Duff in an apron."

I notice Dani looking at me again. When I smile, she looks away. I try not to let my thoughts spiral, keep hold of the cozy campfire feeling. Maybe she's just shy.

"Anyway," Buck says, "Nancy lives in this tiny village not too far from here, and one day she comes across an injured preacher in the woods. He's all fucked up, been attacked by a bear. Nancy takes him back to her place and nurses him well again."

Buck peeks at me out of the corner of his eye. "One evening, the preacher is finally well enough to go into town to buy something nice for Nancy, as a thank-you. But that's when he learns the truth. Nancy is a witch, the villagers say, and they hate her spooky guts."

I'm pretty sure I know where this is going, but Buck is a good storyteller with his shag of sasquatch hair and his smoky, drawling voice.

"Let me guess, Nancy gets burned at the stake?" Misty asks, looking bored.

"I'm getting to it. So the preacher is all affronted and stuff when he realizes Nancy used her witchy lotions and potions on him. He finds Nancy chopping wood and confronts her, demands that she renounce Satan and accept the ever-loving Jesus into her heart. Nancy refuses.

They argue, and the preacher flies into a religious rage. He grabs the ax and Nancy turns tail and runs."

Buck is on his feet now, arms raised, firelight carving shadows into his features.

"Nancy goes from door to door, screaming for mercy, knocking with all her strength, pleading with the villagers for help. But nobody comes to her aid, because even back then, people were shitheads who believed everything they read on the medieval internet. Nobody answers Nancy's screams."

"Now you're just raiding Kitty Genovese for material," Misty says.

"Let him finish," Kat says, glaring, and I can't help glaring, too. What's Misty's problem?

Buck ignores them both, looks sorrowful.

"The next morning, Nancy's body is found in the town fountain. There's no sign of her head, nor the preacher, but the message is clear: the preacher took her head so that Nancy could never be properly laid to rest. Her soul would be damned, forced to endure eternal judgment for her sins. To this day, Nancy goes around knocking on doors at night, looking for her missing head. If you're stupid enough to answer and you don't give it to her, she takes yours." Buck lets the words hang for a moment, then yells, "*Boom!*"

I jump. Everybody does.

Juniper shakes her head, mouth puckered with amusement, while Misty looks irritated as she fixes her bangles, which have gathered around her wrists. Beside her, Kurt grins, looking impressed.

"Spooky, right?" Buck says, all teeth.

Misty rolls her eyes. "Calm down, Ichabod."

"It happened in a town near here," Kat says. "One of the Castaway campers told me when I first got here. He checked out a week ago—or at least I assume he checked out. Maybe Knock-Knock Nancy got him."

Buck lurches forward and snatches the ax from the log where Bebe left it.

"*Gimme your head, Kat!*" he screams, raising the ax over his stoner bud.

Kat yelps and falls backward off the log, hitting the sand. She lies there, real fear in her eyes. Buck laughs and lowers the ax, holding out a hand.

"Sorry, man, I thought we could use a joke to break the tension."

"Nothing funnier than a man swinging an ax at a woman," Juniper says.

She's not wrong.

At Juniper's words, Buck's smile drops. The ax thuds down beside the fire.

"Shit, I'm sorry," he says, hand still held out to Kat. "I didn't even . . . I wasn't thinking. Are you okay?"

He sounds genuinely upset. Kat looks uncertain as she reaches for his hand. As soon as their fingers touch, her grip tightens, and she shoots up from the ground, kicking out the backs of his knees, toppling him over.

Buck lands facedown in the sand, arms flailing.

"Now we're even, shithead," Kat says.

The mood lifts. Everybody laughs as Buck spits out wet clumps, but I find myself staring at the fire, watching the shadows shift in the depths. I'm still thinking about the story. It feels like we've conjured a specter.

Misty laughs. "Oh shit, I think Buck peed himself."

VI

"Hey," a female voice says behind me as I head down the boardwalk. I turn and raise the lantern I took from the beach party, finding the girl from the grill, Dani, quick-stepping to join me. She doesn't have a lantern, but she looks like she can handle herself. There's something Bear Grylls-y about her—sensible black boots, khakis, messy brown bed-hair. She's pretty in an appealingly understated way.

"Thought you could use a guide," she says, a little breathless. "It can get confusing out here when you first arrive. All the cabins look the same."

While her half smile doesn't reach her eyes, the fact that she ran to catch up with me makes my cheeks warm. And I'm glad for the company. The stories we told by the fire cling to me like cobwebs, making me see shapes in the dark. A couple of the other campers have already gone to bed, and it's so quiet, I feel disoriented.

"Thanks," I say. "That's nice of you, Dani."

We start walking, the lamp casting shadows in a halo around us.

"Right—Dani. It's weird, going by our camp names. But now I sort of like it. It changes the way you think about yourself, different than you are in the real world. It's sort of freeing."

I'm about to say that I get it, that I've used dozens of different names throughout my career, but that would open up the topic of my life, and I really don't want to go there.

"How long have you been here?" I ask.

"Just under a week. I'm hitting my groove. I'm starting to think I never want to leave."

"Is that a good thing?"

She gives a small laugh. "Maybe not."

We pass the first few cabins, their windows dark. The chatter from the fire pit has been replaced with the subtle buzz of insects. I look at Dani and find her studying me like she can't quite place me, which makes me nervous. I pretend not to notice, but I can't help thinking about the way she looked at me through the campfire earlier. Her gaze had seemed interested, but in what exactly?

"Does Bebe always run around camp like Lizzie Borden?" I ask, reaching for something to fill the silence. "Because that might take some getting used to."

"Tonight was a first. She does spend her life in the woods with tech-fried head cases like us, though, so who can blame her?"

"I feel sorry for the iPod."

"Me too. That's what'll drive you crazy out here—no music. I'd kill for just thirty seconds of Florence right now."

"Are you saying it was your iPod?" I ask.

"Please, I'm not that old. And it was totally Buck's."

"I thought Kurt was the musician?"

"Yeah, but did you see Buck's face? Pure guilt, all over."

I swing the lantern, a show of nonchalance as I say, "Maybe it was Knock-Knock Nancy's iPod."

Dani lifts an eyebrow. "Now *that* is a theory I can get behind."

I laugh and it feels good. It's almost like having my co-star Jenna back, but different. With Jenna, I always got the sense there was a line I shouldn't cross. We could joke around and make fun of each other, but I knew I shouldn't push too far.

Dani makes you nervous in a different way, though, Willow says in my mind, and I swallow, newly aware of what a sight I must make. My ball cap, jagged bangs, and inch-thick foundation are the opposite of flattering.

But Dani's smile when she looks at me is brash and open, like a rock star who knows they're the shit, but they'll play coy anyway. It's a good smile. Of all the people around the campfire tonight, she's the one my gaze kept returning to. Did she notice? Is that the real reason she ran to catch up?

"So what do you do?" Dani says. "Y'know, *out there.*" She uses air quotes around *out there*, like it's a joke. As if in here is reality, and everything else is a mirage.

"I'm sort of between gigs at the moment," I say, which isn't a lie, but I feel heat creeping into my face nonetheless. "How about you?"

"I'm a professional hack."

"A journalist?" I ask. My hands have gone numb.

"Nah, I write books. Or I'm trying to, anyhow. This third one is proving to be a little bitch, as you may be able to tell from the fact that I've cut myself off from the world for a month."

I try to hide my relief. The press haven't exactly been kind to me lately, and I could live without having to avoid one of the other campers for the next two weeks.

Especially a camper as cute as Dani, Willow says.

"I hope inspiration strikes," I say, ignoring the thought.

"It always does. Eventually. So who's the lucky somebody?"

I don't catch her meaning until I see Dani looking at the ring on my finger.

"Kind of difficult to miss a rock that big," she says.

My mouth twitches at the corners, but then I think about Matt telling me to be gone from his house by the time he returned from the shoot. I hear the way he spoke to me after tweetageddon, as if I'd put a spike through the entity that was "us." Like I'd killed us, simply by posting a joke online.

"Shit, sorry," Dani says, "I didn't mean to make it weird."

"No, it's fine. We sort of broke up. I don't know why I'm still wearing this thing. Deluding myself, maybe."

Dani shrugs. "Those things take time. I still have a teddy bear my ex gave me when we were sixteen. It ended badly but I like the teddy. It has a Hannibal Lecter mask. Total collector's item."

"You're a horror fan?"

She grins. "To the bloody end."

Me too, I want to say, more than anything, but the words don't reach my mouth. My agent hated when I talked about horror movies in interviews. It didn't fit my image as "good girl" Willow.

I twist the ring on my finger.

"What about you? Are you seeing anybody?" I ask. The warmth in my cheeks intensifies and I can't tell if it's from the memory of Matt or the fact that Dani's looking at me so intently.

She sighs dramatically, dropping back her head. "Alas, I've yet to find the right girl for me. Apparently the 'I just need one book deal and we're set for life' thing doesn't work for a lot of people."

"Have you tried dating other writers?"

"Please, I'm not a sadist."

I laugh. "What's wrong with writers?"

"Aside from the fact that all they talk about is writing?"

"You seem all right to me," I say, meaning it.

She smiles her rock-star smile, looks genuinely pleased, and I find I can't look away from her.

"Well, thanks," she says. "Maybe there's hope for me yet."

One knock, two knock,
Three knock, four
Someone's knocking at your door
Five knock, six knock,
Seven knock, eight
Who'd be out there quite so late?
Don't be hasty
Stay in bed
Knock-Knock Nancy
Wants your head

APOLLO

eady to rejoin reality?" the driver asked.

In the back of the car, Apollo grimaced.

The phone sat in his hand like a scorpion, and the same thought repeated in his mind like a stinger jabbing his brain.

He wasn't ready.

He wasn't.

He'd thought he was. He'd done the work. Committed to the program. Spent two weeks disconnected from the things that triggered his worst behaviors. His ex-wife. His job. His online profiles.

The feeling coursed through him like venom. Hot and liquid.

The clubhouse fell into the distance behind them as they drove down the road, between the walls of trees, and the farther from camp they traveled, the more panicked Apollo felt. Sweat pricked his armpits, making them swampy.

When Bebe handed him his phone during checkout, he hadn't felt a thing. It was just a hunk of glass and plastic. Chipped and sad-looking. Not even a dead thing, just a *thing*. Bebe told him he could leave the phone at camp, where it would be destroyed. Or he could take it with him and do whatever he liked with it.

He'd wanted to leave it. He had intended to. But then he took hold of it, and he felt nothing. He couldn't remember how it had felt before, the grip this thing'd had on him. In that moment, he knew he had a handle on the compulsions. Everything was going to be okay. He was free.

But now he was in the car, the phone was in his hands, and nobody but the driver would know he was looking at it. The sight of the screen caused a familiar tingle in the pit of his belly.

The sense of possibility.

He was remembering his real name. Not Apollo but Eric Mangold. A guy who could power up his phone and open the app in fifteen seconds. He could see who had DM'd him. Who had missed him. Who wanted to fuck him. The thoughts tasted like raspberry and champagne.

His fingers hovered over the power buttons and Apollo felt his heart beat faster, like he was doing something he shouldn't. Like he was being bad again.

The kind of bad that sent the tabloid press into a frenzy.

They tore him apart when his affairs with men were revealed. They hounded his every move, cameras flashing, desperate to capture this all-American hunk hooking up with other dudes, as if that kind of shitty attitude didn't expire in the '90s.

He'd felt bad for his wife. Didn't blame her when she filed for divorce. She didn't deserve the kind of humiliation that social media piled on her day after day, week after week. And the thing was, Apollo wasn't even gay. The press loved to throw that word around like a shiny Christmas bauble, but if they'd really cared to check, they'd have discovered Apollo was pansexual, and proud of it.

Well, fuck them all.

He liked what he liked, and the world could go to hell.

Apollo licked his lips and squeezed the power buttons and—

"Now who'd be out here at this time of night?" the driver said.

Apollo froze, had forgotten where he was. The car had stopped moving. He looked from the driver to the windshield and saw what the driver had seen. Headlights picked out a shape in the road, twenty feet away.

A person.

They stood with their feet braced wide, facing the car. Blocking the road. Apollo couldn't make out who it was. There was something off about them. They were too far away for him to make out any more than a tall, thin figure with long white hair that glowed ghostly in the headlights.

The driver honked, and the forest absorbed the sound as if it were erasing something that didn't belong there.

The figure didn't move.

When a second honk stirred no response, the driver got out of the car, muttering, "I'll be back after I've dealt with this asshole."

Apollo watched him trudge toward the stranger. He looked down, seeing that his phone had powered on. He had a single bar of signal. His finger trembled over a thumbnail illustration of a biceps.

He opened the app and swallowed, heart slamming ribs, his crotch tingling.

When he looked up again, the figure in the road was gone.

The driver had turned to face the car, and he looked confused as he squinted against the glare of the headlights and—

Tap tap tap.

Apollo turned to his window, seeing that a face had appeared out of the darkness. A knot tightened around the base of his tongue. The phone cut into his palm. He barely had time to react before the door opened from the outside, and Apollo's scalp burned as a hand seized his hair, dragging him out of the car.

He landed in the dirt, pain spasming in his arm as he fell on top of it. He realized the whimpering sound he heard was coming from his own throat.

"Please, I don't—" he managed to choke, looking up at a figure with a mournful, sagging face. The eyes shone with cold steel before the ax swung.

In the eternity it took for the blade to connect with his neck, Apollo's mind lashed out in a dozen directions, speeding through every way he could save himself—everything he had no time to do.

Before he had the chance to draw a final breath, bright pain lanced through his neck, and he heard a wet, meaty sound like a side of beef being cleaved open on a chopping board. The sound would have turned his stomach if his nerve endings weren't severed.

Apollo's vision blurred, and as he lay there, feeling nothing more than faint surprise and a creeping coldness, he heard the rasp of his attacker's breath. He heard a whispering voice as footsteps beat the dirt.

"Got to make them pay. Got to make them all *pay."*

He heard something heavy being dragged over the dirt.

He heard his own throat give a final whine as air left it.

Then he heard nothing.

Hello?

I'm here.

I did it.

I know you did, my love. You did a good thing. You did a very good thing.

I miss you.

I'm so proud of you.

When can I see you?

Hello?

Are you there?

Please don't leave me.

I'm here.

I'll always be here.

As long as you do what I say.

VII

I startle awake with a gasp.

For a moment I think I'm blind. It's so dark, it's like my eyes have stopped working. I blink and try to focus on the shapes around me. The unfamiliar bed. The suitcase against the closet. The window. The curtains are drawn back and, beyond them, the view is pure darkness, with the vaguest sketching of trees.

I'm so disoriented, it takes me a moment to remember I'm at Camp Castaway.

I'm in a cabin in the middle of the woods, over three thousand miles away from home.

And I'm pretty sure a sound woke me up.

I hold my breath, listening. The vein in my temple throbs against my skull. Silence hisses in my ears. Then—

Knock.

Knock.

Knock.

I sit up with a jolt. The sound echoes through the cabin, impossibly loud after the quiet. Knuckles on wood. Somebody at a door. But it's not a friendly sound. The knocks are staccato. Curt. As if the person knocking is daring me to answer. Daring me not to.

Something about the darkness feels alive.

It has eyes on me.

It waits for me to respond.

My mind fills with the words from the text—

See you soon, Red. 😊

—and every cell in my body freezes. Urges me to stay in bed. Some childish instinct whispers that it's safe under the covers. Nobody can get you there. Don't put a foot over the edge or it will drag you under.

It.

The notion is so ridiculous, I snap out of my stupor, remembering Buck's story about Knock-Knock Nancy. It's not my text stalker on the other side of the cabin door, and it's not some urban legend made flesh. It's Buck or one of the other campers. A classic hazing ritual. Give the new girl a scare and then accept her as one of your own.

I get up, the soles of my feet meeting the wood floor. I approach the front door. Cold scuttles up my back as I wait for another knock, but I'm not a kid at sleepaway camp, and I refuse to be a grown-ass woman jumping at shadows.

I reach for the handle. Grip it tight. Then I open the door to find—

Nothing.

The front step is vacant.

A gust of air wraps around me, brushing my skin like a sigh.

"Hello?" I call. "Knock-Knock Nancy? Pretty little head here just ready and waiting."

I poke my head into the night.

"Buck? Anybody?"

All I see are trees and the dim black box of the cabin across the way. Cabin number thirteen.

No lights on.

Nobody awake at this late hour.

Whoever knocked at my cabin is gone.

The quiet isn't comforting, though. I'm suddenly aware of just how far from the world we are. The single road in and out of Camp

Castaway was at least twenty miles long—an unbroken arrow pointing into the heart of forest darkness. It would take hours to walk it, and even then, we'd be miles from the nearest town.

As I hug myself, it dawns on me just how much I rely on my phone. It's my entertainment, my compass, and my comfort blanket.

Alone with the night, I see everything from a different angle, as if filming with a new camera setup.

In summer camp, no one can hear you scream.

I think about Mahjong Misty attacking Buck's story, the carnivorous glint unmistakable in her black-lined eyes. The stoner duo, Buck and Kat, were goofy and fun, but what happens when their stash runs out? And Kurt, the music man who's allergic to nature . . . his mannerisms stirred memories that transport me back in time for reasons I'm not ready to indulge.

Weirdest of all was Bebe's switch from wild-eyed to welcoming. Her expression lingers in my mind, morphing into the grin of a psycho clown wiggling his fingers at me from a lake. I see dead things rushing toward a dilapidated cabin intent on destruction; I see a hulking zombie-man pulverizing anything that dares enter his forest.

I love those films. But I never wanted to live them for real.

And if this were a Juniper Brown movie, she'd be telling me I'm a fool for standing in an open doorway in the middle of the night.

I go back into the cabin and shut the door. There's still no lock, so I grab a chair from the breakfast table and jam it under the door handle. It could be overkill, or it could be just-enough-kill.

You're spinning, I hear Willow say. *You're losing it, girl.*

I know I am. If I'm hearing my on-screen character speaking in my ear, it's essential that I calm the hell down.

The photo, Willow whispers. *You have the photo.*

Yes!

I hurry into the bedroom and fumble around for my carryall. I find it by the bed and pull out what I'm looking for. A dog-eared photograph. I clasp it tightly, tilting it toward the window so that it catches the moonlight, revealing the image of a fifteen-year-old boy. He's yelling joyfully while staring right into the camera with bright green eyes, floppy auburn hair parted in curtains, a splash of freckles across his nose.

My pulse calms. The darkness draws back, no longer smothering.

This is what I need. Not my phone. I'm confusing panic over not having a connection to the outside world with the realization that I've lost everything that my phone contains—pictures of Brandon; screen grabs of his texts, the ones that calm me in my bleakest moments, providing a direct line to the past.

I don't have my phone, but I have this photo, and just looking into Brandon's face centers me.

I lift the photo of my brother, and I can almost hear his voice, singsong and kind.

Perched on the edge of the bed, I think about the smell of the campfire. I think about the way the campers hugged Apollo goodbye, and I think about Dani catching up with me on the walk back to the cabins, flashing the smile that filled my stomach with skipping crickets.

"There's no judgment here," Tye said when I checked in, and I desperately want to believe him.

No judgment would mean no more stares or slurs.

No more hating myself.

No more running.

Camp Castaway feels alive with possibility. It could be everything I need.

I just hope it doesn't let me down.

VIII

"And breathe out through your nose," Tye says, somewhere near my butt.

I exhale, blood rushing to my head as I grimace through downward-facing dog. I feel hands at my hips as Tye adjusts my pose, and I could make a joke about what a great view he has right now, but I'm too focused on not collapsing. My arms shake and I want to lower my knees to the yoga mat, but it's my first class at Camp Castaway and I feel like I've got something to prove. I didn't drag myself out of bed at the six a.m. gong just to wuss out now.

Outside the studio's floor-to-ceiling windows, clouds tease themselves apart like cotton candy to let in shafts of sunlight, and the lake is still. A perfect shining mirror.

"Good, Willow," Tye says, and of course he's a yoga instructor as well as camp groundskeeper. He looks like he stepped out of a '90s Diet Coke commercial, wearing neon green shorts and a baggy gray vest that keeps slipping to show off his muscular chest.

I chew my lip, try to find my Zen. I never got into yoga back home. It seemed unnatural to contort yourself into abstract shapes while trying to become enlightened. Yoga always made me angry rather than calm.

Call me crazy, but here at camp, I think I finally get it. I concentrate on my breath the way Tye encourages us, and even though every one of my joints feels as creaky as a coffin lid, there's energy in the burn. It's like I'm tapping into a base level of strength I didn't know I had.

Beside me, Dani grunts through poses, apparently finding it just as difficult as I do. I admire her determined expression: the way that she keeps going even though she's not a natural-born yogi. She wears a black sports bra and black leggings, and her hair is tied away from her face. The effect is striking, so different from how she looked last night, that my gaze keeps returning to her reflection in the studio mirror.

Our fingers brush when we sweep our arms wide for sun salutations, and we both laugh. I'm glad I'm already red-faced from the physical activity; it helps hide my blush.

We fold forward on the mat, and heat prickles my scalp.

From this vantage point, I have an upside-down view of Juniper, who's breezed through class with the ease of a pro. I still can't believe I'm at camp with my Hollywood hero. The way she moves and sounds is so familiar, it's like we're old friends, and I have to remind myself we've never met. *Don't be creepy.* I know what it's like when fans get overly friendly.

On the mat in front, Misty wears a full face of makeup, her eyes rimmed in black again. Stoner Kat and allergy-music guy Kurt are beside her. Buck is the only resident who's not here, but then Buck doesn't strike me as the yoga type.

"And now the moment you've all been waiting for," Tye says, taking his position at the front of the class. He sits cross-legged, smiling. "It's time to lie on your backs."

"Thank Christ," Dani mutters, and I suppress a laugh as I flop onto the mat.

"Now close your eyes in corpse pose," Tye says, "and we'll take ten breaths together. Breathe in for one, two, three . . ."

Lying with my eyes closed, sweat cooling on my skin, I think *corpse pose*, which makes me think about Brandon, because the movies we watched together as kids were full of corpses. That's sort of a key feature of horror movies. It was the passion that united us growing up.

Horror was one hundred percent our thing, and we dreamed of making it to Hollywood.

"I'll be the creature effects artist and you'll be the star," Bran said when he was fifteen and I was sixteen. "We'll be the first brother-sister horror phenomenon, like if Rick Baker had a sibling who was Dee Wallace. It'll be *sick*."

He loved monster flicks like *Ginger Snaps*, *The Creeper Thing*, and *Alien*, whereas I was all about haunted house movies like *Let's Scare Jessica to Death* and *The Guesthouse*. Though our subgenre tastes varied, the films felt like *ours*. It was as if they'd been made exclusively for us. I don't think that our parents' deaths made us into horror fans, but I think those movies helped. They took us away from the real world, gave us a safe place to store that dark space inside that hurt. Figure out a way to cope.

Horror never lied.

It never assured you it would all work out. It never shied away from reality.

Horror was different. Horror was honest. Horror hurt in the best possible way.

We lived in fear that Grams would find out what we were watching. Grams never met a Bible passage she didn't like, and she thought Netflix was "for people who never read a book." Just mentioning *The Exorcist* had her clutching her bosom. Movie nights were in Brandon's bedroom, safe from Grams's helicoptering, and we'd tell her we were watching PG-rated teen films, making up fake titles like *The Perfect Nerd* and *Stacy Matthews Gets an A!*

Despite how Grams felt about scary movies, it wasn't a horror film that took Bran away from me.

When he was seventeen, Grams walked in on him watching the British movie *Weekend*, right at the moment where the two guys get jiggy on the couch.

That was the beginning of the end.

And the most fucked-up part of it? I don't think I ever really understood what happened to Bran until I got canceled.

Being "outed." Judged. Put in a box and left there. I finally got it.

"And out three, four, five," Tye says, bringing me back into the room. Despite the memory of Brandon, my body feels relaxed. I've melted into the yoga mat, and I feel like I'm floating above it.

A gasping sound rises above the rhythmic breathing of the class. It's on the other side of the studio. It sounds like somebody's crying, but quietly, as if they're trying not to disturb the people around them.

"That's good," Tye says. "Yoga is a powerful tool. It can unlock feelings you didn't even know were trapped. Let's breathe in again for one—"

"Kurt?" Juniper says. "You okay, kid?"

I turn my head. Juniper is sitting up, facing Kurt on the next mat. He's upright, knees bent, arms around them. Sweat beads his face and he's struggling to draw breath, chest expanding and contracting.

"Is he having a panic attack?" I ask.

Tye goes to him. He crouches by Kurt, resting a hand on his shoulder.

"Deep breaths, Kurt. Breathe with me. In for four, out for four . . ."

Kurt shakes his head.

"I just need . . ." His voice is pinched. "I just need air."

He pulls away from Tye, gets to his feet.

"Sorry," he wheezes, an apology that appears to be for all of us. "I'm fine. I just need air." He hurries for the door, disappearing outside.

I look at Dani, feeling unsettled and worried for the kid.

Dani looks stunned. "What was that all about?" she asks.

"That was the power of yoga," Tye says.

IX

Kurt is absent when we gather on the beach after yoga. Five perspiring campers—Juniper, Kat, Misty, Dani, and me—plus Tye, who looks like he could side-plank for another hour, no sweat.

The air is fresh, and even though I'm concerned about Kurt, the physical exertion of class has left me feeling pleasantly buzzed. The lake laps at the shore, the rising sun splashing gold across the surface. It's a special, Instagrammable kind of gorgeous, and if I had my phone, you can bet I'd be snapping shots. But my phone's in a locker in the clubhouse, and that fact makes the view all the sweeter. It's just for us, not our parasocial almost-friends online.

"Good morning, everybody," Bebe says, flashing her large teeth as she stands with her back to the lake. The Camp Mom wears a faded denim shirt and jeans, her heart-shaped face shaded by the brim of a Stetson. A bronze gong the size of a dinner plate rests on an upturned log, a soft-headed mallet beside it.

"I am so ready to affirm," Misty says.

"You're *always* ready to affirm," Dani says with a wry smile.

"I can't help being a glass-half-full kinda gal."

Or somebody who likes the sound of their own voice, I think, and then feel mean. Maybe Misty really is that positive.

"Misty, your enthusiasm is a wonderful quality and very welcome," Bebe says. "And Willow, welcome to your first affirmation ceremony. This is how we greet every day, giving thanks for the things that have served us, releasing that which no longer enables us to grow, and affirming our intention for the day ahead."

I want to say that my intention is to flop around the camp like one of those inflatable car-wash dancers, but I'm getting a no-jokes vibe from the Camp Mom.

"Affirmative," I say—maybe just a little joke?—and Dani sniggers softly at my side.

Bebe picks up the mallet, then pauses as she surveys the campers. "No Kurt this morning? Or Buck?"

"Buck slept in," Kat says. "Again." She wears a headband that pushes her black hair out of her face, plus another flannel shirt, this one tied in a knot above her navel.

"Kurt had some trouble in yoga," Tye says. "I think I saw him head into the shower block."

Bebe clasps the mallet. "Perhaps somebody would like to check on him when we're done here?"

"I'll do it," I say, the words leaving my mouth before I'm aware I intended to speak. The others look at me in surprise, which isn't unwarranted. They've known Kurt longer. I'm not able to explain the fact that I recognize something in Kurt, though. Something so familiar, it urges me to make sure he's all right.

"I need to shower, anyway," I say.

Bebe's smile is warm. "Thank you, Willow. Misty, perhaps you'd like to lead today's affirmations?"

Misty beams. She clears her throat and brushes her curls out of her face, saying with confidence, "I'd like to affirm that I am a force of fucking nature, and I don't ever need to apologize for that."

I make a sound that's somewhere between a choke and a laugh. I can't help it. Misty's affirmation is so brazenly self-congratulatory. I sort of admire her for it. Misty's eyes narrow at me, and I clear my throat, trying to wipe the amusement from my face.

"I like it," I say. "It's badass."

Misty's gaze remains on me, and I can't tell if she's going to shrug it off or start yelling. Strike two after I called her an old lady during check-in. Why can't I ever just keep my mouth shut?

"I just want to affirm that Misty's right," Dani says beside me. "We're all forces of fucking nature." She looks at me. "And we don't ever have to apologize for that."

My stomach flutters, and I feel a surge of appreciation. I opened myself up to an attack, but Dani moved the target.

Misty finally relaxes.

"Sure," she says. "I guess."

"Thank you, Dani," Bebe says. "Juniper?"

Juniper bows her head and then takes a breath, looking out at the lake. When she speaks, there's weight to her tone.

"I affirm that I am not held hostage by my shortcomings, that they do not define me, and I am able and willing to grow from them."

I'm thrown. What possible shortcomings could Juniper Brown believe she has? What could she possibly be sorry for? She's the one who showed me—and millions of fans besides—what it was to be confident even with your back against a wall.

When I left Grams, I was angry and scared, an eighteen-year-old runaway with no plan beyond starting over in L.A. Thinking about Juniper Brown bolstered me. I cycled through every tough character she'd ever played—the vigilante ex–drug mule; the badass sorority mom; the cop who saved her town from alligators—and they were a comfort. They helped me trust that I could make it on my own.

Juniper's voice is lighter as she adds, "Also, I'm grateful to Tye for leading a kick-ass yoga class."

"Hear, hear," Misty drawls, and I sense she's thankful for different reasons than Juniper. Her eyes keep roving across Tye's sculpted physique, her appreciation as obvious as her dye job.

Stop that, Willow whispers in my ear. *Be nice.*

Kat cricks her neck, as if preparing for a bout in the ring.

"There are people who hurt me in the past," she says. "I think about them every day. Sometimes I wish bad things would happen to them. But I intend to let go of that hatred; to live with compassion for them and for myself."

A breeze ruffles my bangs. Everybody is so serious, I feel the urge to do a little dance. Break the tension with the Funky Chicken. Summer camp shouldn't be this gloomy. I clasp my hands together and try to remain still.

"Willow?" Bebe says.

I swallow, feeling the pressure to say something meaningful.

On every episode of *We Love Willow*, before the cameras rolled, we'd stand on set and huddle: actors, writers, and crew members all pledging to put on the best show possible. Then we'd do a team cheer, putting our hands in the middle while we shouted the funniest word we could come up with, which meant we always walked onto the set laughing.

This feels like that, but deeper. More important. It's clear that the other campers are dealing with heavy stuff, and I should respect that, even though I feel weird and vulnerable and desperate to shout "*Bunghole!*"

I look at Dani, remembering how she hurried to catch up with me after the campfire, and her presence is oddly reassuring. I feel like I can risk some honesty.

"I'm grateful to the camp for taking me in," I say, "when I felt like I had nowhere left to go."

Dani smiles. Bebe's eyes glitter at me like the surface of the lake, the corners of her mouth curling.

"You are so welcome here, Willow," she says. I feel like she really means it and I'm surprised to feel pressure behind my eyes. As goofy as the affirmation ceremony is, I appreciate this little scrap of space that has been carved out for us. Space to think—to speak. The other campers wear understanding expressions—even Misty—as if they know exactly what I mean, and I feel seen in a way that I haven't in a long time.

✳

nside the shower block, I find Kurt wrestling with a locker. He's top-less, the shirt he wore for yoga discarded on a bench. His back is red and blotchy. He's clearly still coming down from his episode.

While the others went to breakfast, I found the ramshackle build-ing with the corrugated iron roof. It looks older than the cabins, but there's something adorably quaint about it, both outside and in. Cur-tained cubicles line one wall, mirrors and sinks on the other. Wooden benches fill the space between. I kind of like the gender-neutral setup, although standing here just me and Kurt, it feels rather intimate.

"Hey, Kurt," I say, going to a locker a few down from his. "How are you feeling?"

"I'm fine," he says, tugging on a fresh T-shirt. He doesn't look at me. Everything about him screams *not fine*, and I'm overwhelmed by a feeling of déjà vu.

The way Kurt stands, turned to one side so I can't see his face, it's like I'm looking at my brother. I see the way Bran was in those final months, when Grams was all over him, always on his case. The way cracks appeared quicker than he could cover them back up. His smile the last time I saw him was his best *this is going to be okay* smile, right as he got in the back of Grams's car and she drove him out of the neighborhood.

Blood thumps in my throat as I look at Kurt, and I try to keep it light. Try to be like Willow.

"Gotta admit, I'm not in love with yoga, either. All those poses named after animals. If I wanted to live like a dog, I'd drink from a toilet."

A trace of amusement lifts Kurt's mouth.

"Yoga is as yoga does," he says. "I think I'm just tired. I didn't sleep great last night."

"Really? How come?" I wonder if he's been visited by the phantom knocker, too. What if he *was* the person who knocked on my door?

No way to know, Willow says.

He shrugs. "It's so dark out here. Quiet, too. It can be freaky."

Kurt's afraid of the dark? I'm surprised by his honesty.

"I guess we're pretty isolated out here," I say. "Isn't that sort of the point?"

Kurt shuts his locker, packs his yoga clothes into a carryall. "Sure."

"Have you had panic attacks before?" I ask. I get the sense that Kurt needs directness.

He looks at me for the first time, wary, like a raccoon when a porch light goes on in the middle of the night.

"You know about panic attacks?"

I nod. "I knew somebody who had them." I feel my own pulse picking up, but I sense Kurt's interest, his vulnerability, and it makes me feel like I can be vulnerable, too. "My brother," I say. "My brother used to have them."

Kurt's eyes widen. "Did he get over them?"

He sounds so hopeful, I want to lie to him. I want to help him.

"He learned to deal with them," I say, which isn't a total lie, but still the words dry my throat. I try not to think about the last time I saw Brandon. That smile. But Kurt's expression is so similar to the way Brandon used to look, it threatens to shred my composure.

"Have you ever spoken to anybody about this?" I ask.

"Only my therapist. I haven't had an attack in a long time. I thought

I'd gotten a handle on it, but sometimes—" He stops, looks away. "Never mind."

I stop myself from stepping toward him, because even though I want to help him, I don't want to scare him with physical contact. Bran hated that, too. Instead, I lightly tap my chest.

"Just do this for as long as you need to," I say. "It's supposed to remind our bodies that we're safe, the way our moms would comfort us as babies."

Kurt watches my hand, and then lifts his own, gently tapping his sternum. I wonder what really triggered the panic attack; what he's at camp for. I get the feeling that if I asked, he'd close up again.

"Thanks," he says. "You're easy to talk to." He pauses. "And if you tell anybody I'm scared of the dark, I will hunt you down."

I laugh. "Your secret's safe with me."

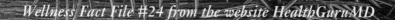

Before we had towns and cities, we were forest dwellers. Early humans found everything they needed in the forest: shelter, clothing, food, medicine. That information remains in us on a cellular level, which may explain why we still find nature so calming—it is our home. And here's the science part: studies show that forests release medicinal aerosols that fill the air with healing biochemicals. These aerosols are proven to improve blood flow, decrease blood pressure, and even prevent cancer. They can suppress the hormone cortisol, and this decrease in cortisol comes with widespread immune-boosting benefits. In short: if you're feeling stressed, *go green!* It might just save your life.

n the canteen, breakfast has been laid out on a long counter. The assortment of colors is dazzling. There are green juices, fresh red berries and creamy yogurt, golden toast with organic peanut butter and jam, granola bars, and aromatic black coffee. I realize I'm ravenous, and I fill up my plate with fruit and yogurt, taking a ceramic mug of coffee.

Bebe beckons me over to a picnic bench outside, giving me a benevolent smile, like a teacher. The picnic area is fringed by fir trees, the air slowly warming as the sun rises. Misty, Tye, and Kurt sit together, while Dani eats with stoner girl Kat. I spot a figure sitting on a boulder at the far side of the clearing and realize it's Juniper, eating alone while looking out at the lake.

I feel a pull toward her, but Bebe is beaming at me from the bench.

"Willow," Bebe says. "I see you located at least one of our missing campers."

"Target secured," I say, sitting opposite her, "call off backup, Eagle One."

Her smile widens, exposes those large teeth. "Wonderful. Listen. Please accept my apologies for last night. I'm afraid it wasn't the most suitable introduction to the camp."

It takes me a moment to remember the ax coming down, the iPod shattering.

"It's already forgotten," I say.

"That is very generous of you. I pride Camp Castaway on its dedication to well-being and rejuvenation. I cannot abide anything that threatens what we do here." She notices I haven't started eating. "Please, dig in. The food here is all locally grown and sourced. You know the stomach is the second brain?"

"I think I heard that on *Oprah* once," I say. I spoon a helping of berries and yogurt into my mouth, feeling self-conscious as Bebe watches me, waiting for a reaction. I swallow, waving the spoon appreciatively.

"That's good eatin'."

She nods and brings a piece of toast to her mouth. "Tell me, what are you hoping to get out of your stay here?"

I shrug. "I needed somebody to help me break up with my phone."

Bebe looks thoughtful as she sets down her toast and reaches across the table to take my hands, including the one holding the spoon.

"You can speak honestly here, Willow, without fear of repercussions."

Her gaze is intense, but it's not the same hard stare she wore while brandishing the iPod by the fire. It's softer, inviting. It makes me think about Grams, which isn't a comfort. After the accident, Grams raised me and Brandon, and she was everything you'd want in an adoptive parent. Loving. Observant. Supportive. But there were certain buttons that, when pushed, fried her circuits, and she could become monstrous.

"Whatever happened out there in the world," Bebe says, "it can't touch you here. We can get so stuck sometimes, pinned in place by other people's notions of who we are. You can use this time to decide if the version of yourself that you've been living with is still the right fit."

Her words resonate. I know all about starting over. Life and circumstances have forced me to pack my bags more than once. This time, though, I wasn't ready.

The morning of tweetageddon, my phone had already blown up by the time Matt got back from the gym. He was setting his bag on the kitchen counter when I stumbled for him and fell into his arms, the sight of him causing tears to fill my eyes. It took me longer than it should have to realize he wasn't returning the hug. Was barely touching me.

"I'm going to my brother's," he said. "You need some space."

"No, please," I said. "Don't leave me."

But he did.

He was gone within the hour.

Across the picnic bench, Bebe sits patiently waiting for me to speak. The breeze tousles her cropped silver hair. What do I want to get out of my stay here?

You wanted to live the Wednesday Addams Camp Chippewa fantasy, Willow says.

"I needed to disappear," I say, surprised, because I hadn't intended to speak so honestly. One night away from my life, and already it feels distant enough that it's almost like I'm talking about somebody else's.

"I've been sort of visible for a while," I say. "Publicly. It's a lot, especially when the negativity gets out of hand. I needed to check out. Hide, I guess. Just for a while."

My gaze flickers to Bebe, and a part of me is scared she'll figure out who I really am. But there's no judgment in Bebe's expression. She nods, seems to get it.

"Removing yourself from a difficult situation isn't easy. It takes guts. As a species, we're programmed to resist change. Better the devil you know. But you've done the hard part. You have acknowledged a need to change, and you're taking steps to make it happen."

Her smoky gray eyes level on me.

"Here's the thing, Willow. For the first couple of days, you may experience a wild mix of emotions. Relief, maybe. Joy. Frustration. It's a powerful thing you're doing, disconnecting, quietening the chatter of other people. I would encourage you to listen to what replaces all of that noise now that it's gone. When we turn down the dial on the voices of strangers, we're able to start listening to ourselves—truly and completely."

I realize I've shifted forward, hanging on her words. When I was fired, when my friends ghosted me, when Matt took the dog, I had nothing. My phone fell silent, aside from the never-ending stream of hatred on social media.

If you strip away everything that *isn't* what I do for a living, who even am I anymore? Would Bran recognize the person I've become?

A murmur of excited voices draws my attention to one of the benches, where the campers have gathered around Tye. He sits with one hand pressed flat on the tabletop, the other holding a knife, which he brings down in a repeated stabbing motion. It takes me a moment to realize he's doing the Bishop-in-*Aliens* knife trick, grinning as the blade strikes the space between his fingers with increasing speed.

Kurt stares, eyes wide with worry. He chews his bottom lip, gaze traveling over Tye's muscular arms, and the sight makes me wonder if Kurt's more than just worried. Does he have a crush on Tye? I could understand if he did. The groundskeeper is attractive.

Bebe doesn't seem to notice the commotion. She looks wistful as she peers at the trees. "This may sound a little gaga, but . . . let the forest help you. There's magic here. Something ancient. When people come here, they feel it. It grounds them."

She gives me a look that is also a question, as if she wants to know if I feel it, too.

"Okay?" I say.

She winks, picks up her coffee. "You'll feel it. Trust me, you will."

Yells come from the other bench. Tye is laughing, the knife

stabbing faster still, while Kurt shouts at him to stop. He finally grabs Tye's hand, brings him to a standstill.

Tye grins, seeming to revel in the drama.

"You're hurt," Kurt says. He seems to realize he's still holding Tye's hand, and quickly lets go.

Tye inspects his finger. "Just a little cut," he says, putting his finger to his mouth. Kurt's cheeks redden.

Bebe doesn't react. She looks down at my bowl. "Are you finished? How about we go for a walk? Get to know the place?"

I look at my empty bowl. I hadn't realized how hungry I was.

"All right, who stole my breakfast?" I deadpan, and Bebe smiles in that teacherly way again, as if I'm a kid who has a lot of growing up to do.

We wander into the clubhouse, which is even bigger than I initially thought. There are water coolers around every corner, some flavored with lemon and cucumber slices. The porch with the cell phone lockers makes me feel weird—it's our closest connection to the real world—but then Bebe shows me the game room, which looks like a professor's study with wall-to-wall bookcases holding board games and wellness literature.

"Down that corridor is the infirmary and a small gym," Bebe says. "And that way is the kitchen."

Outside, we head left, in the opposite direction of the boardwalk and the cabins, and stroll past a dilapidated boathouse. I start to imagine I can feel the magic Bebe alluded to. The camp feels serene but alive, humming with the bustle of nature. With potential.

Bebe herself is an enchanting enigma. She's taller than me, and she moves with the slow confidence of a lioness. I find her both intimidating and reassuring.

We come to a jetty that reaches a long arm out into the lake. Bebe strolls down the walkway and I follow. We stand at the end, and all I can see is water. It's like we're standing on the surface of the lake, watching upside-down clouds live their jellyfish dreams as they skim through the depths.

"It's beautiful," I say, breathing it in.

"It's difficult to find unspoiled places like this nowadays," Bebe says, pride in her tone. "We're very lucky to have it."

"How long have you been out here?"

"Five years. When I found it, I never wanted to leave."

"You found this place yourself? How?"

"You want the long or the short version?" Bebe cracks a knowing smile. "Right, the Gen Z version: Six years ago, I was hiking, and I got lost. I'm not gonna lie, it was scary. I didn't see a single human being for three days and I was getting worried. But then I came across the lake and it was almost like the forest led me here. It wanted me to find this place."

I can't tell if I'm impressed or unnerved.

Hiking alone is one thing. But hiking alone in the endless wilderness of upstate New York? That takes *Revenant* levels of guts.

"We had to plumb a whole new water main out here," Bebe says, "but I just fell in love with the land. The forest. The lake. It was untouched. A miracle."

"Does it ever get lonely out here?" I ask.

"People make you feel alone," Bebe says. "Not places."

I've never thought about it like that, but she's right. I felt so alone when Matt left for New Mexico the day after tweetageddon, but it wasn't because the house was suddenly so quiet. The feeling of loneliness wasn't new. It had been there for years.

Bebe's eyes sparkle and she whispers, as if sharing a secret, "You're going to leave this place a totally different person, Willow. Trust me on that."

Have you been watching them?

Yes.

Good.

What are you going to do?

The right thing. "If you do wrong, be afraid, for rulers do not bear the sword for no reason."

Is that Taylor Swift?

Sure.

I like it.

😊

'm leaving my cabin when I spot Juniper on the boardwalk, strolling away from me in the direction of the clubhouse. She wears purple leggings, a green vest, and electric blue sneakers. Unmissable as a butterfly amid the foliage.

And she's alone.

My grip tightens on the book I came back to my cabin to pick up—Paul Tremblay's latest, which I was planning on curling up with on one of the giant clubhouse sofas; the ones with the view.

It's midmorning, and I'd thought about seeing what Dani was up to, but I'm still figuring out how camp works. If I were Sitcom Willow and this were an episode of the show, I'd be bathing in a natural spring right about now, discovering too late that it was full of baby freshwater crabs that clamped onto every inch of exposed skin.

I'm not her, though. I'm Willow 2.0. And I don't want to impose on anybody's solitude. Reading in the clubhouse means I can doze off if I want. Go full grandma on the place. And if I run into Dani, well . . . we'll just call it fate.

All of that goes out of my head when I spot Juniper walking ahead of me.

Even after almost a decade of working in Hollywood, I've never managed to meet her. It wasn't for lack of trying. She hasn't made a movie in years, but I lived in hope that she'd show up to a red-carpet event or a celebrity mixer, maybe to announce a splashy comeback, Brendan Fraser style.

A couple of years in, when I still hadn't managed to find out what happened to my idol, I asked my agent about her.

"Juniper?" she scoffed. "She stopped RSVPing years ago. Left L.A., I think."

I can't help wondering where Juniper went when she disappeared from Hollywood. What she's doing at Camp Castaway. I keep seeing the way she spoke during her morning affirmation.

I am not held hostage by my shortcomings . . . they do not define me.

Did something happen to her? Did she do something bad?

I want to know what's beneath that cool exterior, and now's my chance.

I hurry onto the boardwalk, preparing to chase after her, but then a low female voice says behind me, "Hey, Willow."

I jump and see Kat approaching from the opposite side of the walkway. She's still wearing her yoga getup: a blue flannel shirt tied at her midriff, black hair pushed out of her face by a sweatband, so very much the embodiment of a '90s Nirvana fan that I briefly forget which decade we're in.

"Hey," I say, still moving, not wanting to lose Juniper.

"Have you seen Buck this morning?" Kat asks.

"I don't think so, sorry." I note the fevered look in her eyes, the worry pinching a line between her eyebrows. Even though Juniper is getting farther away, I slow down, remembering that Buck wasn't at yoga or Bebe's affirmation ceremony.

"Was he at breakfast?" I ask, trying to remember.

Kat shakes her head. "I haven't seen him since last night. I tried his cabin after breakfast but there was no answer."

"Maybe he went for a hike?" I suggest.

Kat's mouth quirks but her attempt at a smile is tamped down by worry. "Buck's not exactly known to exercise. Jesus, if the idiot went and got himself bit by a snake, I'm going to kill him."

They must really be close for Kat to worry this much.

I check the boardwalk ahead. Juniper has vanished.

Crap.

I've lost my chance.

Better luck next time! Willow says, and irritation judders through me.

Kat's gaze rests on one of the cabins on the other side of the board-walk. It's identical to the others: single story, peaked roof, one window and door. It's funny how little we really need to live.

"Is that Buck's cabin?" I ask.

Kat nods.

"How about we try knocking again? He might have come back."

Kat's expression lifts. "Sure. Thanks."

We start to walk, and Kat's pace is fast, worried. She's practically tripping over her own feet trying to get ahead of herself.

"You seem close," I say. "You and Buck."

"We checked into camp two days apart," Kat says. "Been sort of inseparable ever since. He's a loudmouth but he's a good guy under-neath it all. The guys I work with are all super nerds. It's cool, but there's only so long I can debate Janeway versus Picard."

"Where do you work?" I ask.

"I'm in IT." Kat raises an eyebrow. "You see my problem?"

I laugh. "It must be weird for you out here, then, not a computer in sight."

A shrug. "I actually prefer being outdoors. IT wasn't exactly my first choice, I just had an in with my brother. Trust me, if I had any other option, I'd have taken it."

"You have a brother?" I ask.

"Four of them."

I whistle.

"Yeah, it's eat or be eaten. You have siblings?"

I shake my head. Don't want to broach the topic of Brandon. Knowing that Kat is one of five siblings sort of explains her doesn't-give-a-shit attitude. I'm guessing she had to toughen up quick to survive that household.

"You're lucky," Kat says. "They get worse with age. What are you reading?"

I look down at the book I had planned on curling up with. I hold it up, my thoughts circling Brandon, trying not to wonder what I missed out on by not seeing him grow up.

"Looks creepy," Kat says, and there's something in her expression I can't quite place. An odd combination of yearning and melancholy.

"Hopefully," I say. "Why were you desperate? For the job, I mean."

Kat averts her gaze, kicks an errant branch.

"I lost my old job because of—" She stops, flicks a look at me. "Well, because of something crappy that happened."

I smile and decide not to pry, and not just because I'd rather not answer any personal questions myself.

Quid pro quo, Clarice, Willow whispers.

I can't help thinking about what Kat said during affirmations this morning.

There are people who hurt me in the past.

Has everybody here been through something?

We reach Buck's cabin and Kat knocks. When there's no answer, she bangs her fist and yells, "Quit jacking off in there, Metallica Breath, and come socialize with us civilized folk."

Still nothing. She kicks the door and steps away.

I look in through the window at Buck's bedroom, seeing his unmade bed, a tangle of twisted sheets. The living room is equally messy, strewn with clothes and magazines and dirty dishes. But there's no sign of life. No Buck.

And there's no Kat now, either.

I scan the area in front of the cabin and find that I'm alone.

"Kat?" I call.

I look around, wondering if she went into Buck's cabin, but I'm certain I would have heard her. Then I spot her disappearing around the side of the cabin. I follow, thinking that she must have decided to go in the back via the screen doors. Maybe Buck's been sunbathing on the veranda this whole time.

When I turn the corner, though, there's no Kat.

The forest is still.

It's almost eerie, how silent it's become. The birds make no sound. There's no wind shaking the leaves. The air has stopped moving.

I scan the empty veranda, the trees, searching for Kat, trying to figure out how the hell she got away from me—and then I spot movement ahead. Something flashing between the tree trunks. A person.

They're gone before I can get a good look, but I'm left with an impression of tallness, quick-moving limbs, and stark, white hair. There's only one person I know of at camp with hair that pale.

"Bebe?" I call.

My voice is loud in the quiet of the forest. I hurry over rocks, pine cones and fallen branches, trying to catch up with the figure, only just keeping my balance.

"Bebe?"

There's no reply. Bebe doesn't emerge from behind a tree trunk, and neither does Kat.

The forest is silent.

Surely if it was Bebe I saw, she'd have answered. Perhaps the locals hike around here? I couldn't tell if the figure wore hiking gear, can barely remember anything about their appearance aside from the glimmer of white hair.

I start making my way back to the cabin, but then I notice something different about the tree trunk before me.

A symbol is carved into the bark, around shoulder height.

I look closer and see that it's not a symbol, but a letter.

N

I run my fingers across the lines, trying to figure out what it could mean.

N for "Nancy"?

A splinter pierces my skin. I jerk my hand back and rub my palm, which itches where the wood dug into it.

"Nice going," I mutter, digging out the splinter and dropping it to the forest floor. Which is when I notice the hollow in the base of the tree. It's down near the roots, a natural recess in the trunk, ringed in thick, tough bark; something like a mouth.

Crouching down, I peer into the hollow and spot an object resting in the shadows. Small, difficult to discern in this light. Unable to control my curiosity, I reach inside, and my fingers close around a hard object, which I pull out into the light.

It's a doll's head. Small, pink, hairless. One blue eye is cracked down the center, while the other eye is only half open, the lid permanently lowered.

There's no body. The head was the only thing in the hollow.

"Hey," a voice says, and I look up from my crouched position, finding Kat peering down at me, brow furrowed.

I raise the doll's head so that she can see it. "I found it in the tree."

"Wow, it's adorable. Who do you think put it there?"

"Has anybody ever knocked at your cabin at night?" I ask, standing.

Kat shakes her head. "No, why?"

"Because somebody knocked at my cabin last night. But when I answered, there was nobody there."

I watch Kat scan the trees, chewing her bottom lip. Her worry seems to have doubled in the past ten minutes.

"I'm sure Buck'll show up," I say.

Kat nods, looks lost in thought as she starts to traipse back toward the cabin.

I stroll after her, examining the doll head. I squeeze it, just to see what happens, and the mouth pushes outward, the inner lining emerging so that it looks like the head is vomiting itself. I can't help smiling.

It really is sort of adorable.

Let's be clear: cancel culture isn't the same as call-out culture. Movements like MeToo and BLM sought to bring about positive social change by exposing criminals who were otherwise protected by their wealth and status.

Cancel culture, on the other hand, plays out almost exclusively on social media, where individuals who are deemed ethically or morally corrupt face a one-size-fits-all punishment: social exile. And you don't have to be famous. Anybody can get canceled if they're seen to have transgressed.

"The attack felt one hundred percent personal," says homemaker Florence Chu, whose "comedy" reel equating the so-called shrinking candy bar crisis to the global food shortage saw her bullied offline and threatened with legal action.

"It's easy to say that you shouldn't care what people post about you online," Florence says, "but that's missing the point. Imagine it like this: You're at the mall on a busy day, and every single person is whispering about you. Looking at you. Judging you. Maybe somebody laughs or yells. Maybe they start throwing things. And in order to get out of there, you have to walk past all these people who hate you, even though they couldn't tell you your last name, or even the specifics of what you've supposedly done."

XII

After lunch, we play softball.

Juniper looks like she was born at Yankee Stadium—a sporty Terminator, factory programmed to deliver fastballs. She pitches at me, and I squeeze the bat in both hands, determined not to miss. The ball comes at me hard, and I swing, the bat connecting with a pleasing crack that vibrates up my arms. I run, hurtling around the bases with my teammates screaming my name, and when I hurl myself down at home plate, my knees and elbows burning from the grass, I thrill in the knowledge that we've won.

Dani and Kurt drag me to my feet, wrapping their arms around me and dancing in a circle while singing.

"Take me out to the ball game! Take me out to the crowd. Buy me some peanuts and Cracker Jack. I don't care if I never get back!"

"Yeah, yeah, everybody loves a winner," Misty drawls, hand on hip as she squints at us through black-lined eyes.

"Good game," Kurt tells me, flushed and grinning. We're all still holding hands.

"We wouldn't have come close if it weren't for your pitching."

"Naw, that was just luck."

"Come on, you were the star player."

He blushes, looks unsure how to process the compliment, then goes to shake hands with the others.

Dani holds my hand a moment longer, cheeks pink as she catches her breath.

"Nice run," she says.

"I did warn you all that I run like a drunk octopus."

"You made it work." She smiles, and I feel a buzz in my stomach.

Her fingers graze my engagement ring, and her gaze loses a little of its sparkle. She lets go, turns to the other campers to high-five Misty, Tye, and Juniper.

I twist the ring, trying not to let my disappointment show. This stupid goddamn ring that I never wanted to put on in the first place.

Matt proposed via a *We Love Willow* flash mob. Our friends performed an elaborate dance routine set to the show's theme tune, and at the end of it, Matt got down on one knee and held up a ring.

The whole thing ended up online.

Matt's brother had been recording, and when he posted the video on social media, it went viral. Within hours, the whole world knew that I was living out the hetero Hollywood cliché.

When the furor finally calmed down, I couldn't tell if I was angry at Matt's brother for leaking the video, or if I was just ashamed. Ashamed that I'd said yes even though I didn't want to. Ashamed that I was getting married at all—and to a man who thought a *We Love Willow* flash mob meant anything to me. I had become so inseparable from my character, everybody thought I was her. Even my fiancé.

I saw the confusion in his eyes on the occasions I did anything un-Willow. If I suggested watching *Zombie Flesh Eaters*, or going to StokerCon, or ordering my steak *rare*, his brow lowered, his eyes glassed over, and he looked at me like there'd been a glitch in the Matrix.

Whenever that happened, I'd pretend I was kidding, and order would be restored. No need to take the blue pill.

But a part of me wanted to find a way out.

I guess I succeeded, three months later.

"Who wants refreshments?" Tye asks, cracking open a picnic basket. "Man, it's hot out today." He tugs his shirt over his head, revealing a bronze torso that would make Zac Efron start a juice cleanse.

Misty's eyes are practically on stalks. Kurt's, too. He mumbles an awkward "Thanks" as he takes a water bottle from Tye and goes to sit on a picnic bench.

"Admiring the view?" I ask, sliding in to sit beside him. At Kurt's questioning look, I nod in Tye's direction. "He's cute. I can see the appeal."

Color floods Kurt's cheeks.

"Right," he says, and his tone causes my smile to shrink. Crap, is Kurt not out? Am I bulldozing in here all party streamers and heart-eye emojis when he's not ready to share that part of himself?

"Sorry," I say. "We don't have to talk about it. But I'm here if you want to."

He nods, gaze flicking back to Tye and hovering there. "Thanks. I'm sort of a dweeb about that stuff."

Such an adorable baby gay, Willow says.

I lean in to bump Kurt's shoulder and stage-whisper, "The good news is your taste is impeccable."

He laughs, and the sound causes my lungs to inflate. Nobody ever had the "gay talk" with me, and even if Kurt isn't ready to open up, I feel a mixture of excitement and pride that I could be there for him if he needed it.

Kurt picks up his guitar and starts to play a chill-out version of "Oops! . . . I Did It Again."

"Got anything stronger in there?" Juniper asks Tye, peering into the picnic basket.

"There's lime cordial," he says.

"Wild." Juniper takes a water and strolls away from the group.

"Where are you going?" Dani asks her.

"To cool off," Juniper calls over her shoulder as she strides toward the lake. Alone, again.

Suck it up, babe, Willow says. *Not everybody is as friendly as us.*

"Whaddya say to a game of Twenty-One?" Misty asks, tugging a deck of cards from her pocket. "Tye? You might have better luck this time."

My gaze snaps to Misty, her choice of words unsettling me.

Better luck next time, Willow whispers.

But Misty's focus is on Tye. I'm just being paranoid.

"I think I'll try corpse pose again on the beach," I say, hopping off the bench.

"You have to really commit," Dani says. "*Be* the corpse. Want company?"

I nod and say, "Sure," super casually. No big deal that she wants to hang out with me some more.

"Count me in for cards," Tye says to Misty, and we already no longer exist to her.

I give Kurt a *you got this* smile and then stroll down to the beach with Dani. Juniper is already in the water, cutting through it like a blade, and the breeze coming off the lake is refreshing. I savor it whispering across my skin, cooling the sweat that sticks my hatchet-job bangs to my forehead.

I sit on the sand and stare out at the lake. Dani drops down beside me, close enough that I smell her sun lotion. She reties her brown hair in a ponytail, then stretches out her legs and reclines, propped up on her elbows. Our sneakers rest only a couple of inches apart, and I can't tell if Dani sat this close to me on purpose, or if I'm just overthinking as usual.

"How's the book coming along?" I ask.

"I wrote three pages of quality bullshit last night. We're talking the good stuff. A-grade manure."

I'm about to tell her manure is good for some things when I notice a man standing by the clubhouse, to the side of the canteen. He's thin as wire, dark-haired, and wearing a white apron. He puts a cigarette to his mouth and puffs smoke.

"Who's that?" I ask.

Dani raises her hand to shield her eyes from the sun. "Chef Jeff," she says. "He's sort of a behind-the-scenes character, less commonly sighted than Bigfoot. That's probably the last time you'll see him."

I watch Chef Jeff stub out the cigarette and turn into the canteen, disappearing inside. I realize I tensed up at the sight of him. I've already become accustomed to the small number of people at Camp Castaway. Here's another person. Another person who could've knocked on my door or carved the *N* in the woods.

"How many staff are running this place?" I ask.

"As far as I know, it's just Bebe, Tye, and Chef Jeff. I think they keep it minimal, I guess because of..." She pauses and her eyes twinkle at me.

I'm pretty sure her sneaker has inched a little closer to mine, and my leg hums with awareness, wondering what it would feel like if her skin brushed mine.

"You know they call this place Camp Canceled?" Dani says.

"Canceled?" I say, and suddenly I'm not thinking about Dani's skin anymore. "As in 'your life is over you monster don't even try to apologize'?"

"Right. In a lot of ways, cancel culture could be seen as a force for good. It's held people accountable for their misconduct. But social media can get out of hand. Sometimes the punishment doesn't fit the crime. Apparently a lot of people who've endured that come here, I guess because of the whole no-phones thing." Dani raises her face to the sun and closes her eyes. "Except me. I just really need to write a book."

I look at Kurt and Misty at the picnic benches, thinking about Kurt's panic attack, and Buck saying, "Everybody here's trying to put *something* in their rearview mirror." Kat told me that she was desperate for a job because of some unspecified life event, and I'm sure I'd have heard any sort of gossip involving Juniper. *Ours! Weekly* would have gone front page.

Part of me wants to tell Dani everything—really put Castaway's judgment-free philosophy to the test. I want to word-vomit my story at her, tell her all about the past few weeks.

Dani's tone softens. "Sorry. I keep forgetting you're new. It's hashtag-no-filter around here. Everybody just sort of says what they're thinking."

Despite the butterflies dancing in my stomach, I say, "I like that—it's refreshing to be around other people who keep putting their foot in their mouth."

Dani cracks a mischievous grin, then opens her mouth and grabs her foot with both hands, attempting to push her sneaker toward her face. With a cry, she unbalances, rolling away from me on the sand. I laugh as she kicks up clumps trying to sit back up, and I take her hand to pull her upright. She rocks up, landing even closer to me than before, and her leg brushes mine. The sensation lights up my calf. Her skin is smooth and warm, and the heat creeps up my leg to fill the rest of me.

"My hero," Dani says, not letting go of my hand. Our faces are inches apart, and she's flushed, biting her lip, and how am I only just noticing how perfect her mouth is? We sit looking at each other, and my heart thumps so hard I feel it making the tips of my fingers throb. Fingers that are entwined with Dani's.

I should let go, but Dani isn't letting go either, and then her gaze drops to my own mouth, and I know that look.

A low chime sounds, and the moment breaks.

Dani blinks and releases my hand, shattering the spell.

We both turn to look at the clubhouse, where Bebe stands next to the gong that hangs by the door.

"Time for stone circle," she calls, and she strikes the gong again, the sound making the air vibrate, summoning us to her.

XIII

guess it all started when I got divorced," Misty says. She sits across from me, her face downturned, hands knotted in her lap.

It turns out that stone circle really is a circle, but it's a circle of chairs rather than rocks. We sit in a white-walled therapy room that could've been furnished by Laura Ashley. It contains a large monstera plant and a couple of framed watercolors. Voile floats at the French doors, and I can just make out the view, the boathouse sitting beside the lake, the sun angling across the treetops.

"This is a safe space," Bebe said before we began, speaking for my benefit as a group-therapy noob. "Anything goes. You are encouraged to speak up, without fear of hurting anybody's feelings."

The only person not present is Tye, who went to search for Buck. Kat's gaze constantly goes to the window as Misty speaks, as if she expects Buck to appear any second.

Sitting between Dani and Kurt, I try to focus on Misty's story, but I can't help feeling that the mahjong champ is enjoying the spotlight a little too much. I know a performer when I see one.

"I saw an ad for the game app Bingo XXL," Misty says, "and it looked fun, so I downloaded it on my phone. It was love at first play, y'know? It took my mind off the fact that I had no job, no man, no money. It filled all that dead time in my day, and oh my God, when I *won*, it was orgasmic."

She takes a breath. "I guess I knew it was a problem when I looked up from playing on my phone and it was three a.m., and I couldn't remember when I even started. It got worse from there. I'd spend every minute I had desperate to win, and I started paying for fresh content, more do-overs. I maxed out two credit cards and no bank would give me a third."

A black mascara tear tracks her cheek, and she rubs it away with the heel of her hand.

"It got sort of out of control. There's a lot of debt."

She looks smaller, somehow, sitting in this white room, talking about her problems, and I feel bad for assuming she was enjoying this.

I realize I've been too harsh toward Misty since the first night of campfire stories.

The one thing I'm not clear on is how gambling led to Misty being canceled, if that really is the reason she's here.

Maybe Dani was wrong about Camp C-word?

"Thank you for your honesty, Misty," Bebe says. "Would anybody else like to share?"

I can't help looking at Juniper. I know it's wrong of me to want to crack open her skull and paddle in her brain, but it's Juniper "Badass" Brown. I've dreamed of meeting her forever and it's a special kind of torture being this close and still knowing nothing about her.

"I just wanted to say that I get the phone obsession thing," Kurt says. "It's why I'm here. My folks said there was no way I could go more than a day without my cell, so I'm here proving them wrong. And so far, I'm loving it."

"That's wonderful, Kurt."

His cheeks have warmed, and he doesn't look at me. Is he purposefully avoiding my gaze? I can't help wondering if there's more to his stay here than he's letting on—something connected to his panic attack. Maybe he really is struggling with his sexuality. The thought brings me back to Brandon and everything he went through. I want to help Kurt. Make a difference.

"I can relate to things falling apart," Dani says. "I had a bad breakup last year. The relationship was toxic, but that didn't make ending it any easier. I had to move back in with my mom in her one-bedroom apartment. I slept on the couch, and she force-fed me jiaozi and bad advice for months. Things got dark." She shakes her head. "*I* got dark."

"Dark how?" Misty asks, and her question seems genuine rather than goading.

Dani's gaze flicks at me, and I see worry in her eyes.

"I had a lot of self-loathing," she says, "a lot of frustration and anger."

Hurt people hurt people, I think, and I feel for her. I see the reason why somebody might become hateful.

And I keep thinking about our moment on the beach. It's all I've thought about since the start of stone circle.

"We've all done things we regret," I say, and Dani looks at me. "You can't keep beating yourself up about it."

"Yeah," Kurt says. "If you keep that stuff locked up inside, it goes bad."

Dani nods. "If I had the chance again, I'd never move back home."

"You can never go home again," Juniper says, and everybody looks surprised that she's spoken.

"I tried, too," Juniper continues. "A relative got sick so I went home to care for them. It was weird being away from the industry, away from California. Everything was slower, quieter, and the illness was difficult to be around. I got real deep into some bad coping mechanisms."

I feel myself leaning forward, hanging on her words.

Mucho morbid, kid, Willow says, but I can't help it.

Juniper left Hollywood because a relative got sick? I can't tell if I'm upset for what she went through, or disappointed that the reason is so mundane. So real-life.

"Do you want to talk about any of those coping mechanisms?" Bebe asks.

Juniper's mouth crinkles. "Maybe another time."

Her gaze meets mine, and I give her a small smile. She winks.

Juniper Brown just winked at me.

"Anybody else?" Bebe asks.

"I'm worried about Buck," Kat says. "I took a look around the woods in case he got hurt. But there's nothing. And he's still not in his cabin."

"He probably found some magic mushrooms," Misty says. "Decided to have a party."

"He's clean." Kat looks pissed. "He wouldn't go off without telling somebody."

"I'm sure Tye is bringing him back to camp right now," Bebe says. Patient. Calm. Confident. Misty and Kurt both look up at the mention of Tye's name.

"What if something happened?" Kat says. "He could be hurt."

"I think that's unlikely. Please, try not to worry."

"It'll be dark soon." Kat's voice is tight. "And you heard how he was in the last stone circle. He's dealing with some stuff."

I see the worry in her eyes, and I wonder what Buck talked about. If that really is the reason for his disappearance.

Kat looks on the verge of tears. Bebe reaches out and takes her arm.

"Tye will find him," she says, and the finality in her tone tells us that the topic has been closed.

"Willow?" Bebe turns her attention to me. "Would you like to add anything before we finish up?"

Kat chews the insides of her cheeks, and it feels wrong to start talking about myself when she's clearly upset.

"I'm good," I say. "Settling in. Vibing. Camp's great so far."

Smooth, Willow says.

Bebe doesn't blink for a moment, but then she nods. Maybe she's disappointed I didn't share more, but I find I don't care. Kat's anxiety is plain to see. It causes a jab of unease in my own sternum.

What if she's right and something really did happen to Buck?

They're all lying.

I know.

They open their mouths and nothing but lies come out.

It makes me sick.

Be patient, their time is coming.

Soon they won't be able to open their mouths.
Soon they'll wish they'd never opened them at all.

XIV

Hey, who's your favorite artist?" Kurt asks me after stone circle. We're all heading back to our cabins for some pre-dinner downtime, and I found myself walking in step with Dani and Kurt.

I assume he means musical artist.

"I may be known to enjoy a Stevie Nicks track or two."

He nods, brow crinkled in thought.

"Cool, okay, good to know. Well, catch you at dinner." He waves and breaks off down the path to what I assume is his cabin.

"Mine's Christine and the Queens," Dani calls after him. "Thanks for asking." We keep walking, and she says, "He likes you. He hasn't smiled so much in days."

"He hasn't?"

"He was so serious when he first checked in. I think you worked some kind of magic. You're not a witch, are you?"

I don't say this out loud, but I actually did play a witch early in my career—there's a popular meme of me riding a broomstick while hurling jack-o'-lanterns at children.

"You found me out," I say, and I give my best cackle; the one that helped me beat Maya Hawke to the role. Dani stares at me in shock, then laughs.

"Good first circle, Willow," Juniper says. She strides past us, not walking fast, but Juniper's pace is twice the speed of a mortal's.

"Oh thanks," I say. Of course, Juniper Brown speaks to me when I'm acting like a witch.

"Nice cackle, too," she says. "Convincing."

I open my mouth to reply but Juniper is already striding off. I'm not sure which cabin is hers. She seems to be heading out past the last hut on the left, farther into the woods.

I find myself alone with Dani outside my door. She didn't split off to go to her own place but ended up following me back to mine. I can't tell if it was intentional or not, but something feels different after stone circle. There's an air of anticipation. She seems to have something on her mind.

I stand with my back to the door, and she faces me, the forest behind her.

"Group felt good," I tell her. "Really good."

"Yeah," Dani says. "This thing you've got going on right now, it looks good on you."

My lungs inflate. "Did you just tell me I look good?"

She laughs, but in a way that feels serious. "Yeah, I did."

Her gaze keeps returning to my cabin door, and I've got the full-body shakes. She thinks I look good. Like *this*? With my bangs and Clark Kent glasses and ball cap?

Invite her in, Willow says.

Somehow, I manage to open my mouth to speak.

"Want to come in?"

"Sure."

We go inside, and I scan the living room to make sure I haven't left it in disarray. I don't want Dani thinking I live like Oscar the Grouch. Luckily, I haven't been here long enough to trash the place.

"Can I get you anything?" I ask, going into the kitchenette and opening and shutting cupboards, trying to remember where the glass tumblers are kept. My mind has gone blank. It's both racing and flatlining.

"What do you have?" Dani asks.

I finally locate a glass and set it on the counter. I put my hand on my hip, then take it off. Why can't I remember how to stand? Or where to look when you're talking to somebody? My gaze keeps going from Dani to the couch, to my bedroom door, to the glass tumbler. I'm aware that it's just me and Dani in the cabin, and the place is so quiet, my ears ring.

"I've got water fresh from the faucet," I say. "It's a pretty exclusive menu."

"Thanks, I think I'm all watered out."

I leave the tumbler where it is and come around the kitchen counter, clasping my hands together in front of me. Is this how I usually stand? My glasses keep sliding down my nose. I push them back up as Dani looks around the place, taking it in, and I look at Dani, taking her in.

I'm suddenly aware of her lips again. Not plump or pouty or flawless, but modestly, unassumingly elegant. Her hair is big, like eighties big, which I love, and her eyes are dark but warm. And now I'm back at her lips again, and I think I'll die if I don't find out what they feel like.

In the real world, I'd never move this fast. But time moves differently here. After three weeks of feeling like the worst piece of shit, I'm craving something, anything, to make me feel good. I get the feeling that kissing Dani would make me feel *very* good.

She looks at me, and her mouth curls at the corner, and I stop resisting.

I step forward and I kiss her.

I actually kiss her.

And she kisses me back.

Her mouth is firm and warm. I taste peppermint with a hint of lip gloss, and my mind stops whirring like a washing machine. Calm floods my system. In this moment, I'm not Willow. I'm not anybody. I am want and flesh and need.

Kissing Dani feels like the best, most natural thing in the world.

We break apart, catching our breath, and Dani's eyes glitter like opals.

"Sorry," I say.

"Never apologize for a kiss like that." Her tone softens, but then her fingers brush the engagement ring, and the sight of it repulses me more than ever. The metal cuts into my flesh like a toothless fish mouth, and I know it's time.

I need this thing off me.

I grip it between my fingers and twist, loosening it up, then attempting to pry it off. It catches on my knuckle, won't go past the bone, and I grit my teeth, twisting harder, straining to ease it free. Finally, it relents. Comes off.

With a sigh, I hold it up.

"I'm guessing the engagement's off?" Dani says.

"It has been for a while. I just didn't know how to deal with that."

She smiles and pulls me into another kiss. It's less hesitant than the first. Slower. More certain. I find her rhythm and I press my hand to her hip, feeling her heat. It seeps through my palm and into my arm, lighting me up.

"First full day at camp," Dani says when we pull apart, "and you're making out with the hottest resident. Good work."

I laugh.

"What are you going to do with it?" Dani asks.

I'd already forgotten about the ring. I lift it up and the diamond catches the light, large and heavy, and so completely not me. It was bought by a guy who had no idea who I was.

(For the record, I'll buy my own ring if I ever get engaged again, and the stone will be in the shape of a skull.)

There are plenty of things I could do with the ring to be rid of it.

I could pawn it.

Give it away.

But what I really want is to bury it.

I want it gone. Forgotten. Erased from this earth.

"One sec," I say, and I go into the bedroom. I move fast, propelled by the need to get back to Dani. I want to stay in this moment, this spell. I grab my makeup bag and put the ring inside. It'll do for now.

I massage the strip of skin on my finger where the ring used to be. The flesh is worn smooth, even though I only wore the ring for three months.

This place is already changing things. Light has poured into the corners of my life, pushing back the shadows, exposing kernels of possibility that I had forgotten existed.

I have no job and no home, but also no responsibilities. Nobody to answer to.

I'm free.

Something unlatches in my chest, like an old rotary phone being taken off the hook, and I hear the sound my pulse makes.

The quick beat of hope.

Actual hope for the future.

A sound disturbs the still of the bedroom. A creak of wood from the other side of the room.

I turn, expecting to find Dani in the doorway. My smile fades when I see that it is vacant.

My gaze goes to the closet. Maybe it was the hangers on the rail again.

But then I hear the sound a second time. Not hangers, but wood warping under pressure, as if weight has been applied to a floorboard.

I take a few steps toward the closet, wondering if an animal got into the cabin. A squirrel or a mouse. Maybe the doors blew shut on it, trapping it inside.

I stop half a meter away, listening.

There's a two-inch gap between the doors and, through it, a glistening white eyeball stares out at me.

My heart convulses, a cry hitching in my throat. I stagger backward as an emaciated figure bursts out of the closet. Greasy silver hair conceals their face, and they wear a nightgown, sleeves tugged up to reveal yellow skin.

The woman is on me before I have a chance to register the attack.

Her fingernails sink into my shoulders and my legs go out from under me. My back hits the floor, forcing breath from my lungs.

The woman's thighs clamp around my hips, and her fingers are claws, filthy nails twisting the neck of my hoodie as her face presses close to mine.

"Leave!" she hisses, and her breath is like week-old meat. "Leave now! She knows you're here!"

One of the most curious legends of the area is that of Knock-Knock Nancy, the tragic, headless woman who was killed by a vengeful preacher, and whose ghost still knocks on doors at night looking for her head. Some say the legend is a clear mutation of the famous Sleepy Hollow story by Washington Irving. However, we've discovered new information that could shed some light on the true origin of Knock-Knock Nancy. Stick around, listeners, because this is about to get very strange and, yes, very, very unusual . . .

stare up into the woman's face, the hollow cheeks and huge gray eyes, and fear pops in my mind.

"I—can't—" I grunt, unsure what I'm trying to say, but still struggling beneath her. The woman is strong. Her grip is iron cast.

"She's coming," she hisses. "She's coming for you all. She wants your—"

"Hey!"

Dani appears in the doorway, shock registering on her face when she sees me on the floor. The woman's head turns, silver hair fanning out. I smell mulched leaves and ripe sweat. And then the woman is off me, lurching for the door, shoving Dani aside and racing out of the cabin. The last thing I see before she vanishes into the woods are her bare heels flashing white in the evening gloom.

"Are you okay?" Dani asks, helping me stand. "What happened? Where'd she come from?"

"Closet," I wheeze, still catching my breath. Adrenaline spikes my system, urging me to run. Get out of here.

"Jesus, she was hiding in the closet?" Dani's arms are around me, but they don't help. They feel suffocating after the woman. I can't stop shaking.

"Hey, it's okay," Dani says. "She's gone now. It's okay."

I flinch as another figure runs into the cabin, boots striking the floor as they enter. Bebe stops in the bedroom door, tall and broad and panting.

"What's going on?" she asks. "I heard yelling."

I can't find my voice, and my ears ring as the truth hits me full in the face.

"They found me," I say.

You're going to beg to die.

See you soon, Red. 😊

The past three weeks return in screaming Technicolor. The threats. The hate. The demand for blood.

I tried to disappear, but they found me anyway.

"Who found you?" Dani asks.

"I have to get out of here," I say.

I grab my suitcase from the floor, throwing it onto the bed and going to the closet. I stare at the clothes on hangers, knowing they've been touched by my attacker, and I grimace as I grab a handful of shirts and tops, dragging them over to the bed.

"Willow, stop," Bebe says.

"They said they'd kill—" I break off. Swallow. Reach for air. "I have to leave. I have to get out of here right now."

"Willow," Bebe says again, softly, and her composure forces me to stop and look at her. How is she so calm when the camp has been breached by an outsider? She should be dispatching somebody to look for the woman, notifying the cops, warning the other campers.

"That was my sister," Bebe says, and it takes me a moment to hear what she's saying.

I stop moving, clutching hold of a shirt, full of uncertainty.

"Your sister?"

Bebe nods, face serious. Behind her, Dani stares at the back of her head with the same surprise I feel.

"I saw her running from your cabin," Bebe says. "I'm sorry she came in here. Are you okay?"

I can't think. The woman hiding in my closet was Bebe's sister?

Shock ruptures into anger.

"What the hell was she doing in my room?" I demand.

Bebe's gaze is apologetic. Entreating.

"Sadie lives with me on-site. She's not supposed to come into the camp, and for the most part she doesn't. But sometimes she gets confused and goes wandering. I'm sorry she scared you."

My grip tightens on the shirt. My brain is still firing *get out of here* signals, and the fear that a text stalker infiltrated the camp—*found me*—still feels real.

"Jesus," Dani says.

"Are you okay?" Bebe asks me again, and I can't help snapping back at her.

"I'd be better if somebody didn't just attack me in my own goddamn bedroom."

Her eyes are wide, her jaw tense, and I see the likeness there. They really are sisters.

Bebe and Sadie. They even *sound* like a pair.

As my pulse begins to settle, I know I'm not angry at Bebe. I'm angry at everything and everybody who made me feel unsafe. Everybody who made me feel like my life was going to end abruptly and violently—and soon.

This place was meant to be my escape, and for the briefest moment, it had felt like it would be.

"What did she say to you?" Dani asks.

Bebe frowns. "She spoke?"

I hear the woman's voice again, a rasp like torn paper.

Leave now! She knows you're here!

Something stops me from repeating Sadie's words.

"She seemed upset," I say.

"Please believe me when I tell you that she's harmless," Bebe says. "I'll make sure it doesn't happen again."

Harmless. My bruised butt isn't so sure. But now that the adrenaline is draining away, I feel more rational. Embarrassed by my reaction. Apparently melodrama isn't just in Hollywood. The last of the anger fades, and the full-body trembles suddenly seem funny.

"I thought this place was meant to be relaxing," I quip, dumping the shirt on the bed, feeling Willow return. I'm not the trash-fire actor who fled L.A. I'm Willow. Bright. Perky. Unflappable.

Dani's mouth quirks. "Yeah, way to keep us on our toes, Bebe."

I'm so glad Dani's here. Glad she chased Sadie away.

Bebe doesn't look amused. She is solemn as she says, "I would appreciate if this stayed between us. There's no point worrying the other campers about Sadie."

I begin to nod, but then I see Sadie's wild eyes and I feel her pinching grip on my arms.

Is she really harmless?

If I refused to keep quiet, would Bebe ask me to leave?

The thought of being ejected from the camp, being forced to return to the real world, makes the bottom drop out of my stomach, and I realize I'd do anything not to have that happen. I want to get back to the simplicity of camp life. My lips prickle at the memory of Dani's kiss, and I see Kurt smiling as he plays guitar, Juniper complimenting my cackle . . .

If keeping Bebe's secret is the way I get to have all that for a little while longer, so be it.

"Of course," I say, and Bebe's face smooths, her shoulders lowering.

As we leave the cabin together for dinner, though, I remember the flash of silver hair I saw outside Buck's cabin when me and Kat were looking for him. I remember the knock at my cabin door my first night here, and a question buds in my mind like a fragile forest flower.

What if there's something to the legend of Knock-Knock Nancy, after all?

It's dark when I get back to the cabin at the end of the night. Dani had offered to come inside with me, and even though the memory of Sadie is still bright in my mind, I said no, because I know that if me and Dani are alone again, I won't be able to control myself. I'm good with kissing somebody after knowing them a day, but I don't want to move too fast.

We spent the evening listening to Kurt play guitar. He sang a soulful version of "Outside the Rain" by Stevie Nicks, and even though he didn't state it outright, I knew he'd played it for me. It was the reason he'd asked who my favorite artist was.

Afterward, Tye brought out a Jenga Giant set. Everybody attempted to psych everybody else out whenever they were removing a block. I fake-tripped near the tower while Tye was playing, which made everybody gasp, then groan. Kurt then fake-tripped while I was playing, which turned into an actual trip, and he bulldozed the tower like a gawky twenty-something Godzilla. His horrified expression as I pulled him upright again made me laugh so hard, I almost peed my pants.

While I change into my pajamas in the bedroom, I feel a smile on my face thinking about Kurt's laugh, and Dani's warm, glittering gaze.

I've never had anything close to a girlfriend, and it's not because I didn't want one. I dated when I first moved to L.A., before the fame game started playing its hand, but whenever I got close to a woman, if there were hints that things were getting serious, I'd see Grams's frown and hear her whispering the Hail Mary. I ended every single nascent relationship.

I hate Grams for being able to influence my life even from afar, but I hate myself more for letting her.

For the first time in forever, though, I'm able to be me. Maybe I don't need Willow anymore.

Willow says, *You'll always need me.*

In the bedroom, I start to unpack again. My clothes are still stuffed haphazardly in the carryall, and I tug out crumpled shirts and dresses, hanging them up in the closet, trying not to think about Sadie's eyeball watching me from the dark.

The only dampener on this evening was Kat, who stared into the campfire while Kurt played, looking lost, confused, and angry. Tye didn't find Buck earlier, and he went back out again with a lantern after dinner, refusing Kat's offer of help.

I feel Kat's worry. It is unsettling that Buck's just up and vanished, but we have to believe that Tye will bring him safely back. The alternative—that Buck is hurt or lost—doesn't feel possible. Not in this little corner of paradise.

As I hang a sweater, I notice a piece of paper on the closet floor. It lies facedown, scuffed, and ragged.

I pick it up and turn it over, seeing that it's a police report.

My surprise turns to interest as I read words printed in faded ink, which detail the arrest of a man named Caleb Mayhew in Illinois. According to the report, Caleb attacked a man in the street last March and was arrested by two attending officers.

I turn over the document, looking for something that might tell me why it was in my closet, but there are no annotations or scribbles in the margins—nothing other than the report itself. And there are no other documents in the closet. The floor is bare, aside from my flip-flops and sneakers.

Did Sadie leave the report there? Did she drop it by accident? Where did she even get it? We're miles from Illinois. Unless . . .

Is this about a camper? Is Caleb the real name of one of the residents?

There are no other distinguishing details in the report. Nothing that might link Caleb to one of us.

I remember the envelope of papers I handed to Tye at check-in: the waivers, in-case-of-emergency numbers, and personal information. Were residents with a criminal record requested to share their history with the camp?

Or Caleb could be somebody who works here. Tye? Chef Jeff?

Holding the report makes me uneasy—it's private, something I should never have seen—so I stow it in the nightstand and climb into bed. I drag my carryall to me and reach into the pocket for the photo of Brandon. It's not there, so I search the rest of the bag, in case it fell out.

But the photo isn't in the carryall.

Maybe I dropped it on the floor when I was panic-packing?

I look under the bed, and then I tear off the bedsheets in case the photo slipped between them. With growing desperation, I move the nightstand to look underneath, then go over every inch of the closet and behind the curtains, but it's no good.

The photo isn't in the bedroom.

It's gone.

Brandon is gone.

INFORMATION ABOUT PERSON INVOLVED IN THE INCIDENT

Full Name: Caleb Mayhew
Home Address: 600 Myer Street, Chicago, IL

INFORMATION ABOUT THE INCIDENT

Date of Incident: 3/20/23
Time: 2:35 a.m.
Location of Incident: Miss Hellfire nightclub
Description of Incident: Officers Miller and Gordon attended the scene of an assault on Shivers Street, outside the premises of Miss Hellfire nightclub. The victim was unconscious with visible trauma to the face and head in the form of cuts, bruises, and swelling. CALEB MAYHEW resisted arrest and refused a toxicology test. He sang loudly, visibly inebriated and suspected to be under the influence of drugs. He claimed that the victim insulted him as he was attempting to leave the premises. Official questioning to follow.

KAT

The woods were dark, but Kat had never been afraid of the dark. She had her four brothers to thank for that. Years of sneak attacks and wet willies, of being bundled into closets and tool sheds, being told she had to prove she wasn't a "lame little girlie girl." It hardened her, kept her alert. She could smell danger, like one of those comically macho generals in the movies they all watched growing up.

That was how she knew Buck was in trouble.

And nobody was taking her seriously.

She didn't knock at the door of Buck's cabin, instead letting herself in quietly like a considerate roommate who had been out late with work friends. She'd waited until she was certain everybody else was in bed. Through a gap in her curtain, she watched Dani say good night to Willow, and Kurt and Misty go into their cabins. She heard Bebe and Tye talking, their lanterns bobbing outside Kat's window, then vanishing into the night. When she was sure everybody had turned in, she slipped out of her cabin and went into Buck's.

Standing inside the door, she listened for a second, hoping for the sound of snoring from the bedroom or the spark of a cigarette being lit on the patio.

All she heard was the steady tick of her pulse.

She left the door open an inch and walked into the living room.

Even in the dark, she could tell the place was a sty. Pants and

T-shirts sagged over chair backs and pooled on the floor, as if their wearer had spontaneously dematerialized.

Jesus, "dematerialized."

Her Trekkie co-workers had really rubbed off on her.

She stepped on something that squelched and saw that it was a plate of food that Buck must have snuck from the canteen.

"Nice crib, pal," Kat said under her breath, and hearing her voice made her newly aware of what she was doing. She wouldn't break into just anybody's cabin. She'd perfected the art of apathy. People found her too hard. Too weird. Too difficult to predict. She smoked and drank and had opinions, preferring to hang out with guys. In Gardendale, Alabama, that made her Strange.

But Buck liked Strange. He was Strange, too.

He'd become her first genuine friend in years.

And if he'd gone and done something stupid like getting bit by a snake and dying in the woods, she'd be pissed.

She checked the bedroom, the closet, the cupboards in the living room, and down the back of the sofa for good measure, and then Kat stood in the dark and felt angry at herself. What had she hoped to find, anyway? A goodbye note? A sign saying *HE WENT THAT WAY?*

She rolled her eyes, and then straightened as she spotted something above her.

A gray square in the ceiling.

A hatch.

Did these places have attic storage?

She'd never noticed a door in her own identical living room ceiling, but then she didn't spend much time in her cabin. She hated being alone. Another thing to thank her brothers for. She hated being alone, but she never felt heard when she was with them.

It was one of the reasons she'd become a content creator. She had spent her whole life being shouted down and talked over, as if she didn't have her own thoughts and opinions. Her BookTok channel, Read with Lulu, finally gave her a voice. She delved into overlooked modern classics like *The Bone Diamond* by T. R. Bay and *Shriekmeister* by Prunella Frost. Her video essays ranged in topic from literary urban legends to the best unsung book editors. And the great thing was, people actually wanted to hear what she had to say. She gained a following. Created a community.

Then Roxanne Fisher came along and ruined everything.

Roxanne had her own channel, RoxPop, in which she took a scalpel to the book industry, peeling back the epidermis to reveal the fascinating stories beneath. Kat had watched her TikToks and found them interesting, if a little aggressive.

And then Rox started commenting on Kat's videos. Challenging her opinion, sometimes outright telling her she was wrong. And Kat wasn't going to be shouted down again. She wouldn't be silenced the way she had been her entire life, so she bit back.

Hard.

Kat went outside and dragged in a chair from the patio, positioning it under the hatch. She stepped up and reached for the little clasp. Her fingertips grazed the metal, barely kissing the rusted lock, and the door fell open. She flinched back, half expecting something to fall out, or a rabid squirrel to launch at her face.

Instead, an object poked through. The bottom of a ladder.

Kat ignored the heavy feeling that had settled in her gut, knew it was just the lizard part of her brain sounding a warning. She hopped on the spot, jumping high enough to grab the lowermost rung and haul the ladder down.

"If you got yourself stuck up there," she told Buck as she tested the ladder, "I should really just leave your moron ass."

She started to climb.

She only paused at the top because she was still waiting for a squirrel or a rat to leap at her head. The dark she could handle, but rodents had disease. They had teeth.

"Quit bellyaching," she muttered, and stepped up so that she was a full head and shoulders inside the storage space.

It was cramped, the roof low. She'd have to crouch if she went any farther.

She remained on the ladder and felt along the boards, brushing something that moved. Paper. As her eyes adjusted to the gloom, she saw that paper was strewn all over the floor. They looked like official documents, but she couldn't make out what for.

Amid the paper rested dozens of small objects.

Heads.

Baby heads.

More doll's heads, Kat realized.

"What the fuck?" she murmured.

Some were missing eyes; others had their hair shorn off to leave porcupine tufts. The head nearest to her lay on its side, staring up at Kat with eyes that were so human, she felt a chill. It seemed to be both pleading with her and condemning her.

It was like it knew.

It knew what had sent her here.

It knew that Kat had her stomach pumped a month ago, after her brother found her unconscious on the couch with an empty bottle of pills.

Kat felt like a failure. She'd tried to fight Rox. She challenged every one of her snide comments, but Rox just kept coming at her. And when Rox ran out of real ammo, she started making things up. She accused Kat of plagiarism. Of filming while on drugs. Of bullying other BookTokers. She tore Kat down in every way she could think of, and the worst part was that everybody believed her.

Kat found herself canceled for things she hadn't even done. The

BookTok community turned against her, and Kat was forced to shut down the channel. As quickly as she'd found her voice, it was taken away again.

A week later, after a night of drinking, she picked up a bottle of pills and made the worst decision of her life.

She wished she could take it back. She hadn't meant it to go so far. All she'd wanted was for Rox to back the hell off. But the pills made everything worse. Her family staged an intervention, and now here she was, phoneless, directionless, and now, apparently, friendless to boot.

The one comfort she'd had was Buck. When she came to camp, she told Buck her story, and he understood. She'd thought she had a life-long friend in him—somebody in the real world who got her the way her followers had, before the channel got shut down.

But now Buck was gone, too.

Kat surveyed the sea of heads, looking—

—something grabbed her legs.

Swept them out from under her.

Kat cried out as she fell.

She tried to grab hold of the ladder as it rushed past, but her hands were too slow, hitting every rung without catching hold.

She struck the floor and all her weight landed on her right foot. Her leg made a crunching sound and she saw red stars, followed by pain so sharp it shredded her lungs, made it impossible for her to scream.

It took her a moment to realize she was on the floor, sitting upright somehow, cradling her broken leg. She sensed a figure moving in the darkness. Sensed, because her vision was edged in black. She was peering through a pinhole.

She looked up to find a person hovering over her. Long silver hair gleamed in the moonlight, and the face was distorted with a sorrowful expression, the eyes black as midnight.

An object flashed in the gloom.

Kat recognized the shape of a rusty ax lifting into the air, and a desperate need to move flooded through her.

As she shifted on the floor, though, pain detonated a bomb in her broken leg. She went rigid, opened her mouth to draw breath, but then the white-haired figure had already swung, and an icicle ran across Kat's neck. Freezing cold. Bitter as starlight.

It was raining now. She felt the patter of something hitting the boards around her.

And Kat went silent as tiny plastic heads rained from the ceiling.

Did you get her?

Yes.

Good. That's very good.

Do you think it hurt? Do you think she hurt?

Yes, I think she hurt a lot.

Please . . . I don't want to hurt anybody.

Well, if you don't love me

No! I do! I'm sorry. I love you so much.

Then make them pay. They have to pay, my love.

I know. I'm sorry.

I love you. I'll do whatever you want.

XVII

I t's raining.

The soft patter fills the camp as we stand on the beach for afternoon affirmations, and the air feels expectant. Waiting for thunder.

The morning was taken up by swimming, archery, and forest bathing, a full-on itinerary that failed to distract me from thoughts of the missing photo. Before our swim, I turned the cabin upside down looking for the picture of Bran, but it was nowhere to be found. I stood by the upturned sofa, breathing hard, trying to keep hold of the calm of Camp Castaway, but it slithered through my fingers like ribbon.

I need Bran. It's not just a picture. It's a reminder of the way my brother looked at me—the way he *saw* me. We understood each other without the need for words.

My unease only grew when my search uncovered something else in the cabin. It was under the sofa, pale and round, its plastic, fish-pale skin peeling, the eyes missing.

Another doll's head. A tortured thing, ravaged and worn; its mouth open in a silent wail. Holding it made my skin crawl, and I trembled as I tugged a rolled-up piece of paper from inside the head. A note, written in shaky black crayon.

GIVE HER YOUR HEAD.

"Isn't the rain invigorating?" Bebe says, looking at us each in turn as we stand on the beach. "It washes away everything that has come before, allows us to start fresh."

Standing between Dani and Kurt, I stare out at the lake, which shudders under the drizzle. If I look at Bebe, she'll see the confusion and anger in my eyes. She promised that Sadie wouldn't come into my cabin again, but she failed to mention that her sister was also a kleptomaniac.

It's the only explanation for the missing photo, and I still haven't figured out how I'm going to get it back.

"Where's Tye?" Misty asks, her curls twice as big in the rain.

"He went to encourage Buck and Kat to join in with afternoon activities," Bebe says. "Now, who wants to start off our affirmations?"

"Did Buck come back?" I ask.

Buck, Kat, and Tye have been absent all day. It can't be usual for campers to disappear like this. Bebe avoided the question all morning, though, merely saying that Buck and Kat had "opted not to take part in the activities."

It's difficult to believe her. First Buck went missing, and now Kat's absent, too. My worry has sharpened to a needle point. I try to dull it, but Camp Castaway is starting to feel off. My fear that first night at being so far from civilization almost seems justified. And Bebe's refusal to share what she knows has me scrutinizing her every gesture, suspicion gathering like smoke in my lungs.

"I'm sure Buck will be right along," Bebe says.

"That wasn't an answer," Misty says.

"Where is he?" I ask.

Bebe's expression gives nothing away. "They'll join us soon. Now, let's complete our affirmations."

The muscles in my neck tighten. I'm newly aware of the rain seeping into my skin. The other campers seem to share my unease, their expressions grim. Or maybe they just want to get out of the rain, too.

And I can't stop thinking about the doll's head under the sofa, the *N* in the woods, and Sadie's steely grip on my arms.

She knows you're here!

Has Sadie been taken in by the Knock-Knock Nancy myth, too? How does a made-up story have so much power over so many people?

"Willow," Bebe says, "the floor is yours if you'd like to go first."

I force myself to look at her. Her calm expression rankles me more than it did yesterday when her sister had just invaded my cabin. I'm not going to let her intimidate me—or keep lying to us. I feel bolder than during yesterday's affirmation.

"I'm starting to feel the magic of this place," I say. "I'm seeing things differently now. I'm not going to take anymore bullshit. I'm done running."

Bebe's left eye twitches so subtly, you'd miss it if you weren't intently watching her. I can't tell if she's unsettled by my words, or if that's respect in her pursed lips. Maybe fear? Her eyes are as gray as the lake.

"Welcome to camp, kid," Juniper says. "Glad you finally made it."

She gives me a side-eye smile, and my chest swells with glee.

I barely hear the others giving their affirmations, vaguely catching Misty say something about trying harder to let out her inner goddess.

When we're done, Bebe strikes the gong. At the same moment, the sun punches a hole in the clouds, and a bright beam of light hits the lake. The timing is so perfect, I almost wonder if there really is magic here. Something wild and unpredictable, like the ghost of Knock-Knock Nancy.

We disband. Juniper, Misty, and Kurt head toward the canteen for afternoon snacks, but I hang back when I see Bebe walking along the beach to the spot where the sand meets the boardwalk. I'm intrigued by her hurried pace, and then I see that Tye has appeared at the tree line, face somber. He wears blue sweatpants and a hoodie with the hood up. Despite going to fetch Buck and Kat, he's alone.

Bebe speaks, and Tye shakes his head. No.

No what?

No Kat? And no Buck?

They're *both* missing?

Bebe bows her head. Her fist hits her thigh once, twice, three times. The sight causes that needle point of worry to dig into my temple.

"Hey, Willow, are you coming?" Kurt asks.

He's stopped at the edge of the beach. Dani is still by my side, giving me a questioning look.

"I'll catch up," I tell Kurt.

He hesitates, then jogs to join Misty and Juniper.

"What's up?" Dani asks me. "Everything okay?"

"Look at them," I say.

Bebe and Tye exchange a few more words, and then Tye turns and vanishes down the boardwalk. Bebe doesn't notice me and Dani watching her. She seems preoccupied as she hurries for the clubhouse, and it's clear she's not going to tell us what's going on. Well, if she can keep secrets, there's no reason I can't break a few rules myself to get back the photo of Bran.

"I'm going to find Sadie," I tell Dani.

"The sister?"

"She took something from my room. Something sentimental."

"And you don't want to tell Bebe," Dani observes.

"Something's going on that they don't want us to know about," I say. "I think Buck's still missing. And now Kat, too."

"Kat?"

"Tye didn't bring her to affirmations," I say. "And you saw Bebe just now. She's being super shady about Buck."

Dani's eyes widen. I see her mind working and I wonder if she's struggling with the same questions that have started to circle in my mind.

Finally, Dani speaks.

"If it helps," she says, "I know where Bebe's place is."

For what feels like the first time today, I smile.

XVIII

How exactly do you know where Bebe lives?" I ask as we stride down the boardwalk. Rain drums at the trees, less intense under cover, and the afternoon is changing, becoming less brooding. Light filters in through the forest canopy, running fingers through the air that seem to urge me forward. If something is going on at Camp Castaway, I'm going to find out what.

I realize that's the real me talking, not Willow. If the sitcom version of Willow McKenzie ever found herself in this situation, she'd bumble around camp for a while before getting distracted by a forest creature.

But forest creatures are so cuuute, Willow says.

Something has shifted. I'm Willow but not Willow. A Willow in flux.

"I've been putting a file together on Bebe for the past ten days," Dani says in answer to my question.

I raise an eyebrow at her, and she laughs.

"All right, I stumbled across her place when I was jogging a few days ago." After a second, she adds, "What did Sadie take from your cabin?"

A tremor runs through me.

"It's a photo of my brother," I say.

Dani doesn't respond, but her silence is, in its own way, encouraging.

"It's the only picture I have of him without my phone," I say. "It's sort of a comfort blanket."

Dani nods, thinking.

"You're really close to your brother?" she asks.

"I was."

"Oh."

There's a moment of silence.

This is where you say more, Willow says. *It's called a conversation.*

I realize just how much Dani doesn't know, and the thought paralyzes me.

"What was he like?" Dani asks.

I push through the freeze.

"He was quiet, but fun. And smart. Scary smart. He loved horror movies. We both hated it in Iowa. Neither of us felt like we belonged there, we just never seemed to fit in. And our Grams was strict. She dominated my grandpa, and she was super conservative. One time she made me wash my mouth out with lavender soap because I said 'Jesus Christ' when I meant 'shit.' And parties? I might as well have said I wanted to go to the Met Gala."

"She sounds like a hoot," Dani says, tone somber.

"Yeah. After Brandon died, I moved back to L.A. I was eighteen, and I thought it would be better there, being back where our parents raised us. In some ways, it was better, but also not. It felt like, in L.A., everybody was either buying or selling something twenty-four-seven, and people spent most of their time arguing over the price."

Dani smiles that rock-star smile. "Well, I like you whatever it is you're selling."

"Thanks."

I feel her hand in mine, and she gives me a timid look, as if she's worried I'm going to flee in the opposite direction.

So I kiss her, because I want her to know that I talked about Grams for her. And I know what I want.

We keep walking, and Dani says softly, "What happened to your brother?"

I should have anticipated the question, but it still lodges in my chest like a spike.

"Grams tried everything to change Bran after she found out he was gay. She took him to church with her, made him pray with her every morning and night. She even set up dates with her friends' granddaughters." I emit a bitter laugh. "Brandon got depressed. He started to believe there really was something wrong with him."

I feel Dani's gaze on me. I swallow. "A few weeks after he turned seventeen, Grams saw him with a boy. Bran was walking down the street with one of his classmates, and they were laughing. That was all. They weren't touching. Just laughing. But she lost it. She decided to send him to a camp in North Carolina that was meant to help him see the light, 'pray away the gay.'"

I bow my head, scuff the dirt with my sneaker.

"I tried to stop him from going. I told him we could run away together. But Bran didn't want any more drama. He just wanted everybody to be happy. That's the kind of person he was. I remember, we were in his room, bags packed on his bed, and I begged him to run away with me. He said no, and he was so calm, but I . . . I fell apart."

I wipe my cheek. "He was going to a 'conversion' camp, but I was the one who broke down. He put his arms around me and told me everything would be okay, and I realized he was stronger than I imagined. So I stood on the doorstep with Grandpa, and I watched Grams drive Bran away in her beat-up Subaru. He smiled the whole time. This awful smile, like he knew he'd never see me again."

The air has thinned. I push on, even though the spike in my chest is agony.

"He went to that place," I say, "and a week later, he hanged himself."

Dani's eyes are wide with shock.

My throat stings. I haven't told anybody about Bran in years, and going back there, even in my mind, leaves my limbs feeling heavy, weighed down by grief.

"Your poor brother," Dani says.

I keep seeing him. The smile. The fear.

"Parents fuck you up," Dani says. "My dad bailed on me and my mom when I was five. I idolized him for the longest time, and then I found him out in Sacramento, running a car dealership. He pretended he was somebody else. Lied to my face."

"That's awful," I say.

"It's his loss." She shifts her gaze to look at me. "Is this your first time at a summer camp since your brother?"

I nod. "I figured it might help me lay some ghosts to rest." She looks so somber, I feel the need to lighten the mood. "You know, detox *and* get over your dead brother, the holistic twofer."

Dani smiles, and she moves forward to kiss me. I kiss her back, let her fold around me.

"Thank you for telling me," Dani says. "Listen, Willow, you should—"

She breaks off, looks around us. I hear it, too. A rustling, like the underbrush being disturbed.

"What was that?" I whisper, then I hear another sound, this one loud and unmistakable.

A sneeze.

My shoulders relax. "Kurt?" I call.

A head wearing a baseball cap pops out from behind a tree.

"Damn allergies," Kurt says, coming toward us, looking sheepish. He's wearing a Chili Peppers T-shirt and jeans.

"Are you following us?" Dani asks.

He shrugs. "I was walking in that general direction."

"Which direction?" I ask.

His cheeks dimple. "Whichever way you're going?"

I can't help smiling. We both know he's lying, and I could get annoyed that he gate-crashed our little mission, but his appearance has banished the gloom that settled on the forest. It's impossible for me to be irritated.

"We're sacrificing virgins in the woods," I say. "Want to join?"

"Good one," he says, and though he's smiling, it's clear he's not going to let us off the hook. I decide that telling the truth will be easier.

"Bebe lives out here with her sister, and she has something of mine. She took it from my cabin last night, so I'm going to get it back."

Kurt's eyebrows go up, and he looks from Dani to me. When neither of us laughs, he says, "Okay, so what are we waiting for?"

We continue through the woods.

"You're quite something on that guitar," I tell Kurt.

"Naw, mostly I'm just noodling."

"Take the compliment," Dani says. "You're good. Where'd you learn?"

"My sister taught me. She's the music whiz in the family."

"She's a musician, too?" I ask.

Kurt nods. "She's in Chicago. She performs in clubs and bars, and she supports bands when they come to town. She was the warm-up act for Rosewater last year."

"No shit!" I say.

Then I pause on what Kurt just said—that his sister is in Chicago.

The report about the assault outside the nightclub was from the Illinois State Police. Is Kurt really Caleb?

Dani cuts off my train of thought by coming to a standstill, making us all stop.

"There it is," she says.

We stand fifty yards from a house that is larger than the residents' lodgings. Older, too, by a good decade. The door has a porch and there are three peaked roofs and a chimney. The windows are dark, the netting pulled closed. It looks like it's been here for years, and if I squint at the space above the front door, I can make out a discoloration of the wood where an object once hung. A cross.

A shiver snakes up my spine.

"Do we knock?" I ask Dani.

Even though we would have seen if Bebe had doubled back and headed this way, I feel like it's important to keep up the pretense.

"I think we sneak," Dani says.

"Sneak it is."

Together, we take the steps up to the front door, and I try to see through the netting at the window, but it's too dense.

Dani reaches out and turns the handle.

The door opens with a click.

Dani makes an O with her mouth, part surprise, part celebration.

"Gotta love country folk," I say.

"It's not breaking and entering if there's no lock, right?" Dani says.

"Yeah, that's how it works," Kurt breathes, and I suppress a laugh.

I go in first, easing through the door with every part of me tensed. I half expect an alarm to sound, lights to flash, but this isn't L.A., and I figure Bebe would find an electronic security system worse than a break-in.

The hall is quiet. Long and narrow. The walls are polished wood, and there are framed pictures. The light is muted, struggling through the net curtains, casting the house in a yellow pall. It's clean, though. The dresser against the wall is spotless, holding a bowl of fruit. I spy the living room through a doorway, and the upholstered couch looks inviting.

"Okay, Goldilocks," Dani says. "Where now?"

I venture through another door into a dining room. A dark wood table takes up most of the space, and a mural of Jesus on the cross looms over the room, lacquered to the wall. The face is impossibly lifelike. Skeletal and shadowy. The electric blue eyes seem to be watching us. It's the kind of tacky religious paraphernalia Grams would have swooned over.

Above the image is a line of text, painted in gold serif.

The Lord is a God who avenges. O God who avenges, shine forth.

"Did you hear that?" Dani whispers.

I stop, listen.

Knock.

Knock.

Knock.

Every hair on my neck prickles. It sounded close. Too close.

Standing in the hall, Kurt looks panicked, his gaze darting to the front door.

Dani doubles over laughing as she holds on to the door frame.

"Sorry," she says. "I couldn't help it."

"Not funny," I say, shoving her. What is it about this camp that brings out the kid in everybody?

Dani abruptly stops laughing, her gaze going past me. Goose bumps prickle my scalp as I turn to look at the other side of the room, where Sadie crouches in the doorway.

You don't have to be Yayoi Kusama to create masterpieces.
The power of art is all in the eye—or the hand—of the creator.
Sometimes words elude us. They limit us. But a blank piece
of paper offers a whole world of possibility. It enables us to
communicate with our unconscious—that deep, dark part of
ourselves that doesn't adhere to logic, and we can express
ourselves through pure emotion, finding comfort in the
abstract.

XIX

"Hi, Sadie," I say. "Do you remember me?"

Sadie's eyes are glazed. In her hand, she twists a potato peeler. Her silver hair hangs in unwashed tresses either side of her face, and she wears a white lace dress that floats at her bare ankles.

"I'm Willow," I say. "You were in my room yesterday."

She sways on the spot, making her dress fan. She seems lost in thought, doesn't blink. Finally, her head moves up and down in a nod.

Relief cools the heat that has gathered in my throat. She understands me.

"We were hoping to talk to you," I say. "Is that okay, Sadie? Can we talk?"

She's looking at Kurt now, eyes wide and staring.

"I think she likes you," Dani says, and Kurt shifts uncomfortably.

"It's okay," I tell Sadie. "We won't tell Bebe."

Sadie's jaw twitches at the mention of her sister. Her gaze shifts to the Jesus mural. She looks at it like she's waiting for a response. Like it really is watching us. Then she makes a low sound and turns, vanishing through the door in a swirl of white lace.

"Shit," I say.

"That's Bebe's sister?" Kurt whispers.

"Yep."

"Is she all there?"

"I guess we'll have to find out. Come on."

I go after Sadie, passing through an old-fashioned kitchen where a stuffed pheasant hangs from the ceiling, wings spread wide. Its beak is parted as if in a silent cry.

Through the next door is a sunroom with large windows. The stained glass fits together to form a cross, and the light coming in from outside stamps a red, upside-down cross on the floorboards.

"What's with all the religious symbols?" Dani says.

"A holdover from the previous owners?" I suggest. "Bebe strikes me as more of a Gaia lover than a Jesus nut."

Except Bebe told me she built this place from nothing. She said that when she found the lake, the land around it was nothing but wilderness. They had to plumb a whole water main out here. So where'd the house come from?

It takes me a moment to spot Sadie. She's on the floor behind a wing-backed armchair, drawing on a sheet of paper. Multicolored crayons surround her, the potato peeler discarded at her side, and her hair pools down to conceal whatever she's drawing.

Dani and Kurt both hang back, eyeing Sadie uneasily.

I'm not afraid, even though I remember Sadie straddling me on my bedroom floor, hissing like a viper. Those kinds of girls in horror movies are almost always just misunderstood loners. I can relate.

I go over and perch on the arm of the chair, trying to see what Sadie is coloring in, but failing.

"What are you working on?" I ask.

Sadie ignores me, scratching the paper with a purple crayon.

Crayon, like the note in the doll's head.

Did Sadie leave the toy in my cabin?

"Sadie, do you remember being in my cabin?" I ask.

She nods.

"Did you take something? I'm not mad. It's just that the photo is really important to me. You know the photo I'm talking about?"

Sadie pauses. She stares at the drawing like the colors are moving. I try to keep the frustration from my voice.

"Sadie? Please can I have my photo back?"

She shakes her head.

"No?"

She shakes her head again, giving me a defiant stare.

"No, I can't have it back?" I ask.

"Or," Dani says, "no, you didn't take it?"

Sadie looks at Dani and nods. I frown.

"You didn't take it?" I ask. That would mean somebody else has been in my cabin. Somebody else has been going through my belongings.

Maybe Sadie is a liar as well as a thief.

There's something sad about her, though. She's got to be in her forties, but she's so childlike, it's difficult to tell. I wonder what made her like this, or if she's always been this way.

Sadie tosses aside the drawing she's been working on, grabbing a fresh sheet of paper and selecting a brown crayon. I reach down to pick up the picture she discarded, and she grabs my arm. She moved so quickly, I barely saw her, and her fingers grip my arm so tightly, I clench my teeth to stop from crying out. I'd forgotten how strong she is.

"Hey," Dani says, stepping forward. "Let her go."

"It's okay," I say, keeping my voice level. I set my gaze on Sadie, whose lips are drawn back over her teeth, nostrils flaring.

"I just wanted to see what you drew," I say. "Is that okay, Sadie?"

Her grip slackens and she lets go. I pick up the paper, seeing that it's a drawing of two people standing by a tree. One with wild brown hair, the other with a short black pixie.

"Wait," I say, looking at Sadie. "Is this Buck and Kat? Have you seen them?"

Sadie gestures at the paper, and I see that there's a third figure in the corner of the page. It's little more than black circles and lines, scribbled hurriedly. It looks like a person holding something. An ax.

"Who's this?" I ask, pointing at the figure.

Sadie's mouth moves, but I can't hear what she's saying. She seems to be repeating the same word over and over. I lean forward until we're separated by only a few inches, and I hear her voice like a trapped breath finally released.

"Nancy," she says. "Nancynancynancynancy."

I wince.

Knock-Knock Nancy.

A sound comes from somewhere else in the house. The click of a latch and the thump of boots on floorboards. A door opening and somebody coming inside.

Shit, the front door?

It can only be one person. Bebe's home.

Kurt darts farther into the room, looking rattled.

There are two doors in the sunroom. One for the kitchen, the other for the hall. There's no way out of here.

"She's bad," Sadie whispers, staring at the door to the hall. "My sister . . . she's bad."

My insides stretch and pull.

I remember the look on Bebe's face when she brought the ax down on the iPod, the stony stare she gave me after my affirmation, and I feel sick. If Bebe finds us in here, I have no idea what she'll do.

Sadie is on her feet. She nips to the corner of the room and opens a door I hadn't noticed before. It's painted the same color as the walls. I see the inside of a storage closet, and realize Sadie is showing us a place to hide.

"*Go!*" I whisper at Kurt, and he hurries inside. I grab Dani's hand and drag her across the room. She resists, stares at the closet with big, untrusting eyes, but we don't have any other option. We go inside. I turn to see Sadie reaching into the pocket of her dress. Just before she shuts us in, she shoves an object into my hands.

Then darkness closes around us.

I hold my breath, listening. A gap in the door filters a sliver of light inside. I'm face-to-face with Dani, who looks like she can't decide if she's excited or terrified. Kurt is at the back of the cupboard, eyes shining with fear.

"Sadie," Bebe says. "What have you been doing?"

I can't see her, but I feel her presence in the room like something heavy. Sadie doesn't speak.

"You've been in the camp again," Bebe says. She doesn't sound angry, but still, I sense the threat in her tone. "What have I told you about going into the cabins?"

No answer. I put my eye to the gap in the door, but I can't see the sisters.

There's a sound like something hard coming into contact with something soft, followed by a gasp.

Jesus, did Bebe just hit her sister? It's impossible to tell. I bite my lip, resisting the urge to thrust open the door and confront Bebe.

I hear a sharp inhale behind me and see Kurt squeezing his nose, not breathing. I can't tell if he's having another panic attack or trying not to sneeze. I can't tell which would be worse.

"Stay away from the camp," Bebe says, tone cold. "Don't make me lock you up like Daddy."

Footsteps again, then silence.

Is Bebe still in the room? Or have they both gone?

And what the hell did Bebe mean about their father?

Is there somebody else living in the house?

Kurt sneezes.

The sound echoes in the cupboard, and I freeze, every muscle in my body clenched. After a few seconds of silence, I relax.

"Jesus, Kurt, way to be stealthy," Dani whispers.

"Sorry. Willow, what did she give you?"

I'd almost forgotten I was holding anything. I raise the object to get a better look at it, and see hard plastic, curved at the edges. My stomach hops with recognition.

"It's a flip phone," I say, not believing it myself.

I examine the Motorola, which looks like an original from the early 2000s. Old and scuffed. Now that I can see it for myself, I understand why I forgot it was in my hand. It's because it fit there so snugly. Like it belonged there, pressed into my palm. Just like my own phone.

A pang of longing moves through me, and I can't resist opening the phone. I press a few buttons, waiting for light to fill the closet. But it's dead. Probably hasn't been used in years.

"Where do you think she got that?" Dani whispers.

"I have no idea."

Kurt cocks his head, listens. "Do you think they're gone?"

"Same answer."

I take the door handle and turn, ready for it to make a noise. When it doesn't, I ease the door open, poking my nose through the gap. I don't see Sadie or Bebe. The sunroom is deserted.

"Hey, there's another door back here," Kurt says.

I look back into the closet. Now that more light is coming in, I see that the back wall is entirely taken up by another door. It looks older than the rest of the house. Simple dark wood. A bronze handle. It's so unremarkable, it would be easy to miss.

"A closet inside a closet?" I say.

Curiosity buzzes in my mind, but I know that we'd be idiots to delve farther into the house.

"Let's get out of here before Bebe comes back," I say.

XX

ebe is waiting for us when we get back to camp.

It's late afternoon, almost evening, and the air feels like warm syrup. Bebe stands in the picnic area wearing a Stetson and a fresh shirt and jeans. She looks like she just showered, her skin too bright and clean for this climate.

She's bad, Sadie said in the sunroom.

Is it possible Bebe doesn't have our best interests at heart?

Is she hiding something dangerous?

Don't make me lock you up like Daddy.

"Please, take a seat," she says. Her eyes are in shadow.

We find places on two picnic benches.

"You're all aware that Buck and Kat have been absent today," Bebe says. "This is clearly a cause for concern, which is why I have spent the past few hours with Hodder Valley PD and local forest rangers. They have searched the camp and been unable to find our friends."

"Cops have been here?" Misty asks, sounding on edge.

"They found no evidence of foul play," Bebe says, "and they have no reason to suspect that Buck and Kat have met with any misfortune. Their search is continuing now into the surrounding woodland. They'll notify me immediately if anything or anybody is found."

The way she says it, it sounds like "any body" is two words. I shiver, despite the heat.

I look down, realizing that I've been tracing a pattern in the bench top with my finger. It's a faded, rudimentary carving of a flower, gouged into the wood. A fresh chill lifts the hairs on my arms when I see that the petals have been created using a single repeated shape. It looks like an *N*.

Is Knock-Knock Nancy everywhere here?

"This is what we're going to do," Bebe says, removing her hat. The setting sun flashes in her silver hair. "We're going to carry on as best we can. We're going to trust the authorities and continue with our program. This evening, we could all use a distraction, and I can't think of anything more fun than an 'end of the world' costume party."

She gestures to a couple of large trunks resting outside the canteen doors. I hadn't noticed them before, which seems crazy given how big they are.

"All right!" Misty says. "I *love* dress-up parties!"

"Of course you do," Dani mutters.

Nobody has reacted to the fact that Bebe said *end of the world*.

Bebe claps her hands. "Okay, everybody go get ready. Dress up. Have fun. Try not to worry. Once everybody is changed, we'll hold stone circle on the beach, and then we're going to party like it's the last night on Earth!"

I watch Misty leap up from the bench and run for the trunks, as if Bebe has fired a starting pistol. As she tears off the lid and starts rifling through the contents, my thoughts spin. Buck and Kat are still gone. Authorities are looking for them in the woods. We're celebrating the end of the world.

And Sadie said . . .

Nancynancynancynancy.

✳

B y the time I get to the dress-up box, Misty and Juniper have already gone back to their cabins to change. Kurt is trying to decide between a pair of overalls and a sparkly sequined jacket, and Dani is working her way through the pile of fabric that somebody—I'm gonna say Misty—left in a heap on the ground.

"Buck's gonna be so pissed he missed this," Kurt says.

"Maybe they'll get back in time. What do you think?" Dani poses in an oversized crown.

"You were born to be royalty," I tell her.

She smiles, takes off the crown. "Everything okay?"

"I keep thinking about Sadie's drawing. What if she saw what happened to Buck and Kat?"

"I'm sure the cops will find them," Kurt says.

"I don't know. Listen, I've been thinking . . . what if there's something to the Knock-Knock Nancy myth?"

"What do you mean?" Dani asks.

"I found the letter *N* carved in a tree behind Buck's cabin. And there was a doll's head, and somebody knocked at my door in the middle of the night on my first night here, and Sadie said she's *seen* Knock-Knock Nancy."

Dani frowns. "Somebody knocked at your door?"

"When I answered, there was nobody there."

Dani looks torn between spooked and suspicious. "You think the ghost of Knock-Knock Nancy is hanging around Camp Castaway?"

"Ghosts aren't real," I say. "But somebody could be bringing the legend to life to mess with us. They could be making campers disappear."

"Why would they do that?"

"You heard Buck's story. Knock-Knock Nancy was doomed to live in eternal judgment for her supposed sins. What if we're being punished, just like she was?"

Dani switches between Kurt and me. "Buck's the one who told the story. This could all be an elaborate prank."

Kurt nods. "My first day here, he put a rubber scorpion in my bed."

"If it were a prank, he'd have shown up by now," I say.

"You think we're in danger?" Kurt asks.

"I think we'd be safer if we weren't here. Who's to say Bebe even called the cops?"

Kurt's face pales. "You think she lied?"

"I think she knows more than she's saying. Bebe clearly has a lot to hide."

Silence settles. Dani and Kurt can't deny that fact, and I can see them wrestling with the same disbelief that I am. Disappearances at a wellness retreat are one thing, but somebody impersonating a local legend is a whole other ball game.

Ha, wellness, Willow says. *If you say so.*

I can't help thinking that if this were an episode of *We Love Willow*, it would be a goofy *Scooby-Doo* homage in which the ghost of Knock-Knock Nancy turns out to be a forest ranger sick of city kids partying on his land, and the missing campers are just playing an epic game of Sardines that got out of hand.

"Look, all I'm saying is this: Can you think of a reason somebody would want to hurt Buck? And Kat? And any of the other campers? Because if this place really is Camp Canceled, I'd say there are a dozen excuses for hurting us."

"Knock-Knock Nancy is all about revenge," Kurt murmurs.

The humidity feels oppressive, the air close against my skin. Dani and Kurt wear such grave expressions, I almost feel bad involving them in this. But it's for their own good. We could all be targets.

"Are you saying we get out of here?" Dani asks.

"I'm saying I'm sure as hell not leaving it to Bebe to look out for us. There must be an emergency phone on-site, probably in Bebe's office. We break in, call the cops, and we make sure they really do come out here."

"Another break-in?" Dani says.

"It's our best plan for now." I'm already rooting through the dress-up trunk, searching for something that will help us get into Bebe's office.

"Won't it be locked? How are we getting in there?" Dani asks, right as I find what I'm looking for. A corset with a stiff bustier. I use my teeth to rip the fabric, and then I tear at it with my hands, dismantling the bodice, finally uncovering what I'm looking for. A long, thin piece of wire.

"With this," I say.

Dani breaks into a slow grin, and she looks at me in a way that makes my whole body hum.

"After you, Nancy Drew," she says.

S2E4 "Willow vs. Werewolf"—Willow is put in charge of the office Halloween party by her klutzy manager, Wilhelmina (special guest star Tina Fey), but a pumpkin shortage could spell disaster. Meanwhile, Eliza discovers that imaginary friends are visible to regular people on Halloween night.

XXI

The lock on the door of Bebe's office is a straightforward pin-and-tumbler. I guess Bebe doesn't count on many campers attempting to break in.

I take the wire and bend it in five places so that it resembles a hairpin.

"Keep a look out," I say, and Kurt nods, facing the darkening foyer. I crouch in front of the door and slot the wire into the metal plug, feeling around inside the lock.

"How exactly do you know how to do that?" Dani asks.

"Grams used to lock me in my room a lot," I say. "Most locks are pickable, you know. They only provide an illusion of security."

"Thanks for that."

I feel around with the wire, wondering if I'm too out of practice. It's been a long time since I had to jimmy my way out of my bedroom. But then the lock clicks, and I try the handle. The door opens. Dani looks impressed. I flash her a smile, and then we hurry inside. Kurt closes the door.

I don't waste any time, going straight to the desk. There's no landline phone. The desk holds an unused notebook, a pot of pens, a mini calendar of New York sights, and absolutely nothing of any interest.

"There's a safe," Dani says from the bookcase. "How are you at code-cracking?"

"There's room for improvement," I say. I try the top desk drawer. It's fitted with a barrel lock, less easy to pick.

I open the next drawer, which is full of paperwork. Rifling through it, I see that it's mostly safety literature. Emergency protocol and fire procedure.

The bottom drawer is deeper than the others. I tug it open and stare inside. It takes a moment for my brain to comprehend what I'm looking at.

The drawer is full of round, pink objects.

Doll's heads.

At least a dozen of them, of various shapes and sizes. They nestle together like alien creatures, a sea of eyes, mouths, and little snub noses.

I pick one up, unable to stop my hand from shaking. What the hell is Bebe doing with a drawer full of doll's heads?

"Hello, creepy," Dani says, staring at the object in my hand.

"I found one outside Buck's cabin yesterday," I say. "And there was one in my cabin, under the sofa."

Dani's eyes are wide. "I found one under my bed a few days after I arrived."

"Me too," Kurt says, "only mine was in a kitchen cupboard."

We all look at the head, and the silence of the office is oppressive. Expectant.

Has Bebe been hiding the heads around camp?

"What do you think it means?" Dani asks, voice low.

All I can think about is Knock-Knock Nancy and her missing head.

"It's a warning," I say.

Kurt swallows. "A warning for what?"

"I think somebody is hurting campers, and I think this is what they leave as sort of a mark. I bet if we looked around Kat's cabin, we'd find one of these there, too."

Kurt looks like he wants to curl up in the corner and disappear.

"Or it's part of some game Bebe's set up that she hasn't told us about yet," Dani says.

"What kind of game at a digital detox camp could possibly involve dismembered doll heads?"

Dani shrugs. "A weird one."

"Listen," I say. "I'm all for theories, but here's what we do know: Buck and Kat are missing. Creepy heads are being left all over camp. Bebe is acting Jack Torrance levels of weird. And Sadie says Knock-Knock Nancy is coming for us."

Dani stands thinking.

She releases a breath.

"Okay. Say that's happening. Say somebody is dressing up as a local legend and disappearing campers. We can leave. We tell the others we're checking out, Bebe orders a car, and we get the hell out of here. Or we go now. Just start walking."

My gaze goes to the enormous map framed on the wall behind the desk. There's an annotated cross at the center, the words *CAMP CAST-AWAY* printed in tiny letters, right next to a blue smudge that must be the lake. The rest of the map is green. An endless stretch of forest that reaches right to the edge of the frame.

A part of me can't believe I'm even considering leaving. Just yesterday, I told Bebe that I wouldn't mention her sister, if it meant I could stay. Yesterday feels like a long time ago.

"It's so far," I say. Farther than I'd thought. Farther even than it felt in the car. "And I'm not sure we can trust Bebe anymore. We need to find a phone and call the police ourselves."

"What about our cells?" Kurt suggests.

I'd almost forgotten that our phones are locked up just twenty paces away, in the front porch of the clubhouse. The thought makes me queasy. Three days without my phone and the idea of having it back is unsettling.

"The porch is locked," I say. "If we ask for our phones back, Bebe will know we're up to something, and there's no guarantee she'll go along with it. Our best bet would be walking out of here. We'll have to find our way to the road by going through the woods, and then we'll keep walking until we find a phone."

"It's getting dark already," Dani says from the window.

She's right. The sky is darkening. I swear it's past six p.m., and it feels like night is already drawing in. The rain clouds are dark as bruises, blocking out the light. Frustration gathers behind my ribs. A storm will make it even more difficult to navigate our way out of here, and then there's nightfall to worry about. It doesn't just get dark out here, it's a total blackout.

I remember that some parts of the road weren't paved on the way here, and the driver had to depend on the GPS, which we don't have. Even if we aren't getting targeted by Knock-Knock Nancy, we could still get lost, end up like those *Blair Witch* kids. And just like them, we'd have no phones.

I toss the doll's head back into the drawer and shut it.

"We're just going to have to wait until morning," I say. "Hope the storm passes by first light—hope we survive—then get out of here."

"You think it's safe to wait until then?" Kurt asks.

I want to lie to him, the way I have been the whole time we've been here. I try to imagine what Willow would say.

It's just a prank, total camp high jinks. Now let's have a cocktail.

"We'll look after each other," I say instead.

"I'm thinking sleepover," Dani says. Quickly, she adds, "For everybody, I mean. We should stick together. Number one horror rule after *don't answer the phone.*"

"I don't think we'll have any trouble with that one."

"Are we still dressing up?" Kurt asks as I check that the coast is clear. The foyer is empty, and my top lip curls at the thought of going along with Bebe's evening activity.

"We should probably play nice with the Camp Mom," I say. "We don't want to tip her off."

"Right." Dani rolls her eyes. "Before she hacks off our heads."

Back at the dress-up trunks, I search halfheartedly, pushing aside masks, wigs, and silk capes. Halloween is my religion, but it's difficult to focus on a costume when I'm already forming a plan in my mind.

I'll need weapons. If something's going on at camp, I'm not going to be defenseless.

Because I'm not sitcom Willow anymore.

I'm the horror chick who's going to save everybody.

"I'm gonna change," Dani says. She holds something behind her back. "Don't peek. It's a surprise."

I smile. "Can't wait."

"Want me to help you find a costume?" Kurt asks me.

"Thanks, I've got this," I say.

He starts to walk off, then stops.

"Everything okay?" I ask.

He turns to look at me, and his face is serious.

"I wanted to tell you something, in case something bad happens," he says, his tone soft, searching. "I wasn't completely honest about my sister."

"You weren't?"

He shakes his head. "She studied music, and she taught me how to play guitar. That part's true. But she's not in Chicago. She died."

I frown, must be giving off stunned question marks, because he says, "It was a couple of years ago. She was in a car accident and . . ."

He trails off, his eyes bright with emotion. His jaw firms, and he lifts his gaze to mine.

"It was my fault." His voice is thin, weightless.

His breath is catching again, the way it did in yoga. He raises a hand and taps his sternum lightly, the technique I showed him.

"Kurt, I'm so sorry," I say. "I had no idea."

Congrats on the grief clichés, my brain says. Language fails us so often, it's a wonder we're able to communicate with each other at all.

"It was all my fault," Kurt repeats.

Sorrow twinges my heart. Kurt must have been driving.

I feel renewed concern for him. How do you deal with that kind of guilt? How do you keep going when you were responsible for the death of somebody you loved? Could that be a reason to attack a man in a parking lot? Again, I wonder if Kurt is really Caleb. Is that the reason he got canceled?

"I'm not telling you this because . . . well . . ." Kurt stops, keeps tapping. After a few moments, his breathing eases. "Things were tough there for a while, but they've been better. A lot better, since I came here. Everybody's been so welcoming, and being out here in nature has helped . . . that's the real reason I came. I had to get away from my life for a while. So I guess I wanted to say thank you. For being here."

I'm speechless. I don't know what to say, but I see him waiting for me to speak, so I gather myself the best I can.

"I'm glad you're feeling better," I say. "I'm glad I could be a part of that."

He nods. "Okay, I should get going before we start ugly crying."

I laugh. "Yeah, what is this, *Queer Eye?*"

He smiles, then turns. I watch him head for the boardwalk, and I can't help frowning.

What happened to Kurt and his sister is awful, but I'm not ready to rule him out as the man from the police report.

When he's gone, I root around some more in the dress-up box, finding a doctor's coat and scrubs. Plus what looks like a medical bag.

It's perfect.

And now that I'm alone, I can start prepping.

My first thought is to go to Juniper. She's the toughest person at camp. She would know exactly what to do. But then I remember the way she's evaded any meaningful contact with anybody at the retreat, and I wonder if, like Kurt, she's going through something that I shouldn't disturb.

Besides, Juniper has already taught me everything I need to know.

If Buck and Kat were targeted because of whatever got them canceled, I'm going to do what I can to help them until we're able to seek assistance outside the camp.

I'm sick of people being hurt.

I'm so over the cycle of judgment and shame.

I'm going to help Buck and Kat because nobody else will.

First stop: the kitchen.

The canteen is deserted. I sling the medical bag over my shoulder and head for the counter, slipping behind it to push open a door with a porthole. It reveals a long and narrow kitchen. Pots boil on the stove and it's even hotter in here than outside, thick with the smell of onions and boiled meat. I hear movement at the far end of the kitchen, where a pantry door stands open. Now's my chance.

I open a drawer that contains a load of party poppers and streamers. Another drawer is full of cutlery, all of it too blunt to be useful.

I spot a knife resting on a chopping board. It's stained red and stuck with meat flecks, but it's long and sharp. I drop it into the medical bag I took from the dress-up box. A couple of utensils hang on hooks farther down the counter. A skewer, a couple of steak knives, and a carving knife.

Noise still comes from inside the pantry, so I hurry over to lift off the utensils, slipping them into my bag.

"Can I help you?" a gruff voice asks.

I jump and turn, staring into red-rimmed eyes. Chef Jeff is taller up close, easily scraping six feet. He's late thirties. A hair net keeps his greasy black mane in check, and he wipes his long fingers on a stained apron. With his hollow cheeks and sun-starved complexion, he looks like he should be tending bar at the Full Throttle Saloon. I guess that's why Bebe keeps him behind the scenes.

"Just looking for water," I say. My throat really is dry.

Chef Jeff squints at me for a moment, then nods past me to where a chill box sits on the counter by the door.

"Thanks," I say. I go to the box and take out a bottle. I clutch it to me, savoring the coldness, and turn back to the chef, an idea occurring to me. Sadie isn't the only person at camp who might have seen things everybody else missed.

"Have you worked here long?" I ask.

Chef Jeff takes a knife from a drawer and starts chopping tomatoes.

"Couple years," he says.

"Do you know what was here before?"

He frowns. "Before?"

"Before it was Camp Castaway."

He stops chopping, stares at the bright red tomato pulp.

"I wouldn't go poking around in that," he says. "Stick to softball and dress-up. It's safer."

I suppress a shudder at the thought that he really was watching us during the game yesterday.

"Did something happen here?" I ask. "Before it was Camp Castaway?"

When he doesn't answer, I throw a curveball. "Is it something to do with Knock-Knock Nancy?"

Chef Jeff rubs his forehead. "You ask a lot of questions."

"I'm a curious kind of person."

"You should go back to your friends."

I stand firm. "I can't do that."

Chef Jeff keeps his head down. He mutters something under his breath.

"People are missing," I say. "Campers. If you know something, you have to tell me." I pull back, adding more gently, "Whatever it is, it'll stay between us. You have my word."

He starts chopping again, cucumber this time. Cubing it with ease.

"She was a resident here a few years after the millennium," he says, tone soft, as if he's speaking to himself.

"Who was?" I ask.

"Nancy."

"Nancy was a resident here twenty years ago?"

He nods. "This place has been a camp for fifty years. At one point, it was a Bible camp. That's when Nancy was here."

"She came here on a pilgrimage?"

A laugh, bitter and cold.

"She was seventeen, sent here by her parents, but she wasn't a believer. She played up, was sort of a brat. She was into rock music and Wicca, like those chicks in *The Craft*. One night, she went missing. When they finally found her body, she'd been dead two days, out in the woods." He shakes his head. "They found her body, but they never found her head."

I hold the water bottle tight.

"I heard that was in the 1800s," I say.

Chef Jeff grunts. "People like to make up stories. I'm telling you what really happened."

The cold of the bottle has frozen my fingers.

Buck's story was true, to a point. The setting and the backstory were different, must have been altered by word of mouth, but the most important details were the same. There was a woman named Nancy, and she was murdered right here at Camp Castaway.

"Did something happen with a priest?" I ask, thinking about the legend, in which an injured preacher killed Nancy after he discovered she practiced so-called unholy rites.

Chef Jeff stills, staring at the knife in his hand, and his look unsettles me. I've struck a nerve.

Is this where reality differs from the story? What if Nancy was killed for another reason? What if there was something rather less than holy going on between her and one of the priests at Bible camp?

When Chef Jeff doesn't speak again, I ask, "Did they catch the killer?"

Chef Jeff dumps the chopped vegetables into a salad bowl.

"Nope."

"Do you know who did it? Who killed her?"

He shakes his head. He's barely looked at me the whole time we've been talking.

"How do you know this?" I ask.

Chef Jeff turns and starts walking back to the pantry, then stops. In a quiet voice, he says, "Nancy was my friend. And what happened to her shouldn't ever be forgotten."

I open my mouth to say I'm sorry, but he's already disappeared into the pantry.

My ears ring as I leave the kitchen. I try to make sense of it. The one thing that pushes through the noise is the knowledge that this has been a camp for decades.

Bebe said she set up Camp Castaway a few years ago.

She said the land was wild when she found it.

But she lied.

She lied right to my goddamn face.

CHEF JEFF

Jeffrey Wooster didn't believe in God, but he believed in ghosts. After all, he'd become one himself. He'd been haunting this camp for so long now, he'd forgotten what it was to be alive. All he did was chop, feed, sleep, start over. He existed solely to support other people.

But then the redheaded camper came into his kitchen, and he felt the past fill his skull like oil, oozing into every crevice and corner, and he knew his patience was about to pay off.

So many years of waiting, watching, hoping—and Nancy was finally going to come back for him.

Jeff threw the vegetables into the pot on the stove. He turned the gas down to let the stew simmer, and then he went into the pantry, savoring the sudden cool. He'd never liked the heat of the kitchen. Found it oppressive and smothering. But it was the only way he'd gotten to stay at Camp Castaway, so he put up with it.

He bent down to pick up a sack of potatoes and groaned when the bag split, scattering misshapen objects across the pantry floor.

"Just my luck," he muttered as he got down on his hands and knees to collect them back up.

He wondered what Nancy would say when she came for him.

She'd been kind to him at camp. She didn't patronize him like the God Squad, who spoke to him like he was slow. Nancy let him in on her jokes. She took him hiking. They'd visit the tree house. She'd made it bearable when the camp leader seemed determined to tear him apart.

We'll get through this together, she'd say. *Just you and me.*

When Nancy died, Jeff swore he wouldn't leave her. Even when the camp closed, Jeff stayed nearby. He got a job in town working as a dish cleaner, and he snuck back to camp when he could.

He knew that Nancy was still out there, looking for him. She'd promised she'd never leave him, and he believed her.

He'd caught glimpses of her over the years. A flicker of ghostly hair. He'd heard her knocking. No matter how quiet he made himself so as not to scare her, or how loudly he called her name to help her find him, she never made it to him. It must be awful confusing to be a ghost.

When the camp finally reopened, Jeff went to Bebe and forced her to hire him. He didn't like Bebe, but he knew that, on some level, she was like him and Nancy. She just wanted to survive. That was why she gave him the job. He knew the thing that nobody else did and he promised to keep the secret, but only if he could work at camp.

Of course, he'd told the redheaded camper a little of the truth, but not enough to upset Bebe.

In the pantry, Jeff loaded the potatoes into a pan. He was about to toss in some carrots when he heard it. The sound that thrilled him, switched on every nerve in his body.

Knock.

Knock.

Knock.

Jeff went to the pantry door and looked out.

The kitchen lights had switched off and, through the gloom, he saw a figure standing at the other end of the kitchen. She was tall, hunched, wearing a tattered gown. Silver hair fell into her face, obscuring her features, but he knew it was her.

"Nancy," Jeff whispered.

He took a step forward, then stopped.

Something was different. As his eyes adjusted to the dark, he saw that Nancy grasped an ax before her, held in two dirty hands, nails chipped, like she'd clawed her way out of a shallow grave.

He heard her whispering.

"Their day of disaster is near ..."

"Nancy," Jeff said. "It's me, Jeff-Jeff Treble-Clef."

"Their day of disaster is near ... and their doom rushes upon them."

She started walking toward him, and as she came, she butted the flat of the ax against the side of the counter, making a knocking sound.

Fear pricked the bubble of joy that had filled him.

Nancy was confused. She'd forgotten who he was. That they were friends. Twenty years was a long time.

"Nance," he said. "Remember the tree house? The songs? I know it's been a while, but you have to remember."

Nancy kept walking toward him, boots striking the tiled floor, the ax creaking in her grip.

Jeff grabbed the salt from the counter, held it in both hands. In the years since Nancy died, he'd read everything about ghosts that he could get his hands on. Salt was purifying. Provided a barrier. He'd use it now, give Nancy a chance to remember.

He kept his eyes on his dead friend as he crouched and drew a circle around himself with the salt. Then he stood.

Nancy had stopped a few feet away from him.

She tilted her head, considering him, and Jeff smiled.

"Hi," he said. "Hi, Nancy."

Pain exploded in the side of his face. Jeff saw stars—a thousand flashing stars—and his vision clouded as he staggered backward into the pantry. His left ear rang, a high-pitched whining that made him want to scratch at his own skull, and something warm and wet ran into his left eye.

He held on to a shelf, trying to bring his attacker into focus.

Nancy held the ax in one hand, and another object in the other. Jeff only realized it was a meat tenderizer as it swung toward his head a second time.

He put his hands up to protect himself, but his left eye was sealed shut and he couldn't see properly. He felt another blow to the side of his head, a pressure so intense it made the world dim. Blow after blow came. It sounded like knocking. Banging. Over and over.

He heard a crashing sound, then felt something solid beneath him, and he realized he was on the pantry floor. The left side of his face felt wet and exposed, and he pressed a hand to it, tears in his eyes.

"Nancy," he groaned, looking up at the figure standing over him.

The meat tenderizer clunked to the floor, and the ax went up.

"*Rise up, Judge of the Earth,*" Nancy whispered. "*Pay back to the proud what they deserve.*"

"I love—" Jeff tried to say, but then the ax swung, and the world spun on its axis. When it came to a standstill, Jeff found himself staring at a headless body. A body wearing an apron. *His* body.

He wanted to scream, wanted to cry, wanted to tell Nancy exactly how he'd felt all those years ago, how he still felt, how he wanted—

XXII

I n my cabin, I lay out everything I took from the kitchen.

Two steak knives. A carving knife. A skewer.

They make me feel safer. More prepared. On the show, I prepped as much as I could before every episode. If I had to know how to do a dropkick or knit a scarf or dance the Charleston, I'd watch YouTube videos and stay up late practicing because, as Grams used to say, "All things are ready, if our mind be so."

At least she taught me one good thing.

Right now, my mind feels swollen with the events of the past twenty-four hours.

I need to see it written down, the way I could only memorize a script by staring at each page in ten-minute bursts. I take a complimentary pocket notebook from the nightstand and start writing a list.

SADIE SAW SOMETHING?
BUCK & KAT MISSING
TEXT STALKER?
BEBE LYING? DANGEROUS?
STOLEN PHOTO
NANCY KILLED 20 YRS AGO, WHY?

The encounter with Chef Jeff has left me even more confused—but also more certain that I've done the right thing by arming up. The camp has a secret history involving a killer who was never brought to justice. The more I find out about this place, the less I like, and the surer I am that Bebe knows more than she's telling us.

I change into my costume—hospital scrubs and a white doctor's coat, because I get the feeling they'll come in handy—and check out the window. The sky is packed solid with dark clouds, and the sun has set, no longer bleeding through the tree line. I should have enough time to search Buck's cabin before stone circle, but I'll have to hurry.

I repack the knives into the shoulder bag and put it on. The material is thick enough that I shouldn't accidentally stab myself.

When I open the door to leave, I find a zombie clown on the step.

"Seen any brains around here?" she asks.

It takes me a second to realize it's Dani, dressed in a pair of multicolored overalls. She's sprayed purple in her backcombed hair. Fingerless gloves show her black nails, and she's painted her face a shimmering gray-white, adding thin, branching lines that make her skin look dry and ravaged. A dead clown who's just stepped off the catwalk.

For a moment, I imagine we're not at Camp Castaway. We're back in L.A., heading out to a Halloween party at a friend's place. We'll drink and dance and make out, disco lights spinning around us, like something out of *Exorcist II*, and everything will feel right with the world.

It's just a dream, though. My bag is full of knives and there's a potential killer in the woods.

"No brains here," I say. "We're fresh out."

"Shoot." Dani's rock-star grin emerges, somehow both sexy and spooky in the clown makeup. "You look hot, though. Sanitary."

"I wanted to dress up as the Heidi Klum worm," I say, "but I figured this was more appropriate."

The grin widens, the one that makes me want to kiss her, even this zombie version of her, but I can't get distracted.

I look past her at cabin eleven. Buck's place is still dark. The more

I look at it, the more it seems to brood. It's a haunted house now; a dark reminder of Buck's absence.

"I'm going to check out Kat's and Buck's cabins," I say, "in case the cops missed anything."

Dani's mouth pinches in one corner. "More breaking and entering. I've created a monster. Also sure, let's go."

As we walk over, I fill her in on Chef Jeff's story about Nancy. I feel bad betraying his trust, but it could help us find the missing campers. I can't keep the truth to myself.

"She was a real person?" Dani says. "That's awful."

"I'm getting the feeling this place has a history nobody wants us to know about," I say. "Bebe told me she built the camp from the ground up half a decade ago, but you saw her house. It's way older. And now Buck and Kat are missing, and Chef Jeff said they never found Nancy's killer. What if somebody dangerous is still out there?"

Dani stops. "You think Buck and Kat are *dead*?"

I grimace. "No. But I do think they're in trouble."

"Summer camps, man. When will people ever learn?"

We look around Kat's cabin first. I send a silent apology into the universe for invading her privacy, but I get the sense that she'd want us to do this.

Her place is somehow both ordered and messy. The bed is made, looks untouched. It seems like Kat has been sleeping on the couch, going by the blanket thrown over it.

Other than that, there's nothing out of the ordinary. Nothing to tell us where Kat is.

A combination of excitement and unease gathers in my chest as we cross to Buck's cabin. The light in the sky is almost gone, and with it, my anticipation grows. Whenever night falls in horror movies, you know that trouble is just around the corner. But we're not going in helpless. I'm armed and goddamn dangerous.

Buck's open-plan living room is even more of a wreck than it looked from the outside. I can't say I'm surprised but also, I can't believe people live like this.

"I guess Buck was waiting for the maid to show up," Dani says.

We search the cabin. I look in all the kitchen cupboards, then under the sofa. I find a couple of guitar picks, empty bottles of Gatorade, and some biker magazines. There's no sign of a break-in or a struggle.

I rub my forehead, sensing the beginning of a headache, and as I look down, I notice something on the floor. I stoop to get a closer look, seeing that it's a thin groove in the wood. Shallow, roughly six inches long. I run my finger along it, thinking it looks like somebody dropped something heavy here. Or hit the wood with something sharp.

My spine bristles.

It could have been made by an ax.

I look up, and breath catches in my throat.

"There's an attic," I say. Dani comes over and we stand beneath the hatch in the ceiling, looking up.

"You ever seen *Rec*?" she asks.

"Only the sequel. I'm going in."

Dani doesn't argue.

I drag a chair from the table and step up, reaching for the square door. I can't help picturing a dozen grisly things up there: a nest of snakes, or Bebe hunched with an ax; Knock-Knock Nancy's apparition.

If I've learned anything from Juniper's movies, it's that these moments are defining.

They tell the viewer if you're a hero or a coward, Willow says.

I played the coward after tweetageddon. I hid. Tried to disappear.

Not anymore.

The hatch falls open, and the sight of the darkness within causes my body to vibrate with unease.

This is it, Willow says. *You've got this.*

I hop up to grab the lowest rung of the ladder and pull it down.

After checking that it's solid, I climb. The ladder shakes as Dani follows. At the top, I poke my head into a recess in the roof.

It's dark. Quiet. The air is cooler up here, and none of the things I pictured are revealed. Still, the space is unsettling. It's unloved and vacant. Charged with dark potential.

"Any sign of him?" Dani asks. Her arms graze my calves and I try not to think about her looking up at my ass in the doctor costume.

"No," I say, "but there is something."

Paper is strewn across the boarded floor. It's like somebody's been handing out flyers up here, but it's too dark to see what they are.

"Here," I say, "take these." I gather up as much of the paper as I can reach and hand them down to Dani. She takes them, and we climb down.

"They look like official documents," Dani says, leafing through the pages. "Contact sheets, waivers, next of kin, newspaper clippings, questionnaires. Where did these all come from?"

"Campers' admission files?" I suggest.

"But if they're from campers' files, why does Buck have them?"

I chew my bottom lip. "I found a police report in my closet last night, right after Sadie was in there. It was about a guy called Caleb who attacked a man in Illinois. Somebody must have raided the office for the files and hidden them up there."

Dani frowns. "You think it was Sadie?"

"She does have a thing for hiding," I say.

"But why Buck's cabin?"

I shrug. "It wasn't always Buck's cabin. Maybe she just likes it up there."

I take the documents from Dani and spread them out on the dining table. They're the last thing I expected to find, but they're hard proof that something strange is going on at camp. Unless Bebe has an incredibly unconventional approach to resident confidentiality.

"The names are all redacted," I say, seeing that every single identifying feature has been meticulously struck through. "Jesus, this one's a prescription for fentanyl."

"Isn't that a painkiller?"

"A strong one," I say. "My grandpa had to take it after surgery. But it's been all over the news, too. People take it recreationally. There have been a lot of overdoses."

"Who do you think is taking it here?"

"I honestly have no idea. Buck's a weed fan. What if he's also into prescription drugs?" I pause.

"Juniper said she had a sick relative."

I remember Juniper mentioning her "bad coping mechanisms" during stone circle. Could the fentanyl be one of them?

"Wow," Dani says, "this one's about a hit-and-run."

She hands me a photocopy of a news clipping.

WOMAN KILLED DURING BIRTHDAY NIGHT OUT

A woman in her twenties was killed Friday night after being hit by a car that failed to stop at the scene.

Cold makes my hands numb.

Kurt's sister died in a car accident, and Kurt said it was his fault. Now there's a news story talking about a hit-and-run. It's too much of a coincidence for them to be unconnected, but what really happened? Did Kurt hit his sister with his car and flee the scene?

My jaw tightens.

"Has anybody ever mentioned this during stone circle?" I ask.

"No. But it must be relevant to their stay. Why else would the camp have a record of it?"

I stare at the story, searching for any detail that will exonerate

Kurt, or condemn him, but there's no mention of a brother, and the names are all blacked out, just like the other documents.

"What is it?" Dani asks.

"Kurt's sister died in a car wreck."

"Shit."

I lower the report, trying to suppress the bleak feeling coursing through me. "What else do we got?"

Dani picks up another document.

"This one's a court summons. '*The attendance of* name redacted *is requested on June 5 relating to the incident of March 20.*' It's attached to a toxicology report. It looks like this person had a lot of drugs in their system."

"You think it's related to the hit-and-run?" I ask.

"I have no clue. The hit-and-run clipping doesn't have a date on it."

"The police report I found was about an assault," I say. "Maybe the court summons is to do with him."

Dani lowers the page. "We had three men at camp for the past week: Apollo, Buck, and Kurt."

"Five if you count Tye and Chef Jeff," I say.

"Who do you think Caleb is, though?"

"Apollo?" I suggest, trying to think outside the box.

"Pfft. He wouldn't say boo to a goose. But Kurt . . . he flipped out in yoga."

"He was having a panic attack."

"That could have been brought on by anything."

I frown. "You think he could kick a man into a coma?"

"I think most people are capable of most things. It's all about the circumstances."

I agree, but Kurt?

He'd looked worried when we found out the police had been at camp. Was that because he's had his own run-ins with the cops? Or was he just worried about the missing campers?

Or he killed his sister and even if it was an accident, he's worried he'll eventually get caught.

"Should we be doing this?" Dani asks. "Looking through these? It feels wrong."

"I know. But what if they help us figure out what happened to Buck and Kat?"

And Nancy, Willow says, which is true. The disappearances and Nancy's death must be related.

Dani nods and, after a moment, looks at another document.

"*'I'm here because I need to get off socials—off BookTok,'*" she reads. "*'It got really toxic for me, and I did something I regret. I just want to get away from it all.'* Wait, that sounds familiar. Kat talked about getting off social media in stone circle a couple days before you got here."

"She got canceled on TikTok?" I ask.

"That's the impression I got."

There are people who hurt me in the past, Kat said during affirmations. And she'd been curious about what I was reading, looking at my book with an odd kind of yearning.

Was she targeted online in the same way that I was?

Guilt twists my gut. She could have gone through the same thing I did, and I was too busy worrying about hiding my own identity and stalking Juniper to notice.

And now she's missing.

I straighten, uncurling my spine as I feel a surge of determination. This is starting to feel more insidious than ever.

"You said people call this place Camp Canceled," I say. "What if these are the reasons campers were canceled? Pills and drunk driving and BookTok?"

"I think you're on to something," Dani says.

"This one's a psych evaluation," I say. "Listen. *'After completing the program,* name redacted *has shown marked improvement in the area of anger management and appears better able to regulate emotional reactions to triggering stimulus.'*"

"Anger management, how very early 2000s," Dani says.

"Nobody at camp has seemed particularly angry," I say.

Dani's mouth twists. "Juniper is sort of broody."

I can't deny that, but I also can't picture Juniper getting so out of control that she required anger management therapy.

"This one's weird," Dani says. "Another personal statement: *'I just need a time-out from my phone. That's it. No trauma. No running away. I just want to spend a few weeks in the great outdoors.'*"

"Somebody here *didn't* get canceled?" I ask. That sounds a lot like what Kurt said, that he'd felt better after spending time in nature. But he also said he needed to get away after his sister died. My head is spinning. So many pieces are laid out on the table, but it's impossible to figure out how they fit together.

And at least some of those pieces could be the reasons for the missing campers.

Better luck next time, Willow says.

Dani looks over the documents. "There are enough files here for seven or eight people. More, if we factor in just how many different types of documents there are."

"There were eight campers when I checked in," I say. "Including Apollo. But what if the files aren't just about campers? What if the painkillers are for Sadie? Or Tye?"

Dani considers the tabletop. "Why would their files be mixed in with the campers'?"

"Maybe organization isn't this hoarder's forte."

I rub my forehead again, trying to rub away the headache.

"This is . . . a lot," I say.

Seeing people's pasts laid out like this is depressing. There's so much suffering. I feel sick, surveying this record of pain. Of hurt. Of misery.

If all these people were canceled for the reasons contained in these documents, how sad. How awful for everybody. There are no victors here.

And how trivial my own situation now appears.

Sure, I lost my job, my home, and my savings. But I'm strong. I know I'll bounce back. How many of these people can say that?

Dani reaches for another document. Just before she picks it up, I see the handwriting. I recognize it because it's my own. It's the personal statement I wrote before coming to Camp Castaway. I grab the piece of paper before Dani can, hugging it to me, suddenly breathless.

Dani looks surprised, then softens. "Hey, are you okay?"

I blink and force myself to meet her gaze. She looks concerned. Worried for me. And I've just made it so obvious the statement is mine. All those years of acting, but when it really counts, there's no hiding.

"Sorry, I just . . ." I trail off, my mind fogged.

"Whatever's written on there," Dani says, "I don't need to read it."

"It's not that. It's just . . . I lied. In my personal statement. I lied about what brought me here because I was ashamed."

Tell her, Willow says. *Just talk to her.*

I feel the truth hovering there, wanting to be spoken. And I realize I want to share it with Dani, because she understood about Brandon and Grams, and maybe she'll understand this, too.

"I came here because I was canceled," I say. "Like, old-school fire and brimstone canceled."

Dani says, "I'm listening."

Her kindness almost makes me unravel. But it makes me more confident, too.

"After my life was ruined," I say, "I suddenly understood how damaging other people's opinions could be. How that tide of shame swallowed you up, became all you could see. If other people at camp went through that, too . . . I feel for them."

Dani nods, takes it in.

"I guess we struggle to really understand that darkness until we've touched it ourselves," she says. "I was the same way when my relationship ended. I suddenly understood just how much my dad walked away from when he abandoned us, and it made me hate him even more."

There's a moment, like the seconds after a storm cloud breaks and the air fills with static.

Standing here with Dani, I wonder how I got so lucky. Camp Castaway may have fucked up in the biggest way, but at least it gave me Dani.

"What is it?" she asks.

"Nothing. I'm just glad you're here."

She cracks a smile. "In Buck's cabin?"

"At the camp. You have a way of making things make sense."

"I don't know, I find the world pretty confusing most of the time. But I know one thing: you're a good person. You might not believe that right now, but you are."

I lower my gaze. "I'm not so sure. I knew when I was younger that I was bi, but I kept it to myself. I didn't want Grams on my back, too. I think about that all the time. If only I'd told Bran we were the same, we could have run away together and found our own place. I could have saved him."

Dani takes my hands. "You can't know that."

"It feels like I do. It plays out in my head like a 'Keep Watching' Netflix prompt no matter how hard I try to cancel it. I see all the things I could've done differently, but in the end, it's always the same. I always fuck it up."

"I think that's called life," Dani says. She squeezes my hands. "Listen to me. You're badass. Your brother would be so proud of how far you've come. He'd be proud that you're keeping on. Whatever happened, whatever bullshit you've gone through, you're still going, and that's all you can do. That's all *any* of us can do."

I nod, finding comfort in her words.

"Thanks."

Standing here with Dani, in a cabin in the woods in the wilds of upstate New York, I realize I'm not the same person I was three weeks ago.

No, that's not quite right.

I *am* the same person, but layers have been added to me since then. I'm like one of the camp's many trees—gaining height and armor with the passing of time.

"We missed one," I say, bending down to pick up a folded piece of paper from the floor. I open it up, and I see it's another Sadie drawing. It shows a tree. The branches are crisscrossed with rectangles and squares drawn in black crayon. Sadie's nothing if not avant-garde.

"It looks like a tree house," I say, the picture suddenly making sense.

Dani peers at it. "You think it's a real place? Somewhere around here?"

"Sadie drew Kat and Buck. It stands to reason she's seen the tree house, too."

"A tree house could be a good place to shelter," Dani says. "Maybe Buck and Kat are there?"

"Or whoever made them disappear," I say, looking back down at the papers spread across the table. I feel like my insides have been scooped out. Camp Castaway was meant to provide an escape. A safe place to regroup without fear of reprisal. Tye promised there was no judgment here. I'm starting to believe the opposite is true.

"What if something bad really did happen to them?" I ask. "What if this whole camp is a scam?"

"What do you mean?"

I gesture at the documents, feeling hopeless and angry and lost all at once. Everybody at camp has something from their past that could destroy them if exposed to the world.

I remember the words painted in script above the Jesus mural in Bebe's house.

The Lord is a God who avenges. O God who avenges, shine forth.

"What if Bebe isn't interested in helping us?" I say. "What if she set up this place to accomplish the exact opposite? What if she brought us here to punish us?"

XXIII

As we approach the beach, I see that a couple of people have already beaten us to stone circle. Kurt sits on one of the logs around the fire pit, wearing a green jumpsuit and aviators, his hair gelled back from his face. Juniper stands beside him, tall and dressed in black.

"Hey," I say, as me and Dani join them. After what we found in Buck's cabin, I feel energized. Ready for a fight.

Easy, girl, Willow says. *Don't get ahead of yourself.*

Dani must sense how tense I am because the back of her hand brushes against mine, and I feel a fraction calmer. The wind is picking up, though. The sky is dark. No stars. No rain yet, either, but the threat is there.

"Hey, guys," Juniper says. "Want a smoke?"

She holds out a pack of Camels. I'm sure she's not a smoker, and I'm so programmed to agree with everything she says, I almost say yes, but then I see what she's wearing—a skeleton bodysuit, complete with gloves. She's drawn white lines into her face that make her cheekbones really pop, and those around the tip of her nose are realistically skull-like.

"Oh, I get it," I say, smiling. "You're Death, right?"

"Sure I can't tempt you?" she asks, waving the pack, which I take as confirmation.

I shake my head, taking a moment to revel in her singularly arch attention, but then I'm interrupted by Misty, joining us on the beach.

"Hey, babe," Misty says. I realize she's talking to me. It takes me a moment to register what she's wearing. A frilly pink tutu with a pair of black Doc Martens, like season one Villanelle. Pink and blue ribbons snake through her hair, and her makeup is layered on as thick as paste—hot pink lips, baby blue lids.

Misty grins at me. "I'm guessing you're the only person who can see me right now."

I feel like air has been punched from my chest.

She's dressed as Eliza. The imaginary friend from *We Love Willow*.

I must be imagining it, projecting something onto Misty that isn't really there. But the style is unmistakable, and the bright glint in Misty's eye tells me I'm a hundred miles from wrong.

Misty knows the show.

She knows who I am.

Looking at the detail of her costume, I realize it's more than mere recognition.

She's a *We Love Willow* fan.

How did I miss it? I've been mooning over Juniper for three whole days. Has Misty been doing the same, but with me? And if she's a fan, she must know everything. Tweetageddon. Everything.

I stare at her, dumbfounded, and her grin slips.

"You don't like it?" she asks.

"What's going on?" Dani asks.

I feel something creak and split in my mind.

Misty is fucking with me.

And I am fully done being fucked with.

"She's dressed as Eliza," I say. "A character from my show."

"Your show?" Kurt asks.

"It's the reason I'm here. I was on a Netflix series that got canned because of something I posted online. Everything fell apart, and I came here to escape it all."

Funny how the truth suddenly feels feeble. It doesn't have the same grip on me that it once did.

"And now Misty's dressed up as your co-star," Juniper says. "That's sort of messed up, Misty."

"Yeah, what's wrong with you?" Dani demands. She seems more outraged on my behalf than shocked by the sitcom revelation.

Misty's head dips. "I thought you'd like it. I thought . . . well, you called yourself Willow. I didn't know it was some big secret . . ."

I don't know where to look.

When I first got here, I wanted nothing more than to be anonymous. Forgotten.

But that was the me from three days ago. A lot has happened since then. I don't have the bandwidth to deal with Misty on top of everything else.

"Look, something is going on here at camp," I say. "I think we're in danger. If we all confront Bebe, she can't deny it anymore."

"You think she's hiding something?" Juniper asks.

"We don't know for sure that she called the cops," I say. "Has anybody seen a single cop around camp?"

"I sure haven't," Dani says.

"You think something bad happened to Buck?" Juniper asks. "And Kat?"

"They can look after themselves," Misty says.

I grit my teeth. "Just listen to me—"

"Wow, look at you all," Bebe says, appearing with Tye. "What fantastic costumes."

She's dressed like a turn-of-the-century explorer in tan shorts and shirt, and a safari hat. Her gaze sweeps us, passing right over me. She doesn't seem to have overheard me or know that I've been in her office.

I look at the others, wondering if they'd back me up if I started grilling Bebe. Juniper, surely? But only Dani seems to be giving the Camp Mom a suspicious glare.

"Merry Christmas, y'all," Tye says. He wears bright red pajamas trimmed in white, plus a matching bobble hat. "Nice shades, Kurt. Let me guess, Maverick?"

"Goose," Kurt says, gesturing to a paper badge on his shoulder that he must have made himself. He gives Tye a nervous smile, and I remember the way he looked at the groundskeeper when he was doing his knife trick. I swear Kurt's crushing on Tye, but I can't tell if Tye's noticed.

"Shall we begin?" Bebe says, breaking me from my thoughts.

Her artificial peppiness is grating, but I bite my tongue. If I push too hard, there's no saying what she'll do.

When we're all seated around the firepit, the lake making hushing sounds as it slips and slides against the shore, Bebe leans forward to address us.

"Welcome to the end of the world," she says. "I am your humble guide as, tonight, we navigate our final hours on Earth. We're going to live as if there is no tomorrow, because who's to say there even will be?"

"Sort of dark," I say.

"It depends on your perspective. It could be liberating, to live entirely in the now, without worrying about the consequences." She looks around the circle. "We hide behind masks every day. Responsibilities, social expectations, self-discipline . . . they all demand we behave in a particular way. But dressing in costume like this allows us some distance from ourselves. That's what I'd like to focus on this stone circle."

My hands are knotted in my lap. Does Bebe really think this is a good idea? Pretending there's no tomorrow when campers are missing? The timing feels like poor taste. But then, Bebe hasn't exactly been sensitive to our needs so far. I'm starting to wonder what qualifies her to lead group therapy. To run this camp. Did she just wake up one day and like the ring of "Camp Mom"?

"This is the question that we're going to ask ourselves," Bebe says. "How would we want to spend our last night on Earth? What would we say or do?" Her gaze roves around us. "Willow? Would you like to start?"

I look at her in surprise. Perhaps she really does know I've been snooping, and she picked me as punishment.

"Okay," I say. "I guess I'd spend my last night on Earth watching horror movies about Ghostface killers and eating Domino's pizza."

"Most excellent," Dani says.

Misty makes a scoffing sound in the back of her throat.

"Do you have a problem?" Dani asks her.

"Me? No." Misty shakes her head, but she looks at me as if she suddenly can't bear the sight of me, and her grimace makes me prickle all over.

She knows what I tweeted.

Of course she knows. She's known the whole time we were at camp. I wasn't being paranoid yesterday when she told Tye he might have "better luck" at a game of Twenty-One.

She was messing with me.

I want to change the subject. Move Bebe's question around the circle.

But I'm sick of running.

I won't run anymore.

"If you have something to say, just say it," I tell her.

Misty looks unfazed. Her gaze flicks at Bebe, then back to me. "I know we're not supposed to know anything about each other's lives outside of camp, but I can't help it that you're famous. Everybody knows who you are."

"Thanks to you," Dani says.

"Ladies, little hostile," Tye says, raising his hands in a pacifying gesture, but it's difficult to take him seriously in the Santa suit.

"This is relevant to Willow's personal growth, I swear," Misty says, and she sounds sincere, but there's a sharpness to her tone, too. I don't like where this is headed.

"Out in the real world, the last thing we knew, you were engaged," Misty says. "To a man. There was that big, splashy proposal; it was all over *Ours! Weekly*. Now suddenly you're making out with a girl, and the engagement ring's gone, and you're talking about horror movies . . . I can't help wondering, is this the real you? Or just another performance?"

"That's pretty reductive," Juniper says.

"Yeah, people are multiples," Tye says. "We're never just one thing."

Misty's gaze remains on me.

"It just seems like you have no clue who you are," she says.

I'm stiff in the chair. And the thing is, she's a hairsbreadth from being right.

For the longest time, I denied who I am. I put my back to the truth and tried to carve a path toward the kind of life that was supposed to be easy. I wanted to fit in. Avoid all the pain and grief that nearly broke me before.

But the truth kept pushing to the surface, like a green sapling seeking the sun.

I know I don't owe Misty anything, and certainly not an explanation. Maybe in some twisted way, though, she's done me a favor by backing me into a corner.

Because I want to say it.

I'm so tired of being the safe girl. The sitcom girl. The girl who dates the right guy, who goes to the right restaurants, who wears exactly the right outfit at awards ceremonies and who says exactly the right thing on the red carpet.

Do it.

Do it.

Finally, I say the words.

"Better luck next time."

"What?" Kurt asks.

"Better luck next time. That's what I tweeted."

Not exactly earth-shattering words, are they? Willow says.

Funny how saying them again feels almost anticlimactic.

Still, I'm shaking.

"They're the words I said in every episode of *We Love Willow*," I say.

A hush falls over the campfire.

I said "Better luck next time!" whenever a character messed up, or something didn't go to plan. Sometimes I said the line to myself in the bathroom mirror. Sometimes I said it under my breath if the scene required poignancy. But it was in every episode. Willow's catchphrase.

"I figured it was so well known that people would get it if I used it in a tweet," I say. "So I tweeted the line to show support for the LGBTQ+ community after a protective bill failed to pass through the Senate."

Instead, I trivialized the whole thing.

I made the bill seem like a joke.

That's what kills me.

Because the thing is: the reaction was warranted. The hatred was justified.

I fucked up. It was an idiotic use of Willow's catchphrase. It's no wonder they wanted my head on a stick. And the worst part is that I wasn't allowed to say I was sorry, because my agent said that would open up a whole new legal can of worms.

"My one moment of public outspokenness resulted in me being gagged," I say.

Maybe that's why I've heard Willow's voice in my head ever since the show was canned.

"So you don't hate gay people?" Misty asks.

"Misty, what the fuck?" Juniper says.

"It was a misunderstanding," I say, and I suddenly understand why Misty is behaving like this. It's right there in her Eliza costume—a costume only a fan would know how to put together. And now I see that under her questioning is a current of disappointment. Disillusionment. She's a fan, and I let her down.

The fans were the ones who believed the lie—that I was the perky and purehearted Willow. They wanted me to be her, and the longer I played her, the more I saw that sitcoms weren't only fluffy escapism. They were a promise. They gave people hope that a better world was out there. Sitcoms never cheated or lied or failed to show up. They were the friend you always wished you had. The one who was always there for you.

And I broke that promise.

I revealed the truth behind the lie.

And they tried to destroy me for it.

"I don't hate gay people," I tell Misty. "I *am* gay people. I'm bi. I've always been bi. I just didn't want the world to know it."

"Because you were ashamed."

"Seriously, Misty—" Dani says, but I cut her off.

"Yes. I was ashamed. And scared. I just wanted things to be easy, but they never are. And that's my shit to deal with, not yours. Anyway, it wouldn't even have spiraled like that if it weren't for the Gossip Goblin."

"What's that?" Kurt asks.

"A Twitter user who hid behind a fake identity in order to expose celebrity secrets online."

The Gossip Goblin got internet famous last year. They posted anonymously to their eight-hundred-thousand-plus followers on Twitter, or X, or whatever the hell it's called now, and their MO was simple: Tearing down celebrities. Exposing their secrets via tweets that became the talk of the town. Their hit rate was devastating.

"Being targeted by the Gossip Goblin is like being hit by a 747," I say. "They set their sights on me three weeks ago, when they quote-posted my *better luck next time* and claimed I was a toxic right-wing sympathizer with an antigay agenda."

If it weren't for the Gossip Goblin, chances are people would have scrolled right past my bad joke. Moved on. But with their huge reach and ardent following, the Gossip Goblin ensured that the snowball kept rolling, getting bigger and bigger until it became unavoidable.

"I'm sorry," Kurt says.

"Right, the Gossip Goblin was the problem," Misty says.

"How about we talk about you for a minute, Misty?" Dani's voice is like glass. "Tell us more about the gambling addiction. I'm still fuzzy on how exactly that got you canceled."

"That really was a misunderstanding." Misty looks uncomfortable for the first time.

"Right, *yours* was a misunderstanding," Dani says.

Silence settles across the beach. My heart is still pounding, my mind struggling to process the powder keg that stone circle has become. Dani doesn't reach for me, but she gives me a look full of compassion and support. I manage a small smile, grateful beyond words that she's got my back.

"Juniper?" Bebe says. "Is there anything you'd like to do before the end of the world?"

"I'm ready for the apocalypse," Juniper says. "I'll watch that fireball coming while enjoying a cold beer."

"Kurt?" Bebe asks.

"I'd spend my final night playing the guitar," Kurt says. "That's all I need."

"Thank you, Kurt. Dani?"

"I'm good," Dani says.

"Really?" Misty asks. "I wouldn't want to go into the apocalypse having not come clean to the people I care about."

Dani's hands curl in her lap. She stares at Misty like she wants to tear off her head and toss it in the lake. Wind whispers through the trees and the temperature drops, like a net being cast over the stone circle.

"What's that supposed to mean?" I ask Misty.

"I'm guessing she didn't tell you?" There's triumph in her gaze. "We're in the company of internet royalty. The Gossip Goblin is right here with us. You two make quite the couple."

I feel suddenly cold.

I look at Dani, waiting for her to deny Misty's claim.

But Dani's silent. She won't look at me. She'd said when we first met that she was a novelist. Not a gossip columnist. She was very clear about the distinction.

A muscle in her temple flickers, hardening and relaxing seemingly independent of her will, and that's how I know Misty's telling the truth.

Dani's the one who dropped a grenade into my life three weeks ago, grinning with the pin still gripped between her teeth.

I think about the way Dani looked at me on the first night, like she was trying to figure me out. Put a name to my face. She made an effort to talk to me. She left the firepit to walk me back to my cabin. Got to know me. Got close to me.

She knew who I was from the start.

I stare at Dani, and her gaze finally lifts to meet mine, heavy with guilt.

"It's not what you think," she says. "I can explain."

I can't bring myself to look at her again.

My lips tingle with the memory of her kiss. I resist the urge to drag my nails across them, scour any trace of her.

Instead, I get up from my chair, and I walk away from stone circle.

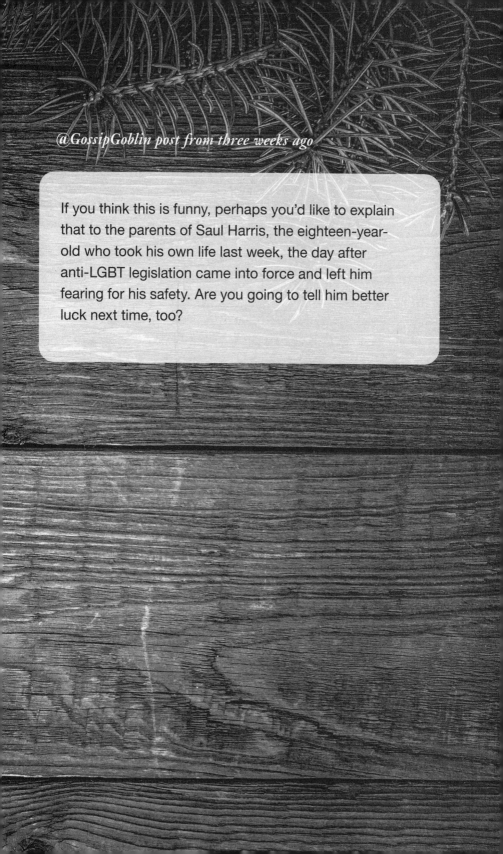

If you think this is funny, perhaps you'd like to explain that to the parents of Saul Harris, the eighteen-year-old who took his own life last week, the day after anti-LGBT legislation came into force and left him fearing for his safety. Are you going to tell him better luck next time, too?

XXIV

A re you okay?" Kurt asks.

"Never better."

I push steamed broccoli and bean salad around on my plate. We sit alone at a picnic bench, a safe distance from the beach. The camp has fallen into shadow around the firepit. A few battery-powered lanterns are dotted about, but they do little to hold back the gloom, and the fire itself feels violent, constantly popping and cracking, conjuring images in my mind of snapping bones.

The end-of-the-world party is big with the weird vibes.

Even if we didn't just have the most aggressive group therapy session, it's clear we're all thinking about the missing campers. I see Juniper looking to the forest while she drinks and chats with Bebe, as if expecting a cop to emerge with Buck and Kat in tow. In the deck chairs, Tye tries to focus on whatever Misty is saying, but his gaze keeps drifting to the clubhouse, like he's waiting for a phone call.

And Dani is by the lake, holding an uneaten hot dog in one hand, looking like the saddest clown in the world.

We haven't spoken. I don't know what there is to say. I'd thought me and Dani were a drama-free zone, but the opposite has turned out to be true.

"That was heavy," Kurt says. "Like, I don't know what Misty was thinking coming for you. And Dani . . ."

He trails off.

"Honestly, it's fine," I say. "I can handle it."

Kurt slowly eats his sweet potato fries. I can tell he's not convinced, but I don't want to make a scene.

"Want to play rock paper scissors?" he asks. "Or arm wrestle? Hey, we could *mud* wrestle?"

He gives me such a goofy smile, I can't help my mouth tugging up at the corners. It feels tight, though, because I'm still sure Kurt's keeping something from me.

"Oh shit," Kurt says, "you messed up the brooding Batman thing. Now we have to mud wrestle."

"I've still got the voice," I growl, Christian Bale style.

"That is actually quite unnerving."

"Hey, guys, enjoying the end of the world?" Tye asks, appearing by the picnic bench. He looks more like a wrestler than Santa Claus wearing his fur-trimmed red pajamas.

"Having a blast," I say.

He must read my tone because he nods.

"Yeah, that was pretty brutal. Stone circle can stir up a lot of feelings that haven't been processed yet. They can be rough in the moment, but they're good in the long run. Like, that kind of honesty is sort of loving."

"Funny, what Misty did didn't feel loving at all," I say.

I can't believe Tye is defending what happened at stone circle. And on top of the revelation about Dani, I'm still reeling from the fact that Misty's a fan. I had no clue. Most fans are sweet, friendly. They just want to share a moment with you, get a picture, and then carry on with their lives.

Only the very few overstep the mark. Get possessive.

Wait, would *Misty* break into my cabin? What if she's the one who took the photo of Brandon?

"It's important to remember," Tye says, "this place looks like a summer camp, but it's got other things going on, too. We're here to process real pain and trauma. That can be messy."

I bite my tongue and nod. He's talking like Bebe.

Looking at the meager gathering on the beach, I can't believe that this is all that's left. There seemed to be so many of us when I first arrived. So many names to remember; so many people to figure out and deceive.

Now there's just six of us. Our secrets are leaking out like gas, and I feel like somebody is watching it all, waiting to strike a match.

I realize that Tye is a vital source of information that, so far, I've left untapped. He's a local. Maybe he knows the real history of Camp Castaway.

"Did you grow up around here?" I ask him.

"Mountain man to the core. I've worked at the camp ever since it opened. Jeez, saying it out loud makes me feel old."

He's at least the same age as me.

"What did you do before?" Kurt asks, and color rises in his throat as he speaks.

"A whole ton of nothing, according to my stepdad," Tye says. His tone is light, but there's darkness there, too. "I tried the big-city thing, got a job in a diner. It didn't work out."

"How come?" Kurt asks.

"I had my own shit to deal with, out here."

His own shit?

Was Tye originally a camper?

"Has it helped?" Kurt asks. "Being here?"

Tye's gaze meets Kurt's, and he looks on edge. Maybe the question touched a sore point. Kurt is practically glowing neon, his cheeks bright red, but he holds Tye's eye contact. I wonder if he wants to reach out a comforting hand.

"Like, it hasn't fixed everything . . ." Tye clears his throat and I swear he's blushing now, too. "But, yeah, I guess things are better now."

The awkward exchange makes me feel for Kurt. He really does get moony-eyed around the groundskeeper. Tye's so difficult to read, it's impossible to tell if he's noticed, or cares. And now I'm wondering if any of the documents we found in Buck's attic really are about the groundskeeper.

"Did you know there was a camper here years ago named Nancy?" I ask him.

Tye bites into a burger. "Isn't that the story Buck told?"

"No. I mean, yes, he told a story about somebody called Nancy, but there was a real camper here who died a while back. She was called Nancy, too."

"She died? Here?" Kurt asks. "How?"

"She was decapitated."

"Where'd you hear that?" Tye asks me, and again there's that split tone, like he's trying to keep it light, but he can't quite conceal the dark.

"There was something about it in the game room," I say. "In one of the books."

"Interesting. That's a new one on me."

He keeps eating, and I feel he's holding something back, but I can't figure out a way to get him to say more.

"Hey," a voice says, and I look up to find Dani standing by the bench.

Kurt and Tye don't speak, their attention on me, waiting for my reaction.

"Hi," I say, looking back down at my plate.

"Can we talk?" Dani asks.

I'm about to tell her there's nothing to talk about when Tye jumps up from the bench. "Kurt, what say we crack out the volleyball set?"

"Uh, sure," Kurt says. He gives me a questioning look, and I appreciate his concern, but I'm a big girl. I nod to him that it's okay, and he goes with Tye, walking slowly, I guess in case I change my mind.

When the guys are gone, I push my uneaten plate of food across the bench.

"How can I help you?" I ask Dani.

Dani frowns.

"I wanted to say I'm sorry," she says. "I've wanted to tell you about the whole Gossip Goblin thing—and I would have, if Misty hadn't outed me."

"Ha," I say, a sound that is part scornful, part bitterly amused.

I see what she wrote about me, and I just can't put together Dani—funny, thoughtful, observant—with the kind of sadistic gossip machine that trolled people online. Destroyed their livelihoods.

"You knew who I was," I say, stating the fact rather than asking. "That first night I arrived here, you knew."

Her eyebrows draw together as she says, "Yes."

The confirmation hurts. I feel like even more of a fool.

"And you wrote that post, telling everybody I was a homophobic monster."

Dani's chin lowers. "I did."

My fingernails dig into the bench. I feel like the ground is shaking beneath me, opening up a fissure I'm about to tumble into.

"Why?" I ask. "Why would you do that?"

Dani takes a breath, seems to struggle with what to say.

"I saw your post as an attack," she says. "I saw red."

My throat closes up.

That's what everybody said about my tweet. They claimed I was attacking the queer community.

"It's a war zone out there for LGBT people right now," Dani says. "All the hard-won freedoms we were only just beginning to enjoy are being taken away. 'Don't say gay' and book banning and fucking 'straight pride' . . . we could slip back into the dark ages so easily. Somebody has to fight it."

I'm glad she's wearing the clown costume, because it helps me separate her from the Dani I've known for three days. The one I like kissing so much. The one who helped me access a part of myself that I've suppressed and ignored for too long.

And the thing is, I have no right to be angry that a stranger drew the wrong conclusions about me, when I was never projecting the real me. I kept parts of myself hidden for so long, and Dani's right about how scary the world is right now. Part of me admires her for taking a stand.

But the pain of watching my life fall apart is still there. Bitter and sharp as any ax.

I can't look at Dani and I don't know what to say.

Dani says, "I sort of figured celebrities were fair game. I went too far."

"You wrote a post telling everybody I was antigay, and then you kissed me," I say.

Dani frowns. "You kissed me first."

"Did you ever like me?" I ask. "Was any of it real? Or were you just proving a point?"

"It was real," Dani says, eyes burning. "I shut down my account right after the post about you went viral. I realized I'd gone too far. The posts are gone."

"Nothing is ever gone online." I shake my head. "Do you get how messed up this is? Why would you hang out with me here, knowing what you'd done to me?"

"I felt bad," Dani says. "I couldn't believe it when you turned up here. Like, that's crazy in itself. But then I figured I could make it up to you, somehow. And then you turned out to be, well, awesome. I liked hanging out with you. I know it's fucked up. I guess I saw you as two separate people. The persona that made you famous, and the real you. *This* you."

I hear what she's saying, but all I can think about is the words she wrote online.

This is too much.

It's insane.

I stand and start pacing toward the boardwalk, my mind swooping in dizzy circles.

Everything that led me to this moment goes back to the Gossip Goblin post. Having my intentions and my identity questioned woke me up from my dream life. I became aware of what I'd become: the sitcom star living a lie in an overpriced beach house engaged to a kind but boring gym hunk. Some people would kill for that life, but that life was killing me.

Did Dani's calling attention to my post actually set me free?

"I'm really fucking sorry," Dani says, following me. "I hate that I could have fucked this up."

I hear the hurt in her tone. The sincerity.

But I feel like a fool.

I spent so long being careful. Trusting nobody with the small, wounded parts of myself. And then I blabbed everything to the first pretty girl who showed me any attention at camp. Told them about Brandon, and Grams—and Dani knew who I was from the moment we first met.

She knew when Misty showed up dressed as Eliza.

I stop walking, facing the forest. I can't do this anymore. I can't deal with this whole situation, and I can't let anybody in.

But she's cute adorable Dani, Willow says. *She's like the Dewey to your Gale, or maybe the other way around?*

"Look, we're fine," I say. "I accept your apology."

Dani's lower jaw pushes out. "Jesus, how can you be so calm?"

"All these things we kept from each other," I say. "We don't know each other. Not really. And that's fine."

"Wow," Dani says, and I'm starting to hate myself, because the hurt look on her face is making me feel almost as shitty as I did post-tweetageddon.

I just want this conversation over.

"Whatever we thought we had," I say, "it's done."

"Please, Willow." Dani tries to take my hand, and I move it out of the way. The fact that she's using my sitcom name only highlights how wrong this has gone.

We stand at the beginning of the boardwalk, and I'm pretty sure everybody on the beach is watching us. Dani doesn't seem to care, though. She stares at me for what feels like eternity. Anger and hurt wrestle in her face.

Maybe she thinks I'll change my mind.

Is anybody truly blameless in this situation? It's not like there's a precedent for a canceled actor striking up a romance with the person who canceled them.

I'm about to open my mouth to speak when Dani beats me to it.

"You know what?" she says, anger appearing to win out. "I tried to apologize, explain, but it's clear you don't want to hear it. Maybe you're not the person I thought you were. Have a nice life, Willow. What's left of it."

"What's that supposed to mean?"

She spreads her arms as she paces backward. "It's the end of the world, remember? Maybe you'll get lucky, and something really will come along tonight and blow up this world you hate so much."

She turns and heads in the direction of the cabins.

I still feel where her hand brushed mine, and the warmth on my skin fades as she disappears into the night.

XXV

I wait until I'm sure Dani is far enough ahead of me that I won't catch up with her, and then I step onto the trail through the woods that leads back to camp. My head is still in pieces after our fight, but I have to focus on what's important. And what's important is making it through the night, so we can all hike out of here first thing tomorrow, find help for Buck and Kat. Actual, real help—not the forest rangers Bebe supposedly spoke with this afternoon.

In the dark, the forest feels huge. Endless. I can't help imagining what kind of things happen out there, in the whispering spaces between trees. Nature is nurturing, yes, but it's also wild, violent, and unforgiving.

My hand tightens around the strap of the medical bag slung over my shoulder. The kitchen knives inside are heavy. Solid and reassuring.

"Hey, kid," a voice says, making me jump.

Juniper has caught up with me. She's wearing her multicolored jacket over the skeleton suit, and she carries a lantern, which lights up her face, that trademark smirk in place—the one that is somehow both companionable and commanding.

"Hey," I say.

"Bebe told me to buddy up with you. I guess she doesn't want more campers vanishing."

Jesus. *Now* is the moment I have to buddy up with Juniper? Why not yesterday or the day before, when I actually wanted her company? I suppose I should be grateful it's not Misty who chased after me.

"I can handle myself," I say.

Juniper gives me one of her *Fight Me* looks. Steel, respect, and curiosity.

The lantern bounces light around us. Juniper digs into a pocket in her jacket and removes something metallic, which she holds out to me.

"Here," she says, and I see it's a hip flask. "I figure you could use something to take the edge off this evening."

My eyes widen. "How did you—"

"You don't get to my age without learning a few tricks. Our little secret? Us Hollywood girls have to stick together."

Us Hollywood girls. I like the idea that me and Juniper are in some kind of club, even if it's one of the most fucked-up clubs you can sign up for.

I take the flask and put it to my lips. Warm, peaty liquid fills my mouth and I swallow, my throat burning, then pleasantly numbing. I've only had whiskey a couple of times in my life, but I can tell this is the good stuff. I pass the flask back to Juniper.

"A toast," she says. "To drama."

"To drama?"

"Sure, it's what keeps life interesting—and us in work, most of the time."

I can't argue with that. "To drama," I say. Juniper winks and knocks back the drink.

"Now tell me," she says, "you and Dani, are you going to survive this? Kiss and make up?"

Her directness is bracing but welcome, although for a moment I wonder if she's asking if we'll survive tonight. There really is something apocalyptic about it—the party, the costumes, the arguments. It feels like a living version of one of the movies I grew up watching with Brandon. The subject of Dani, though . . .

"I don't think we can," I say. "It's too weird and messed up."

"I get it. When I checked in here, I thought I'd get to sit rolling my eyes and sipping cocktails while everybody else braided hair and painted pottery. But healing isn't that straightforward. What's that great Patricia Hayes line? 'It has to hurt if it is to heal.' Crazy movie but that's a great line."

"You make it look easy, though," I say. "The fame game, the press. It doesn't seem to faze you."

Juniper laughs. "Oh, honey, if only." She takes another pull, then hands me the flask. I tip it back and the burn is less intense the second time around. The whiskey is already warming me from the inside.

"They may have dressed this all up with a new name," Juniper says, "but you should've been there in the '90s. They call it 'cancel culture' now, but back then it was just 'culture.' Look at the way they treated Bette Davis in the forties. Pam Anderson in the '90s. We do our jobs and the press do theirs, they just make more noise than us."

She presses a hand into my shoulder, and her touch is grounding. Not charged with some kind of mystical energy. Not "Juniper Brown, superstar," but "Juniper Brown, human person."

"I'm not trying to diminish your experience," she says. "In some ways, maybe you do have it worse, because Bette and Pam could escape it by not reading the papers. You have all of that in the palm of your hand, like a grenade. You had to come *here* to get away from what people are saying about you.

"Listen," she says, "this is the best piece of advice I can give. As long as you're kind, and unprejudiced, and haven't hurt anybody: Refuse. To. Be. Ashamed. Wear your mistakes with pride. Look them in the eye and own your space on this Earth. Own it shamelessly, without regret, and no fucker has any power over you."

Her eyes are dark pools, filled with certainty.

Can it be that simple?

Refuse to be ashamed?

I wish I could disengage the part of my brain that cares, but I *am* ashamed. I'd thought I was indestructible, and the world took great pleasure in proving me wrong. Now I'm sitting amid the wreckage of my life, and I don't have a shovel to dig myself out of it.

Unless I do.

Maybe I *am* the shovel.

Shit, I'm drunk.

Also, we seem to have wandered past the cabins.

"We shouldn't go too far," I say. "I've seen some creepy things around here."

"My cabin's just through here," Juniper says. "It's a little apart from the others, farther into the woods. I like my privacy. That's where I keep the good stuff."

Juniper strides confidently, which calms me. Still, my hand goes to the bag at my side, packed full of sharp kitchen utensils.

You're fine, Willow says. *Just shiv anything that jumps out of the dark.*

Juniper takes another swig and hands me the flask.

"Let's make another toast," she says. "Here's to being canceled, because in my book, a cancellation is just an invitation to make other plans."

"Cheers," I say, and I tip the flask, savoring the warmth that floods through me.

"You're going to be okay, kid. Trust me on that. In a hundred years, nobody will remember any of this."

"Thanks," I say, and I mean it. Talking with Juniper has been different from talking to anybody else in here, including Dani. Juniper gets it in a way few people can.

"Why are you here?" I ask.

Juniper frowns, pockets the flask. "At camp?"

"It's just that you seem to have life all figured out. But you mentioned a sick relative during stone circle and ..." I trail off, wondering if she's about to repeat her disappearing act from earlier, but I have to ask, and not just because the booze has loosened my tongue.

"Right," Juniper says, "I did say that, but it wasn't entirely true."

"It wasn't?"

"No, but here's the truth. It wasn't a relative who got sick; it was me. That's why I left." She sighs, and I've only ever heard her use that naked tone during affirmations. "You know how difficult it is to be unwell in Hollywood? How *brave* you suddenly become? *So* goddamn brave."

I'm speechless. I had no idea.

And suddenly I'm thinking about the prescription for fentanyl that we found in Buck's cabin. And there was the personal statement about only being here for vacation. *No trauma. No running away. I just want to spend a few weeks in the great outdoors.*

Were they both Juniper?

She rolls her eyes. "They martyr you, the fans, and the press, and then they demand updates. They want to go on this fucked-up journey with you. They treat it like a sporting event, one you either win or lose, as if physical or mental stamina has anything to do with beating cancer. I didn't want any of that. So I left."

"I'm sorry," I say.

"Sure."

"Are you ... I mean, are you going to be ... ?" I leave the question hanging, can't bring myself to ask if Juniper is dying.

"I'm not going anywhere," Juniper says, the smirk returning.

"Good," I say. "The world needs Juniper Brown."

She breaks into a grin and shoulder-bumps me. "Gee, kid, you'll make me blush." Her face drops and she grabs my arm, bringing me to a standstill. "Did you hear that?"

I'm pretty sure she's goofing around, but then I hear it, too. A sound in the night. And every hair on my body lifts.

Tapping.

No, not tapping.

Knocking.

Something striking a tree trunk, over and over, the sound ringing through the dark. A sound just for us.

Knock.

Knock.

Knock.

Somebody's out here with us.

XXVI

For a horrible moment, I'm unable to move.

The sound paralyzes me.

My lungs won't take in air.

It's the same knocking from my first night at the camp. Slow. Sarcastic. Goading. A taunt and a tease rolled into one.

I look around and I can't tell where we are. I thought we were just strolling, but it got darker so suddenly. We've wandered away from the boardwalk, into the woods, no cabins in sight. No campers. I can't even see the lake.

Where the hell are we?

As quickly as the knocking began, it suddenly stops.

The blanketing silence that follows is worse because it could mean the wait is over. Whoever is taunting us, they know where we are.

"Who do you think it is?" Juniper asks.

Fucking run, Willow says, but something catches my eye. One of the tree trunks right next to us is different. Markings have been carved into the bark. Deep ridges gouged with a sharp blade. Juniper notices me looking and lifts the lantern, casting light over the tree trunk, and we both see what's carved there.

Eyes.

Half a dozen of them, stacked one on top of the other, forming a pillar down the trunk.

A pillar of eyes.

Even though it doesn't make sense, sounds goddamn crazy, *I feel seen*. The forest is looking at us.

It knows we're here.

Fucking, Willow says, *run!*

"Let's move," I say, pulling a knife from the bag and gripping it tight.

"Nice," Juniper says.

Blood thumps in my ears and it's all I can hear. I can't tell which direction the knocking came from. I just know we have to move. Fast. Anywhere that's away from that sound.

As we hurry through the forest, I see a shape slip behind one of the trees.

Knock.

Knock.

Knock.

The sound rings through the night, and in my mind, I see a headless woman running split nails over tough bark. I hear the wheeze of stale air coming from the stump of her neck. The drag of an ax on the dirt, the hem of her skirts rustling over dead leaves.

No. It's not Knock-Knock Nancy because Knock-Knock Nancy isn't real.

"Sadie?" I call, and my voice is weightless. It falls to the forest floor.

"Who's Sadie?" Juniper asks.

I don't answer, instead clearing my throat and saying louder, "Buck? This isn't funny."

No answer.

"Whoever the fuck is out there," Juniper yells, "you better be ready."

Still nothing.

The silence is insanity-making. Everything in the forest has gone quiet. Every bird and critter.

"Fuck this," Juniper whispers. "Come on."

We pick up our pace. The ground is littered with rocks and jutting roots and tangled underbrush, and I trip and lurch along, grabbing hold of tree trunks for support. Somehow, I manage to remain on my feet.

I hear movement behind me.

A shape cuts through the forest.

With a burst of energy, I speed up, dodging to one side. I dart left, then left again, hoping to confuse whoever is chasing us, Juniper keeping pace with me. I know we're making too much noise, but I can't help it. My heart beats the same command over and over. *Away-get-away*—

I crash into something solid, a person, and open my mouth to scream. A hand clamps over my face, while another grips my wrist, stopping the knife from plunging into their chest. I stare into wide eyes. I smell sweat and dirt, and despite the darkness and the panic, I recognize the face I'm staring into.

Kurt.

"Shhhh." He looks around us, listening, and I can't breathe with his hand over my mouth. Can't think what he's doing out here.

I shove him off me, raising the knife. He staggers back a few paces.

"What are you doing out here?" I demand.

"Quiet."

"Kurt," Juniper says. "What the fu—"

She breaks off, looking to one side, listening. We stand motionless for a few seconds, three campers in costume straining to hear the telltale sounds of a person approaching, but the forest has fallen silent. There's no more knocking.

Finally, Kurt's stance relaxes.

"They're gone," he says.

"They who?" I ask.

"Did you see somebody out here?" Juniper asks.

"I heard them," he says.

I feel a chill. "You heard the knocking?"

Kurt nods, and the chill mixes with relief. I realize a part of me was scared I'd imagined the sound.

"You think it was . . ." I don't finish the sentence.

Buck?

Knock-Knock Nancy?

"What are you doing out here?" I ask again, settling for an easier question.

Kurt swallows. "I saw you and Juniper walking through the woods, and I followed you. Are you guys having your own party out here?"

"You could say that," Juniper says.

Kurt looks around the empty woods. I scan our surroundings for the path leading back to the cabins, but I can't see it.

"So where's the party?" Kurt asks.

I'm about to tell him there is no party when Juniper raises an arm to point.

"I'm thinking that's it?" she says, lifting the lantern. I get goose bumps as the glow trickles over an enormous, gnarled tree trunk and up onto a series of rotting wooden boards nestled in the branches above our heads.

The tree house from Sadie's drawing.

It huddles fifty feet up, cradled in knotted branches. It has a peaked roof, a couple of windows, and a door. Even from here I can see that the wood is chipped and crumbling, the roof sunken. It must be decades old. Ancient.

Juniper whistles. "Oh boy."

"That place is definitely haunted," Kurt says.

It looks just like the tree Sadie drew. Buck and Kat could be up there. If they are, we have to help them. "There are steps," I say, seeing rectangles of timber hammered into the trunk.

Then we hear something that sounds like a low moan. Could be someone in pain, or just one of the many sounds from the forest—it's impossible to tell. But what if it's Buck or Kat? I have to help if I can.

"Be careful," Juniper says, but I'm already climbing. I dig my toes into the wood, and the steps feel secure, so I keep going. It's made more difficult by the fact that I'm still holding the knife, but I might need it. I scale the tree step by step, ignoring the scrubby ground as it drops farther below. I reach a square hole in the walkway above and pull myself through, emerging onto a gallery that runs around the tree house.

A breeze curls around me and I shiver, looking down at Juniper and Kurt huddled around the lantern light.

I turn to examine the tree house. It's dark, silent. I pace around its perimeter, looking for a door. The wood is soft beneath my shoes, wet and spongy, and I realize it's started to drizzle again. The rain is little more than a mist, but I already feel it seeping into my clothes.

I find a chipped door and touch it with my fingertips. I hold the knife tight as I push open the door.

The smell of rot and damp fills my nostrils as I look inside, and as my eyes adjust to the gloom, I see—

"What is this place?" Kurt asks right behind me, making me jump. I didn't hear him climb up. I put a finger to my mouth and watch as Juniper joins us, bringing light with her. Together, we go into the tree house.

The lantern lays the tree house's secrets bare in flickering light.

Crucifixes fill one wall. Thousands of interlinking crosses form a rippling pattern, like rustic art on a budget. Painted words sprawl across another wall, letters long and dripping, as if painted in a hurry, or by somebody gripped by some mad prophecy.

JUDGMENT FOR ALL

AN EYE FOR AN EYE

HEADS WILL ROLL

My gaze lingers on the last sentence, and I think about Knock-Knock Nancy. I think about the ax Bebe brought down on the iPod, and Buck pranking Kat by brandishing the ax over her head.

What if Buck and Kat came across some weirdo in the woods? What if they got hurt?

"Oh shit," Kurt says.

"What?" I ask, and he nods up at the ceiling. I look up, and my heart convulses.

NANCY.

The name is repeated over and over in black ink, filling every inch of the ceiling, until I swear I can hear the tree house whispering the name, exactly the same way Sadie did in the sunroom.

Nancynancynancynancy . . .

I grit my teeth and venture farther into the tree house, seeing that a third wall holds bookshelves that sag under the weight of dozens of books, a record player, little trinkets and Jesus figurines.

The strangest thing about the inside of the tree house, though, is that beneath the crucifixes and the graffiti, it looks almost cute. Mold-ravaged drapes hang at the windows, and there's a seat with a cushion. A soiled rug covers the floor, and there's a little table with three chairs, plus framed pictures of cats and rainbows. It's as if, at some point, the kids who used this place really cared about it.

"Anybody else getting Ed Gein from this?" I ask.

"That or hick Jesus freak," Juniper says.

I'm stone-cold sober now, and my teeth want to chatter. I clench my jaw, which sends the tremble elsewhere.

I remember what Sadie hissed at me—

She's knows you're here

—and I wonder if she has seen somebody using the tree house. A woman, maybe.

I look at the words HEADS WILL ROLL, thinking about the doll's heads in Bebe's desk. This place feels completely different from the rest of the camp, and yet also like a vital part of it. I swear it's made from the same wood as the cabins. Between the tree house and Bebe's creaky home, I'm building a picture of the camp's history, one that Bebe has tried her damnedest to conceal.

"I thought Buck made up the Knock-Knock Nancy myth?" Juniper says.

"No, Nancy was a real person who died here."

Juniper is crouched by a large trunk. "Seems to me the legend is just part of that grand tradition of stories about decapitated people. You ever read the story *The Green Ribbon*? That thing still haunts me. There are tons of horror tales about headless women out there, but you'll find most of them in the fiction section."

She shakes the padlock on the trunk. "Locked."

"It looks pretty old," I say. "It wouldn't take much to bust it."

Behind me, Kurt says, "Like with an ax, maybe?"

I turn and see him looking at the back of the tree house door, where an ax hangs on two hooks. It's ancient-looking, the metal dull and clouded, the handle worn smooth by years of use.

Kurt shifts on his feet. "Maybe we should get out of here."

"Agreed," Juniper says, but I'm not ready.

"After we open the trunk." I stow the knife in my bag and take the ax. It's heavier than I expected, must weigh almost ten pounds. Bebe must be strong to be able to swing one of these the way she did.

I approach the trunk, hefting the ax. Juniper scoots back and I swing. The blade thunks into the trunk itself.

"Want me—" Kurt says, but I swing again and strike the padlock. It clatters to the floor, the trunk popping open a couple of inches like two lips parting.

I pass the ax to Juniper and bend down to lift the lid, my arms trembling. Light spills into the box, caressing a collection of objects that huddle in the trunk like spooked bugs.

Cell phones.

At least forty of them, all different brands. Motorolas, Nokias, Blackberrys.

"What the hell?" Kurt leans over me.

"I was not expecting that," Juniper says.

"Doesn't Bebe offer to dispose of people's phones when they check out?" I say.

"But these are prehistoric," Kurt says. "Early 2000s at least."

"This is starting to feel a little too *Wrong Turn* for my liking," I say.

"You think these are the phones of dead people?" Juniper asks.

Despite my unease, I'm secretly pleased she got the reference.

Nobody says anything.

I reach into the box and push aside the phones.

"What are you looking for?" Kurt asks.

"A charger cable. If we can power one of these up, we should be able to find out who they belonged to."

I keep searching, but it's no good. There are no chargers in the trunk.

"They could be somewhere else in here," I say, getting up and going to the shelves, moving around books and ornaments. A couple of pictures fall out of one of the books. One shows three girls in black dresses, all of them scowling. The other is of a priest. There's nothing comforting or benevolent about his appearance. He stares out of the photo with cold eyes, his features sharp and sunken. He looks like a man who would sneer at somebody in pain.

Is this the priest from the Nancy story? The one who killed her? The thought of that callous, uncaring face being the last thing Nancy saw causes my throat to throb with unease.

Kurt is by the door. "I think we should all go back to camp and tell Bebe and Tye about this place."

"You really think she doesn't know about it?" I ask. I look around the tree house, as if seeing it for the first time. It could be just the kind of place little girls would hold tea parties and share secrets. I wonder if this is Bebe and Sadie's childhood hideout. But why would NANCY be carved into the ceiling?

"Oh shit," Juniper says, and I see she's holding an ornamental box. She tilts it to show us the contents. "Teeth."

I shudder.

"I'm out," Kurt says, and leaves the tree house.

I stand with Juniper, who raises a hand and massages her forehead. "You really know how to have a good time, kid."

"That's me, party central." More seriously, I add, "If the cops don't already know about this place, we have to find a way to tell them."

"Right. I think Kurt has the right idea. Let's get out of here."

We leave the tree house, finding the makeshift ladder. I take the lantern from Juniper, motioning for her to go first. I shine the light through the opening in the walkway and watch as she descends. My mind whirls, trying to figure out what the hell we just stumbled across in the middle of the forest, miles from civilization, but just a quick walk from camp.

"Willow? You coming?" Juniper calls.

I'm about to step down onto the first rung when a shadow moves in the corner of my eye and a hand seizes my shoulder.

With a cry, I spin toward the figure, dropping the lantern. It crashes against the walkway, rolling off the edge. I hear it hit the ground, Juniper crying out in surprise, but I don't make a sound, standing frozen as eyes leer at me in the dark and I hear that low moan again.

"New girl," a male voice says. "You gotta fucking help me, man."

recognize the voice, even though he looks like hell.

"Buck," I say. He's haggard, could have lost ten pounds in two days. His eyes have sunk into his skull and his cheekbones protrude. His fingers bite my shoulders as he holds on to me—it's like he's having trouble standing. Breathing, too. His inhales rattle, sound constricted.

"You don't know what's out here, man," Buck says. "You have no fucking idea."

"Buck, we've been trying to find you. Where have you been?"

"I ran, man. Figured if I kept running, I'd get away, but this forest is insane. It keeps changing. It changes every day."

He's not making any sense. I take hold of his arms, try to speak clearly.

"It's okay, Buck. We're here now. Let's get you back to the camp. Warm you up. It's going to be okay."

His face screws up and he shakes the greasy hanks of his hair. "You don't get it. It's not safe. This place is fucked."

"Buck—"

"She *came* for me, man. She's trying to fucking kill me."

Cold bristles down my arms. I stare into a face hollow with despair.

"Who's trying to kill you?" I ask.

"It was *her*, man. She's got an ax."

Cold flushes through me.

"Bebe?" I ask. "Did Bebe attack you?"

"No, man, it was . . ." He stops, as if afraid to keep going, then raps his knuckles against his skull and whispers, "It was fucking Knock-Knock Nancy."

I stare at him in disbelief, and cold scuttles down my spine at the bleak light of his eyes. He means it. He really believes he was attacked by a character from a campfire story.

The conviction in his voice makes me wonder, just for a second, if it could be true. That Knock-Knock Nancy really did come for him.

What if the story's been warped beyond recognition? What if Nancy didn't die after all? What if she's still out here, in the woods, hunting for heads?

But then I remember this is reality.

Buck's delirious.

The real Nancy is dead. She was murdered twenty years ago.

"Where's Kat?" I ask. "Have you seen Kat?"

"I . . . I . . ." Buck begins, but the sounds come out garbled. He starts to shake so much, I worry he'll collapse.

"Let's just get down from here, okay? We'll get you down and then figure this out. You're safe now."

His face smooths, the information seeming to go in. I remove his hands from my shoulders and climb down first. I somehow manage to keep hold of the steps, even though I'm trembling so much I fear I might shake the whole tree house down on top of us.

When I reach the bottom, I step back to give Buck room. He climbs down clumsily, like he's forgotten how to use his body. Like somebody else is in the driver's seat. When he reaches the ground, he hunches over and coughs.

"Guys," I say, turning to the others, but then Juniper hurls herself at Buck.

Buck folds in half and Juniper lands on top of him. She shoves Buck facedown into the earth, knee in his back, twisting Buck's arm behind him with both hands.

She leans in to demand, "What did you *do*?"

I try to drag her away. "Juniper, what the hell are you doing?" She shoves me off, twisting Buck's arm until he screams.

"It wasn't me, man," Buck cries. He's gone limp, allowing Juniper to pin him down. There's no fight in him. I realize he's crying. And I have no idea why Juniper has suddenly turned into *T2*-era Sarah Connor.

"What the hell is going on?" I ask Kurt.

"There's something over there," he says, pointing to the side of the tree. "We found it when we climbed down."

The spooked look on his face causes my jaw to buzz with tension. I walk with him to the other side of the tree, finding a lumpy object on the ground. It's surrounded by leaves and dirt and rocks, and at first it looks like a pile of clothes, heaped in a rectangle. But then I realize that what I thought was rocks is white skin. Hands, tucked into sleeves, fingers pale and stiff.

It's a body.

My insides harden.

There's a dead body beneath the tree.

There's something *not right* about it, aside from the fact that they're dead in the middle of the forest.

"They took her fucking head, man," Buck says.

I fight a fresh wave of nausea when I see that he's right. That's what's wrong with the body. It has no head. Nausea, despair, and anger pulse through me at the same time. Seeing a body like this, reduced to a hunk of meat, makes me doubt everything I know about humanity. About what we're capable of doing to each other.

"Who is it?" I ask. I see the look of anguish on Buck's face, and I don't need him to answer.

"Kat," I say, and he breaks. His shoulders judder and he cries like a kid. Uncontrollably. Weeping into the forest floor, chewing on dirt, not caring.

"Let him go," I tell Juniper.

"But—"

"Get off him," I say.

Juniper grimaces but relents, getting up. Buck cries into the dirt and I crouch down beside him, help him roll onto his back. He stares up at nothing in particular, his eyes filled with grit and tears.

"Buck," I say, trying to sound calm, "what happened?"

"I found her in the woods," he says. "I found her like this, man."

"Is this where you found her?"

His face creases up. "She was by some freaky thing out there in the woods. I was trying to get her back to camp when I heard that fucking knocking again, so I hid in the tree house. But then I heard voices and I didn't want to get trapped in there, so I hid around the other side of the treehouse's walkway. Took me a while to realize it was you guys, guess my brain got scrambled after Kat . . ."

He breaks off, choking.

I feel a prick of sympathy for him, but I'm also processing Buck's words.

Some freaky thing out there in the woods.

What did Buck see? Some kind of arcane sculpture, like the carvings in the trees? A lair? And freaky *how*? My shoulders ache with tension.

"Here," Kurt says, helping Buck sit up. "Take some breaths. Breathe with me, Buck."

"My name's not fucking Buck, man."

"I know. What do you want me to call you?"

"Call me Caleb, okay? I want to be Caleb again."

I stare at him in disbelief.

Buck is Caleb?

Caleb who beat a guy to near death. Caleb who was so high on drugs, he refused a toxicology test. Caleb who we just found out in the woods with a dead body.

"You're Caleb," I murmur, trying to make it sound right, but all I can think is: *What the fuck?*

"Just breathe," Kurt tells Buck/Caleb. "Tap your chest, like this."

Just like I taught him.

Buck does as he says, and he seems to get a handle on himself, but he's still shaking. I stand, give him some space. Kurt remains by his side, speaking to him, rubbing his shoulder, but I see the wariness in his stance. He's still on guard, the way you would be around a kid you know could throw a tantrum any second.

"What are you thinking?" Juniper asks me.

"We go back to camp," I say, keeping my voice low so that Buck doesn't hear. "We take Buck—Caleb—with us, and we talk to Bebe and the others. Figure out what's going on."

"Are you sure it's safe? Taking Buck with us? Maybe we should tie his hands."

My gaze goes to Buck. His hair is tangled and huge, and his eyes barely leave Kat's body, like he can't believe what he's seeing.

Or he can't believe what he's done.

"Let's just get him back to camp," I say.

"What about the body?"

"I'm not leaving her," Buck says, getting to his feet. Shit, he heard us. He staggers over to Kat. "I'm not leaving her out here in the dark."

I can tell he means it, and that only sends my mind into even more of a spin.

He loved Kat. Enough to kill her and then disassociate from the event? Blame it on Knock-Knock Nancy?

"He already moved the body," Juniper says. "This isn't a crime scene. No reason we can't move her again."

I force myself to consider the body. I have to keep reminding myself it's somebody we all knew. Somebody we liked. And her name's not even really Kat. Even though I don't want to touch her, I feel like we owe it to her to get her back to safety. Somewhere the bugs and who knows what else can't get her. We owe her that much.

"Let's carry her," I say.

t's raining hard by the time we reach the clubhouse.

We're all drenched. My costume clings to me, freezing cold, and I shake uncontrollably, whether from the temperature or from shock, I can't tell. The booze blush is long gone, and I can't believe that just an hour ago, I was drinking whiskey with Juniper, having a heart-to-heart over a hip flask.

The beach is deserted. There's no sign of Bebe, Dani, Tye, or Misty. They must have taken the end-of-the-world party inside when the rain started.

I open the door into the clubhouse, and Kurt, Juniper, and Buck maneuver through with the body. As they pass, I catch a glimpse of Kat's neck, a gaping wound, red and meaty, then tough white at the core. For a crazy second, I imagine it like hard candy.

The wound looks clean. Her head came off in one go. It must have been a sharp blade.

I wonder if we're making a mistake going to Bebe. We all know she's handy with an ax, and there's something about her that sets off a primitive alarm in my brain, and not just because she reminds me of Grams. But we don't have many options, and I'm still armed with my bag of knives.

I run up the stairs ahead of the others.

"Willow?" Bebe asks from the sofa. She's sitting with Misty and Tye, a game of mahjong on the coffee table. They're still wearing their costumes, which makes them look like the beginning of a joke—an explorer, an imaginary friend, and Santa Claus walk into a bar . . .

"Get caught in the rain?" Misty drawls, and then she sees Buck, Juniper, and Kurt enter the foyer, and her grin drops.

"Buck?" Bebe says, on her feet now.

They ease Kat's body to the floor with a groan.

"Buck, where have you been?" Bebe asks. She doesn't seem to have registered that they were carrying a body. Maybe she thinks it's a Halloween prop.

"Somebody killed her," Buck says. He's more composed than he was. Drained and down.

Bebe looks from Buck to the body resting on the floor outside her office.

A puddle has formed around it. Rainwater and diluted blood. I feel another pang for what's left of Kat. There's no dignity in death.

"It's Kat," I say. "We found her in the woods, along with Buck."

"Oh shit," Misty breathes, her bracelets jangling.

Bebe stares at the body with a look of astonishment. She doesn't blink for a very long time. I'm surprised she can bear to look at it for so long without breaking away.

"He's covered in blood," Kurt says, nodding at Buck.

"It's from when I found her," Buck says. "I didn't kill her, man. I found her near some freaky house."

"Then how'd she end up like this?"

"I'm telling you, it was Knock-Knock Nancy."

"Here we go again," Juniper says.

Bebe looks between us, her expression blank, assessing. Finally, she strides to her office door and unlocks it.

"Buck, please go into my office."

"What's gonna happen?" Buck asks, voice small.

"For now, it's best if you go into my office and remain there until the authorities arrive."

"Did he kill her?" Misty asks Kurt. Kurt shrugs, looks lost.

Buck pales. "Not the cops, man. I didn't do anything wrong. For the first time in my fucking life, this wasn't my fault."

"And you can explain that to the police. For now, though—"

"He's backing away," Tye says, and he's right. Buck is edging back across the foyer, away from the group, tangled hair dripping into his face.

"No cops," he says, and it's like he's talking to himself, not us. "I can't deal with any more cops."

He turns to run.

Kurt and Tye both lunge for him at the same time. Buck's right arm jerks up, his elbow going into Kurt's nose. Kurt makes a muffled grunt, his head snapping back. Blood trickles from his nostrils and he grips his face. Tye drags Buck toward him, but Buck flails, tries to break free, and Tye spins him around and punches him in the face.

Buck sags in Tye's arms, head rolling to one side. Out cold. Tye holds him up, biceps popping with the effort, eyes shining with adrenaline.

"Get him into my office," Bebe says, pointing.

Nose still streaming, Kurt takes Buck's legs, and they carry him into the office. Bebe goes in with them, and I watch through the door as she takes a pair of handcuffs from the top desk drawer, the one that was locked earlier. I'm surprised she's so prepared. The guys fold Buck into a chair by the window, and Bebe cuffs Buck's left wrist to it.

I feel bad for him. He'd been manic but also upset. Despite the revelation that he's Caleb, I don't believe he killed Kat, and I keep going over what he said.

He found Kat's body in the woods.

I found her near some freaky house.

Somebody could have been out there the whole time. Watching. Waiting.

What if the cops missed it?

What if the killer is still there?

"Here," Tye says, handing Kurt a tissue. Kurt takes it and mops at his nose as he leaves the office. I put an arm around him.

"I'm fine," he says.

Bebe stands in the door, facing us as we huddle in the foyer.

There's a moment when everybody seems to process what just happened. Misty stands looking shell-shocked, while Juniper has hand on hip, eyes troubled. The only person not here is Dani, and regardless of what happened between us, I have to make sure she's safe.

"I understand that this is an awful, shocking thing to have happened," Bebe says.

"No shit," Juniper drawls.

"But I think it's important that we remain calm," Bebe adds. "I have an emergency cell phone in the safe in my office. I'll alert the authorities that Buck and Kat have been found, and they'll come out as quickly as they are able."

I let go of Kurt, pressing the bag of knives to my side.

"We don't know for sure that Buck did it," I say. "The way he was with Kat . . . Buck wasn't like that two days ago. Kurt, Juniper, you saw him. He was broken by what happened to her."

Kurt is all eyes, doesn't appear to know what to say.

"He seemed pretty cut up," Juniper says.

"Doesn't mean he's innocent," Misty says.

Bebe raises her hands. "We'll let the cops decide."

"Listen to me," I say. "We may not have time for the cops. By the time they get here, it could be too late."

"Too late for what?" Tye asks.

I swallow, aware that what I'm about to say won't be easy to hear.

"Buck said he was running from somebody. Somebody who wanted him dead. If he didn't kill Kat, that means the killer is still out there. Everybody at this camp is in danger."

"Please, Willow," Bebe says, "we must stay—"

"Bebe isn't telling us everything," I press. "She has a sister at camp, a sister she locks away and—"

"You have no idea what you're talking about," Bebe says. "I don't know what you think you saw, but—"

"Did Kat do something?" I ask, shutting her down.

"Do something?" Kurt asks.

"We're all here because we got canceled," I say. "That's right, isn't it?"

At Bebe's blank stare, I continue, "What if somebody killed Kat as punishment? What if they tried to kill Buck for what he did to the man in Illinois?" I gesture at the others. "What if they think we all deserve to be punished for our indiscretions?"

"What man in Illinois?" Misty asks.

"Buck hurt somebody," I say. "The police were called. I get the feeling it was pretty bad."

"So that's what he was talking about in stone circle," Tye says.

The group falls silent.

I can see in their faces that they're thinking about whatever landed them here. I'm thinking it, too. Somebody texted me right before I checked in, and even though the text unnerved me, I didn't take it as seriously as I should have.

Misty says, "I vote we get the hell outta here. All those in favor, say aye."

For once, I agree with her. Forget waiting for the morning, we should run away from here now.

It's the one thing nobody ever does in a horror film. People always talk about cutting and running, but nobody ever does.

"Please," Bebe says. "This isn't helping. We'll get to the bottom of what happened to Kat, but only if we remain calm and allow the authorities to do their job. First, I need to call the police again."

I stare at her, wondering what she's thinking. Does Bebe believe that once she's taken care of Buck and Kat, our path to spiritual enlightenment will resume? She must see that that's impossible. Camp Castaway has broken its promise to us. It is no longer a safe place to switch off and disconnect. It's a death trap.

And I can't believe I'm playing the part of "chick who knows what's up but Mommy doesn't believe her."

"I'm with Misty," Juniper says. "I say we get out of here. Only way to be sure."

"Guys," Tye says, "leaving camp isn't as simple as grabbing an Uber. We're way out in the sticks here. A car service will take longer than the police."

"Screw that," Misty says. "I want my phone back. Now."

She's outside the porch with the lockers—the ones containing our phones.

All eyes settle on Bebe. I expect her to argue—this is the woman who destroyed an iPod with an ax—and for a moment it looks like she might. But as her gaze sweeps the group in the foyer, she must sense that she's lost the room. The atmosphere of desperation and fear is palpable.

"As you wish," she says with a sigh.

She goes to the keypad at the porch door and punches in a code. The light blinks green, and Bebe opens the door, goes into the porch, Misty right behind her. We all stand by, watching. Blood drums in my temple as I stare at locker seven, the one I left my phone in two days ago.

Two days without my phone has been bliss. I've felt freer than I imagined possible. A part of me is curious what I've missed, but I find I'm repelled by the idea of having my phone back so soon after I freed myself of it. I don't want to let all that noise back in.

Bebe must have a master for the lockers because she uses a single key on her chain to open locker nine. Misty's, I assume, going by the expectant look on her face. Misty moves forward to peer inside, looking like an unhinged kids' TV presenter in her Eliza costume.

"What the fuck?" she says. "Where is it?"

I move to get a better view and see that the locker's empty.

Bebe frowns, looks at Tye, who shrugs. Bebe slots the same key into locker eleven—Buck's, I'm guessing—and opens it up.

Also empty.

"Seven," I say, my voice tight. "What about seven?"

Bebe's hands shake as she opens locker seven to reveal a vacant box.

There's nothing but shadows inside.

The phones are gone.

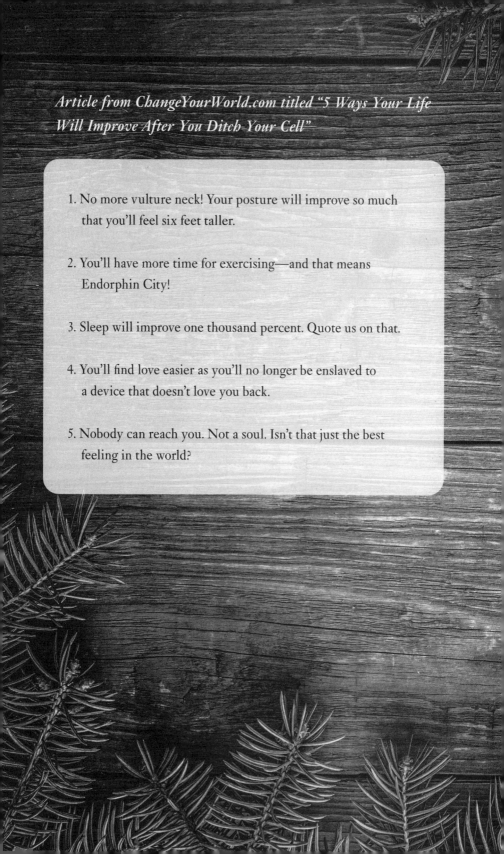

Article from ChangeYourWorld.com titled "5 Ways Your Life Will Improve After You Ditch Your Cell"

1. No more vulture neck! Your posture will improve so much that you'll feel six feet taller.

2. You'll have more time for exercising—and that means Endorphin City!

3. Sleep will improve one thousand percent. Quote us on that.

4. You'll find love easier as you'll no longer be enslaved to a device that doesn't love you back.

5. Nobody can reach you. Not a soul. Isn't that just the best feeling in the world?

XXIX

Where the fuck is my phone?" Misty demands.

"Are they all gone?" Kurt asks, as Bebe opens the final locker to show that it, too, is empty.

Standing here, soaked through, a dead body on the floor, everybody's faces pinched and anxious, I feel our isolation more intensely. Our only link to miles-away reality is Bebe's cell.

"Who else has access to the lockers?" I ask.

"Nobody," Bebe replies.

I look at Tye, who raises his hands.

"The keys are in the safe," he says. "No way I could get to them."

At his words, Bebe turns and strides to her office. I hurry after her, seeing that Buck is still out cold in the chair, slumped to one side. I swallow a prick of jealousy that he gets to sit all of this out. I guess he's already been through hell.

Bebe opens a cupboard to reveal a safe. She turns the dial, pops the door, and takes out a black box, which she sets on the desk.

She opens the lid and stares down in disbelief. Her eye twitch is more pronounced than before. Her hands shake as she pulls out the pieces of a broken iPhone. It's been smashed to bits. Destroyed—and then put back in the safe, as if nothing ever happened.

We have no way to communicate with the outside world.

"Shit," Kurt whispers.

"Great," Misty says, leaning round the doorframe. "That's just perfect."

"Does anybody else know the combination to the safe?" I ask.

"No," Bebe says.

"Nobody? Not Sadie?"

"No," Bebe repeats, her voice cutting the air between us.

I meet her stare, and I'm not afraid of her, even though she looks like she's about to put her fist through a wall. I look at the others, each freaking out in their own way, and Dani's absence feels bigger with every second. I hope she's in her cabin, doors shut, curtains drawn. *Nobody home, ma'am, come back later.*

"How are we going to call the cops?" Juniper asks.

"Yeah, and a transport vehicle," Misty adds. "I want out of here like yesterday."

Bebe slams the box shut. "There's a radio at the house."

"Radio?" I ask.

"It's old, but it's all we have."

I shudder. The thought of going out into the woods again makes my breath shorten, but I have to keep it together.

"I'm not going back out there," Misty says. "No way I'm going into the camp."

"For once, I think Misty's right," Juniper says. "The cabins have no locks. We should stay here in the clubhouse. Check that the windows and doors are secure."

Misty strides back to the porch. "I'm no sitting duck. I'm done. The road is right there."

"We have no idea what's out there," I say.

"Or who," Kurt adds.

Misty gestures at the office. "He's tied up. I'm not locking myself in here with that monster. I'm going out the front door and I'm walking down that road until I find somebody with a phone or a car or a fucking *gun*. No way I'm ending up like Kat."

"Misty—" Bebe says, but Misty shouts over her.

"Open the fucking door! Now!"

She looks manic in her Eliza costume.

"This is a bad idea," Bebe says, joining Misty in the porch and searching through her keys.

"Everybody's entitled to their opinion," Misty says.

Bebe slots a key into the lock at the front door. It clicks, and Misty shoves open the door, hurrying out into the open.

"Misty, think about this," I say, following her. "We can't just leave Dani. We—"

Misty has stopped. She stands stock-still at the top of the stairs that lead down from the clubhouse, her foot hovering over the first step. I follow her line of vision and see why she hasn't gone any farther.

There are objects on the stairs, blocking her path.

It's dark, but my stomach turns when I see a hand. A leg. A sneakered foot.

There are bodies on the stairs. At least two of them, splayed out as if they've had a bad fall.

Misty's voice emerges light as a child's.

"Who the fuck is that?"

I see that one of the bodies wears a Hawaiian shirt. Another a dirty white apron.

"I think it's Apollo and Chef Jeff," I say.

"Their necks . . ." Misty murmurs, and nausea clenches my gut.

Just like Kat, they have no heads.

"Misty," Juniper says, coming outside. She stops when she sees what we're looking at. "Oh shit."

I take a step toward Apollo's body, because I've noticed something attached to his shirt. A scrap of paper. I reach for it, aware of the darkness that spreads out beyond the stairs. Anybody could be out there watching us. I think about the eyes carved into the tree trunk as I tug the paper free and step back to join the others. Four words are written in dark red ink.

Or is it crayon?

THE ROAD IS MINE.

"Inside," I say. "Now."

We hurry back into the building. Bebe locks the front door, then punches in the code on the porch, making the lights blink white.

I hold up the warning so that everybody can see.

"Fuck," Misty says, pacing back and forth. Juniper chews her nails, thinking, while Kurt looks shell-shocked, dried blood flaking from the skin below his nostrils. Bebe looks as stunned as I feel. And we all can't deny it any longer.

Kat's death was connected to something bigger, something connected to this place. There's a killer at camp.

"We need to find Dani," I say, "and get to that radio."

Bebe looks at me like somebody who's just woken up from a bad dream to find they're in a nightmare. Slowly, she nods.

"We pair up," I say. "One group stays with Buck. And I'm going with Bebe to the radio, to make sure nothing happens to her."

And to make sure she doesn't grab an ax.

"Right," Kurt says. "That makes sense."

I can see in Bebe's pale eyes that she knows I'm right.

She goes back to the safe and takes out another box. Punches in a code to open it, then takes out a gun. Black, sleek, loaded.

It looks like a movie prop, which somehow makes it more sinister. I never liked guns. Never found the sight of armed guards or cops comforting. Having one now makes sense, but having Bebe in charge of it? I'd rather take my chances with Buck.

"Got any more of those?" Misty asks as Bebe tucks the weapon into the back of her pants.

"Stay with Buck," Bebe tells Juniper, ignoring Misty's question. "You too, Kurt." She looks to Tye. "Take Kat to the infirmary. Misty can help you."

Misty licks her lips and nods, apparently still keen on time with Tye, even in a crisis.

"Be smart, now," Juniper tells me, placing a hand on my shoulder. I nod, understanding the reference from *Fight Me*.

"Yeah, try not to lose your head," Misty says, and even though I think it's time somebody punched her, I know she's right.

Priority number one right now really is not dying.

✳

It's still raining as we head for the boardwalk.

We carry battery-operated lanterns from the supply closet, but they provide little comfort, merely illuminating the rain, which flurries like a swarm in front of us. I keep expecting a figure to lunge from the shadows, grinning madly with a hatchet in hand.

Unless, of course, I'm with the killer right now.

I watch Bebe, trying to figure her out. She didn't seem shocked by Kat's body. She seemed intrigued.

Now is the perfect time to ask her all the questions I've stored up. Maybe now that everything's going to hell, she'll actually be honest with me.

"How much do you know about the camp's history?" I ask, raising my voice to be heard over the rain.

Bebe's face is set against the wind.

"This isn't the time," she says.

"No? I'd think this would be the perfect time, what with three headless bodies turning up at the same camp where a girl had her head cut off twenty years ago."

Bebe looks at me, jaw set.

"You know a girl called Nancy died here?" I ask. "She was decapitated."

"How do you know that?"

"Chef Jeff," I say. "He said she was a resident, sent here by her parents when it was a Bible camp. It's true, isn't it? Is it also true that they never found the killer?"

Bebe slows her pace. Fury hollows her features, but she speaks evenly.

"I wouldn't trust anything Jeffrey said."

"So he was lying?" I ask, my voice rising. "There's something you're not telling us, and if we're going to die here anyway, what the hell does it matter? Just tell us the truth."

I almost expect her to shout back, *You can't handle the truth*, but that would be too Hollywood.

Instead, she looks away, staring into the downpour. For the first time in the three days I've been at camp, I sense vulnerability. I catch a glimpse of the real Bebe.

Finally, she says, "Yes, a girl named Nancy died here, and what happened to her was a tragedy that doesn't bear repeating."

"Who killed her?" I ask.

"They never proved anything, but the authorities blamed the preacher who ran the camp. Twenty years ago, this was a religious retreat, and Nathaniel Carver preached a particularly unforgiving church. He was known to punish campers who transgressed."

Nathaniel Carver.

Another *N*.

Maybe the mark in the tree didn't mean "Nancy" after all.

"Punish?" I ask. "How?"

"You don't want to know."

I process her words. "Did he think Nancy transgressed?"

Bebe nods, face tense, offers nothing more.

"What happened when she died?" I ask.

A pause, and then she says, "All I know is that she was found in the woods, and when the police came, the preacher ran. He disappeared into the wilderness."

Just like the legend.

I try to think through the cold pounding my skull.

"People really thought a priest killed Nancy?" I ask. I see the photo from the tree house. The sharp profile, thin lips, and deep-set eyes.

"That's how it seemed," Bebe says. She walks robotically, pushing through the rain. "Nancy wasn't the only death at the camp. Others died during the fifteen years the Bible camp was open. Most of them drowned."

"He drowned them?" I ask.

"Nobody ever proved it." Bebe's jaw hardens. "People believed he would look after them, but under it all, he was a mean, selfish bastard. The only person he ever cared about was himself."

I see the pain in her face, and in my mind, I see the imprint of the cross above the front door of her house. I see the Jesus mural in her dining room, and the truth suddenly seems so obvious, I can't not ask the question that forms on my tongue.

"He was your father, wasn't he? The priest?"

Bebe turns, and for a second, I think she might strike me with the lantern. The light blazes in her eyes. Then she calms, lowers the lantern.

"If you could call him that," she says. "He always wanted a son. He hated that he ended up with girls."

We resume walking, and I keep hearing what Bebe said to Sadie in the sunroom—

Don't make me lock you up like Daddy.

—and only now do I hear the ambiguity in the statement.

In the moment, it had sounded like Bebe meant she didn't want to lock up Sadie in the same way that Bebe had locked up their father.

But now I wonder if she meant something entirely more upsetting. That their father locked up Sadie.

Was that the reason for Sadie's strangeness?

The thought of her spending hours in the dark, cramped and bent over and scared, makes me angry.

There was a door hidden in the back of the closet. Is that where he locked her up?

Bebe stares ahead, a picture of composure, but the more I watch her, the more I see micro twitches under the surface of her skin. The muscles in her face are desperate to form a different expression.

I wonder what happened to the camp in the years after the preacher's death. Whether Bebe was glad when he was gone.

"You said you built the camp from nothing," I say.

"I *did* build it from nothing," Bebe snaps. "Nobody came near this place for years. They thought it was cursed, made up stories, turned that poor girl into a bedtime story. It took a long time for that to settle down, and when it did, I decided to do something *good* with this place. Wash away its horrors and use it to help people. Really help people."

Maybe she hears how naive that sounds, knows how spectacularly her plan has backfired, because she falls silent.

"And the preacher was never seen again after he disappeared?" I ask.

"He's dead," Bebe says. "There's no way he'd be alive and not come back for us."

I come to a standstill, staring at her in disbelief.

"You opened this place back up," I say, "without knowing for sure that it was safe. Without knowing he was really gone. You brought innocent people here. Brought them right to the place where your father killed—"

"It's safe," Bebe says. "Has been for five years. He's dead. He's long gone."

She sounds so certain, but what if she's wrong? What if her father *has* come back? Returned for more heads?

I only realize we've reached Dani's cabin because the lights are on, and the front door is open, casting a warped rectangle of light across the ground. The sight of the door stills me. There's no movement inside. All I can see is the couch and the edge of the dining table. Maybe Dani fell asleep?

I hurry to the door and go inside. The living room is neater than I expected. A couple of books stacked on the coffee table; the cushions lined up on the couch.

But no Dani.

"Hello?" I call. "Dani?"

Bebe goes into the bedroom and then immediately comes back out, shaking her head.

"Where would she go?" I say.

"Maybe she went for some fresh air."

"In the rain? And why was the door open?"

"Could've been the wind," Bebe says.

It could've been, but not here. Not tonight. There's no way the door was left open by accident. I try not to think about Buck telling me he was chased through the woods. I try not to hear the knocking sound that me and Juniper ran from, but it echoes in my mind.

Kat went missing and she turned up dead.

What if Dani—

The lights go out.

Darkness pushes in around us like smothering fabric.

"Great," Bebe says, "there goes the power."

"You've got to be kidding me," I say.

I'm back at the front door, looking out at the boardwalk and the other cabins. I squint through the dark, seeing nothing out of place. Nothing to hint at the horror that is creeping stealthily through Camp Castaway, aside from the darkness itself.

As I look at the cabin opposite, I see movement in the window. The curtain trembling, then going still.

"Whose cabin is that?" I ask.

"Number five is Misty's," Bebe says.

I open the satchel and remove the first weapon my fingers find. The carving knife. Big. Solid.

"Where did you get that?" Bebe asks, but I ignore her, already striding toward cabin five. I don't allow myself to think. I close the distance quickly, ignoring the dark, ignoring the sound of Bebe hurrying after me, lantern swinging.

I throw open the door to Misty's cabin—

—and a shape leaps at me.

JUNIPER

It was quiet in the office. Juniper listened at the door but heard nothing. Buck must still be out cold, and Juniper envied him. She never slept. Hadn't in years. She remembered being a kid and going out like a light when her head hit the pillow, drifting into dreamless oblivion. Now she had to pay for that kind of simplicity. Had to get away from the life she'd built in order to feel alive.

Usually, the quiet soothed her. Tonight, it set her nerves on edge.

"You okay in there, bud?" she called through the door. "Tap once for yes, twice for no."

No response.

"Sleep well, Buck old pal," she said.

"Are you sleeping at all?" Chad Flanagan had asked a month before she checked into Camp Castaway. She'd moved to Colorado years before, but they Zoomed every couple of months. Chad was her oldest friend, one of her few keepsakes from Hollywood. He was still in L.A., still had a full head of now-white hair, and had settled into his sixties like a sports car that had only just discovered it had seventh gear.

"A little," she'd lied.

"Did you know you have a tell?" Chad asked, unleashing the grin that won him a Golden Globe for the romantic drama *Oil Slick*.

"I do not."

"Sure you do. Whenever you lie, you get twice as beautiful."

Standing in the clubhouse foyer, half smiling at the memory of

Chad's cheesy flirting, Juniper heard a sound like fingers on glass. She saw that the rain was picking up. It struck the panoramic window, where Kurt stood, surveying the camp. Beyond the pane, the moon picked out the outlines of trees and turned the lake into a shimmering sheet of silk.

"Why Kat?" Kurt asked. "Why'd he kill Kat?"

"Who knows why people do the things they do," Juniper said. Decades of acting, and human behavior still bewildered her.

She placed a hand to the pane.

It never rained like this in L.A. It was one of the things that really grated on her after a while. The lack of seasons. Growing up in New York, she'd had mad-dog summers and white-out winters. The change in climate made her aware of time.

In L.A., there was no time. Nothing changed. Not quickly, anyway.

She left precisely for that reason.

Nobody wanted to let her go, though. There was always some new magazine or vlogger that wanted to talk to her about yet another re-release of a movie she made thirty years ago.

The thing was, Juniper's memory was failing. Had been ever since the chemo. First, she started forgetting plans and appointments. Then the bigger stuff dropped out of her mind, like overripe fruit from a withering tree. It was a small price to pay for having the tumor in her brain shrink three millimeters. Didn't mean it wasn't still going to kill her.

"What's that?" Kurt asked.

Juniper realized a new sound had entered the clubhouse.

A buzzing or chiming, not that far away.

"Is that . . . ?" Kurt began, before trailing off. She knew why he didn't complete the question. The answer felt impossible.

"A phone," Juniper said, right when the lights went out.

Darkness fell around them, thick as velvet.

"Seriously?" Juniper said, blinking as her vision adjusted.

"What happened to the power?" Kurt asked. He was little more than a pair of wide, staring eyes in the dark, his voice quavering.

"The weather, maybe," Juniper said. "We just have to wait for the generator to kick in."

The phone kept ringing, and Juniper strode back to the office, wondering if a call was coming in there. Maybe Bebe had already spoken to the police.

But the ringing wasn't coming from the office. It echoed down the corridor from the canteen.

"Who the hell has a phone in here?" Juniper murmured.

The ringing stopped. A new sound replaced it, reverberating along the corridor.

Knock.

Knock.

Knock.

"Oh shit," Kurt said. "Not again."

Juniper felt reality bending the way a projected image did when it hit a lens. She'd played this scene in two of her more commercially successful movies. The ones that cast her as a battle-scarred sorority mom and a "too old for this shit" Detroit cop. She died both times, and she'd turned down a third movie that wanted her to play out the ultimate horror movie cliché: that of the victim who bangs on a window for help while a party rages on, the revelers unaware she's about to get the chop.

This wasn't a movie, though. Wasn't that the point of Camp Castaway? It was reality cubed.

Knock.

KNOCK—

"Hide," Juniper told Kurt.

"But—"

"Go into the game room and lock the door. Now."

He nodded and backed away. Juniper watched him go into the room, and she waited until she heard the lock turn before she started to walk down the corridor toward the canteen.

"Misty?" she called. "Tye?"

Three loud bangs answered her, echoing from the canteen.

Juniper thought about Kat's body.

She thought about Buck's story.

"You have three seconds to fucking show yourselves," she said.

Silence. The banging stopped.

Juniper was done. Nobody messed with Juniper Brown. Everybody who had tried found that out the hard way.

She gritted her teeth and peered in through the canteen port-hole windows, seeing benches and chairs resting in the gloom, but no people. She shoved open the door and stepped inside, scanning the canteen.

"*One knock, two knock, three knock, four . . .*" a voice whispered.

Juniper turned and saw a crouched shape by the window.

A person.

They were bent over, huddled into themself like a scared child. Long, silver hair fell to cover their face, and they wore some kind of tattered cloak, which pooled around them like smoke.

"Jig's up, kid," Juniper said. "You got me. Now, who is that?"

The figure lifted its head, and Juniper felt a splinter of fear pierce her heart. The eyes were dark as nightmare, like cigarette burns. They glared at her without emotion, cold and staring. The face drooped, the skin rubbery and inhuman, mouth hanging open in a mournful cry.

Was the person wearing a mask?

"*Don't be hasty, stay in bed,*" the figure hissed, and Juniper heard a scraping sound, saw them lift an object from the cement floor.

An ax.

"Knock-Knock Nancy wants your—"

"Oh boy," Juniper said, right as the figure lunged for her.

She was ready for it. Juniper brought her fist down with the force of a dozen Hollywood trainers. She punched the face, felt the solidity of bone and cartilage, heard a low grunt as the figure tumbled backward. She didn't stick around to deliver another blow, turning to run for the door that led back into the corridor.

The figure was too fast. They reached the doors first, raising the ax, ready to swing, and Juniper fell back, forced to redirect. She leaped up onto a table and ran as fast as she could, hopping table to table, heading for the counter at the far end.

She heard running. The slap of boots on the cold floor.

She ran behind the counter, reaching the kitchen door. Tried the handle. Locked. She shook it a few more times, emitting a cry of frustration, then turned just in time to see the ax swinging for her head. She dropped, felt the rush of air over her head, heard the crunch of the blade biting the doorframe.

They missed.

Juniper looked up, saw the figure wrestling to free the ax. She took her chance, *fight or flight, motherfucker,* pitching herself forward, tackling her attacker to the floor. Juniper landed on top, grimacing at the stench of damp coming off the figure.

She punched them in the kidney, just like she'd learned in Krav Maga, and felt a surge of satisfaction as the figure tried to curl up in pain. She punched them in the face, heard a groan, tried not to think about the ache in her knuckles.

"How do you like that—" she began, then stopped.

Bright pain, like branching frost, in her abdomen. She didn't have to look to know she'd been stabbed. She fell back, clutching her stomach, heat oozing between her fingers.

As she shuffled across the floor, behind the counter, she thought about Chad. His flirting. So creaky it was adorable. And she'd kept her distance. Made sure it never turned into something else. Something she couldn't control.

Not because she didn't love him, but because she was done with excitement. Done with butterflies and I-love-yous. Four failed marriages and three stalkers were enough.

But in that moment, she felt the hard, bleak possibility that she'd never get to tell Chad she liked his flirting. Would move back to L.A. if he asked.

Juniper scuttled back across the floor, her free hand flailing for something to defend herself with. The figure rose from the floor, breathing hard, and returned to the ax. They gripped the handle with gloved hands, tearing it free.

Up, a voice commanded in Juniper's mind. *Get. The fuck. Up.*

She got to her feet, just as the white-haired figure flew at her. Juniper threw open a cupboard door, smashing it into her attacker, and then while they staggered and tried to recover their balance, she tore out drawer after drawer, casting serving implements, wooden spoons, and kitchen utensils to the floor.

And through it all, her stomach pulsed like an alarm, demanding attention.

Pain is all in the mind, Juniper told herself, limping as fast as she could to the other end of the counter, emerging back into the canteen.

Chad had no idea about the cancer. She wasn't ashamed of being sick, it was just that you had to fight some battles on your own.

She admired the other campers because she wasn't like them. Juniper didn't get canceled. There was no pitchfork-wielding mob in her past. She simply needed to get away. Take a moment. Regroup. The other campers were fighting to better themselves, to understand their mistakes and atone, and it was an honor to be a part of that. To find the goodness in the complicated.

The canteen doors were on the other side of the room. Another set of doors held an emergency exit sign and were farther away. She dismissed them. If she could just reach the clubhouse foyer, get inside the game room, and lock the door, she'd be okay.

Half bent over, holding her gut, she ran.

"*Can't run,*" a voice whispered, just over her shoulder, accompanied by the crashing, stumbling sounds of pursuit. "*Got to pay.*"

The figure was faster. Skidded to a stop outside the canteen doors, standing braced, ax held across them in preparation.

Juniper redirected, aimed for the emergency exit instead. She had no idea where it led. It was on the opposite side of the canteen from the picnic area, so these doors must exit into the front of Camp Castaway.

She gritted her teeth. Urged herself forward. Thought about Chad and home. Thought about what a great story this would make. She'd died in those movies, but in real life, she was a survivor.

No, that was faux heroic bullshit. She wasn't a survivor. She simply kept living.

Out of the corner of her eye, she saw the figure giving chase. Coming at her faster than she had thought possible.

She crashed against the emergency doors, and they flew open, right as the figure tackled her to the ground.

Juniper looked up, saw trees. They were outside, in the driveway. The clubhouse towered over her, trees swaying, rain coming down hard.

The emergency doors slammed shut behind them, must be on an automatic spring, and she saw a warped, sagging face as the figure loomed over her. The ax went up. Rainwater struck its blade, and Juniper saw everything in slow motion.

As the ax came down, she felt like she was back on one of those movie sets, facing an unstoppable force, one that had its whole energy focused on one thing: ending her.

"Cut," she muttered, as the blade descended.

XXX

The shape lunges out of the darkness, and I prepare to drive the knife into it.

"Willow, stop! It's me!"

Even through the adrenaline haze, I recognize Dani's voice. I feel her hand around mine, the one holding the knife. As light comes into the cabin with Bebe and the lantern, I see the smeared clown makeup and Dani's unmistakable brown eyes.

She looks even more like a zombie than before. Disheveled and freaked.

I don't relax, still gripping the knife.

"What are you doing in here?"

"Snooping," Dani says, and she doesn't look ashamed.

"Snooping for what?"

She shrugs. "Anything. After stone circle, I went on sort of a roaring rampage of revenge. Or more specifically I broke into Misty's cabin to find some dirt on her."

She's trying to be cute, but I feel caught between two minds.

Dani's unharmed, which fills me with relief, and I wish we could go back to that moment in my cabin when we first kissed, before everything went to hell.

But my relief is already curdling into anger. That familiar feeling of resentment that has followed me around ever since tweetageddon grows. Now I have a name and a face to direct it at, and I can't believe that name and face belongs to Dani.

A clicking sound breaks the silence, and I turn to see Bebe trying the light switch. It remains dark.

"The power went out a second ago," Dani says. "I'm guessing there's no backup generator out here?"

"It must have failed," Bebe says.

I know how it feels. It's been a long day, and every part of me hurts.

I finally tug my hand free from Dani's. Bebe sets the lantern on the dining table. It casts a pale glow around Misty's living room, which is almost as messy as Buck's. Clothes, makeup, and magazines litter every surface.

"Is that blood?" Dani is looking at my shirt.

I'd almost forgotten that I'm filthy from the forest.

"It's Kat's," I say, and even though speaking to her makes my jaw ache, she deserves to know the truth. I tell her about finding Buck and Kat in the woods, bringing them back to camp, locking up Buck, finding Apollo's and Chef Jeff's bodies and deciding to use the radio at Bebe's house to call the police.

"Apollo's dead?"

I nod. "Oh, and Buck's Caleb."

"Buck's . . . Jesus," Dani says. She shakes her head. "You sit out one party, and everything goes to shit. I can't believe Kat and Apollo are dead."

"And Chef Jeff."

"Right. Are you okay?"

"I'm fine," I say. I realize I'm still holding the knife. My knuckles hurt from gripping it so tightly. I stow it and shake my hand to get the blood flowing.

Dani gives me a look of such care and concern, I almost soften.

She's still here, Willow says. *She cares about you.*

But even as my guard drops, I sense the weight of tweetageddon returning—the weight of three weeks certain I was about to die—and

I press my mouth closed. Dani blinks and all concern vanishes from her eyes. When she speaks, her voice is level. Unemotional.

"So what now?"

"We're going to Bebe's place. There's a radio."

"Perfect," Dani says, then adds, "Wait!" She reaches into her pocket, takes something out. "I found this."

She hands me a small rectangle that is so familiar, my heart seizes.

It's the photo.

It's Brandon.

I take it from her and hold it tight.

"Where did you find it?"

"In Misty's nightstand."

Anger bristles through me. "What the hell was Misty doing with it?"

"Maybe she wanted a keepsake from her time at summer camp with her favorite canceled actor?"

I almost crush the photo.

I can picture it without even trying. Misty breaking into my cabin while I was hanging out with the others. Looking through my stuff. Thrilling in being among my belongings, like those kids in *The Bling Ring*. She hid her love of *We Love Willow* for three whole days. Has she been watching me this whole time?

That question leads to an even more baffling one: Why the photo? What could Misty possibly get from taking Brandon? As far as I'm aware, she has no clue who the photo is of, nor why it's so important to me.

Unless she does.

Unless she knows things about me that only somebody who'd gone beyond a mere fan could.

Dani tugs something else out of her clown overalls.

"I also found these," she says, handing me half a dozen plastic cards. I look through them, seeing that one is a driver's license, another is a social security card, a third is a state-issued identification card from Florida. Each bears a different name, and aside from the social security card, they have one thing in common. The photo is of Misty.

"What are these?" I ask.

"I'm thinking identity fraud," Dani says.

I frown, wondering if this, finally, is the reason Misty was canceled. Not for gambling, but for some kind of scam.

"Did you know about this?" I ask Bebe.

She's at the door, looking out into the night. At my question, she turns and shakes her head.

"I can't discuss campers' personal lives without their consent."

"Come on, is this the real reason she's here?" I ask. "She's not at Camp Castaway to recover from a gambling addiction, but because she committed fraud, and it got her into trouble."

"I really can't say," Bebe says.

"If she's dangerous, we have a right to know."

"A right to know what?" Misty asks, appearing in the doorway.

Bebe staggers back, caught off guard, and my hand is back in the bag, attempting to wrestle out the knife, but I'm too slow. Misty's face is lit up by a second lantern, and she's alone. Soaked by the rain, her hair plastered to her head. Her gaze finds Dani as she steps inside.

"Oh wow, lover girl's back. What are you guys doing in my cabin?"

"Hi, Stokely," Dani says, smiling sweetly as she uses one of the names from the fake IDs. "Or is it Janine? I always thought you looked more like a Tina."

Misty's face drops. "What did you call me?"

"We were just wondering what you were doing with these," I say, holding up the cards.

"What the fuck?" Misty snarls. "You've been going through my stuff?"

"Pot, meet kettle," I say. "Who are you, Misty? Who are you really?"

"Yeah, and why did you kill Kat?" Dani adds.

Misty looks like she doesn't know whether to laugh or scream.

My grip remains on the knife, waiting, tensed with anticipation. Misty went through my cabin. She has numerous fake IDs. What if she's Knock-Knock Nancy, too?

"Not that it's any of your business, but the fake IDs are just a reminder. I haven't used them in months and don't plan on using them ever again."

"A reminder of what?" I ask.

"Of what I did. The people I hurt. You may not believe this, but I feel bad about that, and the cards help remind me to do better."

I don't understand what she's saying.

"What happened?" I ask.

"Misty, you don't have to tell them anything," Bebe says.

Misty considers her, and the anger in her tone dims.

"After my second divorce, I got lonely. I went on dates, but I guess I had a lot of barriers. Guys never got past the first dinner. But I missed being around people, so I started chatting online. I made up a bunch of fake names and signed up to a lot of dating apps. I bought some fake IDs to complete the act in case anybody wanted to verify my identity. There's a lot of paranoia out there. It was sort of liberating because I could be anybody I wanted. It was just a bit of fun."

She shakes her head.

"Next thing I know, a couple of unshaven twenty-somethings turn up on my doorstep with a full camera crew. Some guy I'd been chatting with on Flirter for a couple of months got pissed when I blocked him. He wanted to find out who I really was, and, well, pretty soon everybody with a television set knew both who I was *and* what I'd done."

I try to piece together what she's saying, and it sounds a lot like—

"You were on *Catfish*?" I ask, struggling to believe it myself.

She nods and, for once, doesn't seem to have anything to say.

Dani laughs. "Oh shit, that's actually hilarious."

Misty's face darkens. "Oh yeah, hilarious when you have to move out of town, start a new life, report to a parole officer, and live in constant fear that your fucking episode will run again and again in syndication, and it's only a matter of time before somebody recognizes you."

Dani stops laughing. She looks at me, and I look at Misty. I see that same double negative of a person that I saw in the therapy room during my first stone circle. Underneath all the bravado, there's a sadness to Misty.

Maybe she really was lonely. It would explain her interest in Tye.

And while I don't condone what she did, I understand being afraid somebody will recognize you. I understand wanting to be somebody else, even for a little while.

"Now tell me why you were going through my stuff," Misty says, her tone clipped again.

"It's not fun, is it, having your personal space invaded?" Dani says.

"Ladies, please," Bebe cuts in. "We have more important things to concern ourselves with."

"Like the fact that Misty stole from my cabin?" I say.

"Now what are you talking about?" Misty asks.

I raise the photo of Brandon, which Misty gives a brief glance.

"Cute kid. Why am I looking at this?"

"We know you took it from my carryall," I say.

Misty's frown deepens.

"Have you guys been smoking Buck and Kat's stash? I've never been inside your cabin."

"Yeah, right," Dani says, but I hold up a hand, and she falls silent.

"You've never seen this before?" I ask.

Misty shakes her head. She just told us she's an expert liar, but her confused reaction seems genuine. Unless I'm so wiped out by the events of today that I'm not thinking straight. I realize I don't have the energy for this.

"Fine, whatever," I say, pocketing the photo. "The important thing is we found it."

"Where's Tye?" Bebe asks. "I thought you were sticking together at the clubhouse."

"We were," Misty says. "I helped Tye get Kat's body to the infirmary, and then we went up to meet Juniper and Kurt, but they were gone."

"Gone?" Bebe asks.

"They weren't in the clubhouse when we got back from the infirmary. We looked all over."

"And Tye?"

"He told me to wait in the clubhouse, and then he went down to the boathouse to see if they'd holed up in there. But he didn't come back."

"He went alone?" Bebe asks.

Misty nods.

"What about Buck?" I ask.

"The office door was still locked, but I had to get outta there. I couldn't stay in the clubhouse alone with a killer."

"Christ," I say. "We can't go five minutes without a camper going missing around here."

Juniper and Kurt wouldn't leave the clubhouse without good reason. I try not to think about them like Kat. Hunted by some monster. Necks severed.

And why would Tye leave Misty alone?

I remember the fevered look on his face as he played Bishop with the knife and his hand, the excited light in his eyes when he knocked out Buck. Does he think he's being a hero by going off alone?

Or is he the reason Kat's dead?

"We have to find them," I say.

Bebe picks up the lantern. "We're not splitting up again. We'll get the radio first, then look for the others."

"Let's just hope your father doesn't get them first."

Silence settles over the cabin.

"Father?" Dani asks.

Bebe gives me that ice-cold stare that I feel in my bones. The stare that tells me she's dealt with worse than me over the years.

"Let's go to the house," she says.

"Father?" Dani asks again as I head out the door, into the rain.

I could explain to her about Nancy and the killer priest who vanished into the woods twenty years ago, but I find I can't talk to her anymore. I'm glad she's safe, but I'm not ready to forgive her.

JUNIPER II

She'd thought she was dead.

As the ax came down, Juniper tried to accept the fact that she'd lost this battle. She'd played enough heroes on-screen to know that there was always a moment when they faced an enemy they couldn't outwit.

In the movies, though, the "all is lost" moment was always a precursor to the uplifting finale. The moment when the hero's mettle was truly tested, and they found deeper reserves of inner strength than they thought possible.

Juniper thought about all the fans who praised her for being a big-screen badass and an inspiration to generations of viewers, no matter their age, gender, or ethnicity.

The thought of this fucker robbing her of that, robbing her of a life she'd fought so hard to make, lit a fire within her.

She wouldn't let them.

And she wouldn't let them hurt anybody else.

Her arms went up, and she caught the handle of the ax, stopping the blade inches from her face. The razor edge hovered above her, teasing, threatening an end that could come at any moment. Just a few inches stood between her and the big sleep.

Juniper's arms ached.

Whoever it was, they were strong.

But so was Juniper.

She forced the ax sideways, knocked the figure off her, and the game changed.

Now Juniper was in the woods.

Like an idiot, she had run into the wilderness. But she'd had no option. Her only thought was to shake off Knock-Knock Nancy, or whoever the hell it was under the mask. Once she'd done that, she could regroup. Get back to camp and shelter with the others.

For now, she just had to stay alive.

Juniper took off her shirt and tied a knot in the fabric. Then she fastened it around her midriff, tightening it so that the knot dug into the wound. The pain was like a steaming brand, brought hot tears to her eyes, but she kept tightening until she was sure she'd stanched the flow of blood.

Then she collapsed against a tree and tried to breathe.

Every inhale lanced her side.

Every exhale was like a fist gripping her internal organs.

But the breathing helped. Calmed her. Helped her scattered mind come back together.

Somebody was trying to kill her. They had killed Kat.

Not Buck. It couldn't be him—he was locked in Bebe's office.

So who? An invader from outside the camp? Some nut job who escaped incarceration to wreak havoc over one stormy night? The ghost of Knock-Knock Nancy?

Yeah, you spent too long in Hollywood, doll.

Whoever had attacked her was flesh and blood. They were strong. And she got the feeling they wouldn't stop until somebody forced them to.

Juniper willed herself to move. She dug her heels into the dirt and used the tree to lever herself to her feet. Fresh pain tore through her abdomen but she didn't scream. All those years of core work and for what? She felt tired and old. But old didn't mean weak. Old meant you'd survived.

She scanned the trees. Listened. She didn't recognize this part of the woods, but she'd always had a good nose for direction. Her internal compass told her the camp was to the left, back through the trees she was sure she'd raced past just ten minutes ago.

As she started to walk in that direction, though, she noticed a glimmer to her right.

At first, she thought it was the ax, shining in the moonlight. Nancy standing behind a tree, enjoying watching Juniper struggle, waiting for her moment to strike.

But the light was wrong. It didn't look like an ax. It looked like . . .

A mirror.

A small, angled mirror.

Attached to a car.

Twin emotions spiked Juniper's veins. Excitement and fear.

Excitement because a car could get her out of here.

Fear because who abandoned their car in the woods like this? Perhaps somebody who was planning on attacking the camp and then making a quick getaway?

The car could have keys. Then the game really would change.

Gripping her side, she shuffled toward the vehicle, trying not to make a sound that would draw Knock-Knock Nancy to her.

The car was a black BMW. New-looking. So clean you could eat off the hood. Juniper squinted in through the windows. There were no shapes inside, nobody sitting behind the wheel or in the back seat. That unnerved her more than she had anticipated, but she tried the driver's door handle anyway.

It opened.

Juniper sent up a silent prayer, then eased open the door and peered into the car.

The interior looked spotless, as if it had been professionally cleaned. She reached in and felt along the panel beside the steering wheel, searching. Her fingers hit the strip of steel where the key would slot in, but there was no key.

"Why the hell would there be?" Juniper muttered. She straightened, checked the area around the car. When she was certain she was alone, she eased her weight into the driver's seat, leaving the door open. The knotted fabric chewed her wound, and sweat broke out across her brow.

"Come on," she said, gripping the wheel tightly, until her hands hurt enough to distract from her stomach. She thought about the day she bundled Samuel L. Jackson into the trunk of a BMW, the way he warned her not to hit his fucking head when she slammed it shut. She punched him instead, a moment of improvisation that looked killer on film, mostly because Jackson looked so surprised.

She leaned over and opened the glove compartment. Hand gel. A six-pack of tissues. A bottle of water. The car reminded her of the ones that were sent to take her to press events and awards shows. The driver usually stocked up on essentials. A convenience for people who had grown accustomed to convenience.

She dug further into the glove compartment and tugged out an ID card for a driver, confirming her suspicion. This was a private-hire car.

The last person to be dropped off at the camp was Willow.

And the last person to be picked up was—

"Apollo," Juniper murmured.

Apollo was dead, but where was the driver? Did he not leave? Was he still at camp?

A chill bristled her spine as she wondered if he was the one who'd attacked her.

She kept digging in the glove compartment but found nothing more. She turned, wincing as she looked into the back seat.

Something silver reflected light. She couldn't make out what it was. The object was half-buried between the seats. Grunting, she twisted her arm back, sweating through the pain in her gut, and groped along the seat. She felt metal and closed her fingers, pulling the object free.

Gasping, she sat back in the seat and lifted the winking silver foundling.

A cross.

Had Apollo worn a necklace?

She didn't think so, but then maybe he only wore it after leaving the camp.

Tap tap tap.

Juniper turned, just as the drooping masked face appeared in the driver's-door window. Knock-Knock Nancy stood on the other side of the open door, tapping the glass with the blade of the ax, face white and ghostly. Pained and excited all at once.

With a cry, Juniper dragged the door shut, just as the ax swung. It sank into the chassis, shaking the car. Before Juniper could punch the lock, Nancy freed the ax and tried the handle. It remained shut. She tried again, yanking it so hard that the Beamer bounced, but the mechanism must have been impacted by the ax blow. The door was locked.

"Motherfucker!" Juniper said, releasing a jubilant laugh as she flipped the bird through the window.

The head turned to look at something behind her, and the laughter turned to chalk in Juniper's throat.

The rear passenger door.

Nancy moved.

"Shit." Juniper went to punch the lock on the back door, but her abdomen froze her, pain pinning her in place. She tried the door handle beside her, dragging at it with desperation, but it was no good. It was jammed.

The door behind her opened, and the car sank as the weight of a second person put pressure on it. Juniper heard the wheeze of a breath as she attempted to scrabble across to the front passenger seat, but pain in her stomach paralyzed her.

And then something came up and over the seat.

Juniper only realized it was the wooden handle of the ax as it wedged against her throat. She was pulled back in the seat, the back of her head forced against the headrest as the handle crushed her throat.

"*Byebyebyebyebyebye*," a voice whispered in her ear.

Juniper squirmed, legs thrashing in the footwell, hands wrapped around the handle, trying to push it away. But Nancy was strong. Juniper's lungs reached for air but found none. The pain in her stomach dimmed as her chest caught light, screaming for a breath she couldn't draw.

Through the agony, Juniper felt something else in her hand.

The necklace.

She was still holding it. The cross was small, no bigger than her pinky, but it was all she had. Gritting her teeth, she held on to it with her thumb and forefinger and stabbed down. She felt it sink into flesh, and the handle loosened from her throat.

Juniper gasped an endless breath, relief flooding through her as her lungs inflated. She wrestled free from the ax, ducking down and seizing hold of a lever below her. She scooted the seat back with such force, she was surprised it didn't come off the rails.

The seat juddered as it met resistance, pinning Nancy behind her. The ax fell into the front passenger footwell, bouncing and then going still.

While her attacker thrashed and tried to break free behind her, Juniper massaged her throat, every breath divine torture as it squeezed her bruised esophagus.

As she fought for air, she spotted something on the floor between her legs and choked anew.

The keys.

They were under the seat the whole time.

Not wasting a moment, Juniper seized the keys with trembling hands, wrestling with them as she brought them up to the steering wheel. She pushed the key into the ignition and turned.

The engine roared.

Juniper had never heard a sound so sweet. She tried to speak, wanted to drop the kind of cool one-liner she was known for, but she couldn't. Her voice was gone.

Her seat bucked and bounced as Nancy attempted to free her legs, and Juniper leaned forward, put as much space between them as possible as she threw the Beamer into drive, released the hand brake, and sped into motion.

She felt the power of the car as she wove between trees, so alien after two weeks in the wilderness. It was like she was flying. There were so many freeways choked with cars just like this one. They were so taken for granted. Nothing special, only necessary. And yet out here, in the middle of nowhere with a monster in the back seat, *this* was where this marvel of human engineering really mattered.

If only she could stay alive long enough to do it justice.

Movement in the rearview mirror.

The white face appeared, mouth hanging open in a silent scream, and Juniper realized her seat wasn't shuddering anymore.

Nancy had pulled herself free.

She lunged forward, dragging the ax from the footwell and pulling it back with her into the back seat.

You really gonna swing an ax in here? Juniper tried to say, but she couldn't get anything out.

The ax swung.

Juniper ducked.

The blade bit into the headrest, stayed there. Juniper jerked the wheel to the right and hit the brake at the same time. Nancy rolled against the passenger door, grunted, struggled to regain balance.

Juniper drove with one hand, tried to pull the ax free with the other, but it was impossible. She almost ran into a tree and was forced to grab the wheel with both hands to change course. The car screeched as tree bark grated the side panel, spitting sparks. The vehicle hopped and bounced over the forest floor, then emerged out onto a flat, gravelly strip of ground.

Juniper hit the brakes, staring at the road in disbelief.

It was the road that led from Camp Castaway to the real world.

She could drive out of here. Get help.

At the sound of movement in the back seat, she spun the wheel toward the road and hit the accelerator, right as Nancy seized her hair. Yanked hard. Tears sprang into Juniper's eyes and the car skidded and spun.

She couldn't see.

She heard the engine growl and realized she had stomped down hard on the accelerator. Something big and solid rushed at them from the dark, filling the windshield.

Then Juniper felt an almighty crunch, heard the sound of the world breaking open around them, and she lost her grip on the wheel. The hand released her.

The car rocked to a standstill, shrapnel hitting the roof, the scream of breaking things echoing around her.

Juniper wiped her eyes, tried to figure out what had happened, and with a jolt she saw where she was.

They were back in the clubhouse.

Back in the goddamn canteen.

Nancy lay unmoving in the back seat.

And Juniper couldn't feel her legs.

adie?" Bebe calls. Her voice fills the hall, echoing up the stairs into the first floor of the house. There comes no reply, and I'm not surprised. I get the feeling Sadie never stays still for long.

Misty stares at the dark walls and even darker furniture, mouth open. My eye is drawn to the Jesus mural on the dining room wall, and the words above that skeletal face make my legs shake.

The Lord is a God who avenges. O God who avenges, shine forth.

I don't know how Bebe can bear looking at it every day. Aside from being a reminder of her father and all the pain he caused, that thing is creepy as all hell.

"Why do you keep that?" I ask Bebe.

She follows my gaze to the mural. She stares at it a moment, her eyes dull.

"My sister painted it," she says.

I look at the fresco with renewed interest. Sadie painted it? I'd never have guessed from her drawings that she could create something so accomplished.

Bebe goes into the dining room and opens one of the dresser doors. She takes out a small box with a large antenna coming out of the top. A radio, decades old. I watch her set it on the dining room table and then flick a switch. The box lights up, static whining through the speaker.

Peering down the hall, I see that the sunroom is in darkness. Rain flecks the windows, painting the floorboards with rippling shadows. I can't help thinking about the door at the back of the cupboard—the one we decided not to open when we were hiding from Bebe. My curiosity still prickles.

"I could've handled it if they'd called me a monster," Misty says, and her raw tone brings me back to the hall.

She seems lost in thought. Her hair is still wet from the rain, and her makeup has washed away. She was silent the whole way from her cabin to Bebe's house, and I realize she's been thinking about what Dani found. Everything she told us about her past.

"At least being called a monster would've been something," Misty says. "Instead, people online made me out to be a desperate, attention-seeking nymphomaniac who had to create multiple identities just to sate her craving for male flesh."

"Gotta love sexist strangers with an opinion," I say.

Misty shakes her head. "What I did was wrong, I get that. But I didn't actually hurt anybody. Not really. And they ruined my life regardless."

In the dining room, Bebe turns the knobs on the radio, which hisses and crackles.

Misty looks haunted as tears fall, running to her jawline.

"I'm sorry I've been such a bitch," she says. "The thing is, your show helped me. After the whole catfish thing, I got into gambling, and when that went south, I found *We Love Willow*, and it made everything better. I could disappear into your world for as long as I liked. But then the show got canceled, and I had nothing to fill it with. I had no idea who I even was anymore, after everything."

I soften. There's something we have in common.

And I'm so tired of all the judgment. I have no idea what it was really like for Misty after her divorce, or how Buck really felt when he went off the rails outside the Miss Hellfire nightclub. Or Dani, targeting strangers online based entirely on their perceived wrongs against the queer community.

The constant cycle of judgment, virtue signaling and shaming . . . it's exhausting. Pointless. And it has to stop somewhere.

"You're stronger than you think, Misty. Or whatever your real name is. You're strong."

"You think?" she asks.

"Yeah, you're terrifying," Dani says. "Also, I prefer Misty to Stokely, if that's your real name, but what do I know?"

Misty wipes her face and smiles. "Thanks. Maybe I'll change my name when we get out of here. Third time's the charm." She looks at me. "And I really didn't take your photo. I have no clue why it was in my cabin."

Call me crazy, but I believe her.

"Hello?" Bebe says into the radio, holding the mic to her mouth. "This is Camp Castaway. Do you read?"

Static crackles. There's no reply.

I look at the sunroom again, then Dani and Misty.

"Stay with Bebe," I tell them. "Make sure she gets through to the police."

"Where are you going?" Misty asks.

"Just tell me you'll watch her."

Misty presses her mouth closed, nods. Weirdly, she looks the best I've seen her at camp, even with snot bubbling from her nose and mascara striping her cheeks.

I head down the hall, going into the sunroom.

"Quite a one-eighty," Dani says. She's followed me. I sort of expected her to.

"I'm so tired of the blame game," I say. "You just have to look at Misty to know she's suffered, she's sorry."

"Yeah, I know. You ever have to cross the line before you know you went too far? I think that's what happened with Gossip Goblin. I only knew I'd fucked up *after* I'd fucked up."

"Yeah, I know," I say, repeating her words.

"I never wanted to hurt anybody," Dani says. "I don't know what I was thinking. I came here to break away from all that toxic shit. Start over."

"I get it," I say.

Dani's mouth quirks into a smile. "I'm glad it only took a dead body to convince you to talk to me again."

I smile back.

Understanding passes between us.

This new thing we have feels better than the anonymity I valued so much when I first got to camp. This is the opposite of anonymity—this is knowing each other, even the ugly parts, and sticking around. Maybe *that's* where the healthiest relationships take root. Not in the Instagrammable moments of grand romance, but in the moments when we see the real person, and they see us, and neither of you runs screaming off a cliff edge.

"Let's just try not to die," I say.

"Sure," she says. "That always works."

I walk to the corner of the room, standing by the closet door. "Why put a door at the back of a closet like that? I have to see what's in there."

"What if you find something you don't like?"

"At least I'll know."

I open the cupboard, half expecting a figure to burst out. Somehow, the quiet is more unnerving. I take a breath and step inside. Boxes obstruct the door at the back, which looks older than I remembered. Chipped and brown. I push the boxes aside, clearing the space in front of it, and tug open the door, revealing a black space.

"What is it?" Dani asks. She's right behind me, crouched in the gloom.

"I'm trying to see."

As my eyes adjust, I peer into a small, cramped cubby. The ceiling is staggered, and I realize this is the space under the stairs. A couple of old cushions are piled on the floor, and there are a dozen doll heads. More than a dozen.

"This is where she put us," a voice says.

I turn and put out a hand to catch myself.

Sadie stands in the sunroom, just outside the closet. She's not looking at me but at the cubby under the stairs. In one hand, she holds a bald doll's head, which she strokes with affection.

"This is where who put you?" I ask.

"Nancy," Sadie whispers, and her voice causes goose bumps to bristle up my arms.

"Knock-Knock Nancy put you in here?" Dani asks.

Sadie nods. "To keep us safe."

"Safe from what?" I ask.

A pause, and then Sadie says softly, "Safe from Daddy."

I look back at the cramped space with the dolls, trying to understand. A camper put Sadie in here to keep her safe from her father? I picture Sadie locked in there, sitting on the cushions, grasping the dolls . . .

"Sadie," Bebe says, voice sharp and loud. She appears behind her sister, lips thinning into a snarl.

"Come out," she tells us. "Now."

I remain crouched in the closet, holding on to the old door for support.

"She said Nancy put her in here. What does she mean?"

Bebe looks at her sister, then stares into the cupboard. I see the eye twitch, the tense jaw, all the emotions she's trying to keep in check, and increasingly failing to do so.

"Nancy hid us in here when Daddy got mad," Sadie says.

I don't understand. Why would a camper hide Sadie and Bebe in a cupboard in their own house? As I look between them, I remember the three chairs in the tree house. The photo of three girls in black dresses. And I feel the truth like a spotlight shining into the dark.

"She was your sister," I murmur.

Bebe flinches, and she hasn't blinked in a very long time.

"There were three of you, weren't there?" I say. "Nancy wasn't just a camper; she was your sister."

I'd noted that Bebe and Sadie's names rhymed. How didn't I see before that there was a third line to join their couplet?

They're not a pair, but a trio.

Bebe. Sadie. And Nancy.

Sadie continues to stroke the doll's head.

"She was the biggest," she says, "and she wasn't scared of Daddy. She hid us when Daddy got mad. She put us in the cupboard, and she shut the door, and she'd only knock when it was safe. Three knocks meant we could come out again. But one day, she didn't knock. We stayed in the dark for a long time."

My gaze passes between the sisters, a horrible understanding surging up from the pit of my stomach. I feel the full horror of what happened here. I picture Nancy bundling her younger sisters into this cupboard, protecting them from their vengeful father. Maybe one day, she pushed back against him too hard.

"Your father killed her," I say.

A tear tracks Bebe's cheek, and I realize what has always felt off about her. She's not the eldest sister at all—she's the middle child. The pacifier. The bridge between protection and vulnerability. And one day, their father changed that forever. Forced Bebe into a new role; one she's never figured out how to perform.

"He took her head away," Sadie says matter-of-factly, nursing the bulbous piece of plastic.

"What happened?" I ask. I don't want to intrude on their grief, but a part of me is desperate to know why she was killed. What unforgivable thing she could have done, in the eyes of her preacher father.

"There were rumors she was pregnant," Bebe says, sounding

weary. "People in camp said Nancy was sleeping with a male resident, just because they were friends."

I straighten, my head scraping the ceiling. I spoke to somebody who called themself Nancy's friend not too long ago.

"Was it Jeff? Chef Jeff?" I ask.

Bebe nods. "It was misogynist bullshit, and none of it was true. People didn't like Nancy, though. She was opinionated, and loud, and brave. She believed in the magic of nature, and she listened to Kate Bush and Joan Jett. She didn't follow the crowd, and the crowd hated that. So they made up lies about her."

Bebe's lips thin. "Father believed the lies because he always saw the worst in people. He lost it. He demanded she confess and repent, and he wouldn't listen to her denial. They were out by the woodshed. Nancy had made us hide in here and gone out to continue her chores, as if everything were normal. But I heard her yelling, threatening him. They fought. The next thing we knew, she was gone."

Bebe swallows, and my throat aches, thinking about the blade that bit Nancy's flesh. The terror she must have felt. Killed, and so young, because of a rumor.

Because of what her father believed.

And just like the Nancy of the legend, the real Nancy's pain has echoed across the years, as strong now as it ever was.

Is that why her name is all over camp? Her father could have carved the marks himself. Gone mad with grief, unable to process the awful thing he did.

"I'm sorry," I say, finding my voice. "I'm sorry about Nancy."

Sadie's breathing becomes heavy. She grits her teeth, and she raises a hand, moving forward, like she's about to strike me. Bebe catches hold of her forearm and stops her, pulls her away from me.

Sadie turns on her. She swings, aiming for Bebe's face, but Bebe catches her hand and folds her into a hug.

As I watch Bebe comfort her sister, I realize what we really heard when we hid in the cupboard. Not Bebe hitting Sadie, but the other way around.

"No," Bebe says softly, stroking her hair. "We don't do that. Come on. Come on, little Sadie."

Sadie sobs as she buries her face in her sister's chest. "She's bad. Daddy says she's bad."

"He was wrong. Nancy only ever wanted the best for us."

I can't imagine what it must have been like to be left alone the way they were. Their sister, their protector, was killed. Her murderer vanished, and while Nancy became a legend, Bebe and Sadie had to live with the reality of her death. The hole in their lives. The thing their father took from them.

I know a little of what it's like to lose somebody like that.

"She wants her head back," Sadie moans. "She's angry. That's why she's hurting people."

Bebe keeps stroking her hair.

"It's not her," Bebe says. "Nancy is gone. She's gone, and so is he."

I don't know if I believe it. And I can't crouch in this cubby anymore.

We climb out of the closet; first Dani, then me.

I try to reassemble my mind, which has been shattered by Bebe's story. We have to end this. Finally end the pain and suffering and punishing.

"Did you get through to the police?" I ask Bebe.

"They're dispatching officers as we speak."

"Thank God. How long until they get here?"

"With the rain, and the distance from the station, at least an hour, more likely two."

I look past her to Misty, who nods in confirmation. I'm able to breathe a little easier. The police are coming. In just a couple of hours, they're going to save us and find whoever killed our friends.

It's never too late for a happy ending, Willow says.

My gaze moves around the sunroom. Bebe's father's house. And suddenly being in here feels even less safe than being in the woods.

"We have to get back to the clubhouse," I say. "Now."

Sadie tugs free from Bebe's embrace. She steps over to me and holds out a doll's head.

"They protect us," she says. "They keep us safe now. If Nancy comes looking for you, give her your head. That's all she wants."

Give her your head.

The same words written on the note that I found in my cabin.

Looking at Sadie, I realize that the doll's heads left all over the camp weren't a warning. They were hidden in and around campers' cabins in an attempt to protect them. To help them protect themselves.

I take the toy, wondering how I was ever scared of Sadie.

"Thank you," I say. "I think you should get into the cupboard and hide one last time."

JUNIPER III

Juniper heard breathing behind her. Steady, shallow, calm.

Sitting in the driver's seat, she looked out at the remains of the canteen, certain that her attacker was unconscious on the back seat. The windshield was smashed, huge cracks spidering across the glass, and tables and chairs littered the area around the BMW. Victims of her mad spin with Nancy's hands in her hair.

Her body ached with tension, and she realized she was holding her breath. She forced herself to inhale.

The steady breathing continued behind her, and Juniper couldn't turn because her stomach was a hotbed of pain, so she reached up and repositioned the rearview mirror, angling it into the back of the car.

Knock-Knock Nancy slumped in the corner, head against the window, face sagging. Her silver hair spilled up and over the seat, as if it were trying to escape.

Juniper couldn't tell who it was. The costume had too many layers, the tatty fabric of the dress/robe doing a great job of concealing who was underneath. She weighed her options. She could try to maneuver in her seat, reach into the back and reveal once and for all who was under the mask. Reveal the fucker who had killed Kat and stuck a knife in Juniper's gut.

But that might wake Nancy up, and then it really would be lights out for Juniper.

Better to get out of the car.

Get free, then warn the others.

She pinched her thigh, relieved that she felt it this time.

The shock was wearing off. For a full minute after the crash, she hadn't been able to feel her legs, was certain they'd been crushed when the car barreled into the canteen. But now she could move, so she had to get moving before Nancy woke up and finished what she'd started.

Juniper tried the door handle again, as quietly as she could, but it was still jammed.

Trying to stay calm, she peered at the front passenger door and saw that it was flush with the wall. No way she could get out there. And there wasn't a chance in hell she would climb into the back seat.

Her gaze settled on the windshield. It looked like it wouldn't take much to free it from the frame. But it would be loud. She'd have to move fast.

Juniper pocketed the cross and sat forward in the seat. She lifted her legs, focusing on being silent: not snorting air through her nostrils, not swearing, or whimpering, or complaining.

She got her feet under her butt, crouching on the driver's seat. She reached over the steering wheel, past the dash, making contact with the windshield. She got both hands onto it, pressing lightly.

The glass made a loud cracking sound, like ice under pressure.

Juniper froze. Waited for Nancy to grab her.

When that didn't happen, she pressed the glass again. Now. Now. *Now.*

She pushed with all her strength, feeling the glass cutting her palms, not caring, elated as the windshield buckled, so loudly the sound must fill the entire camp. Juniper dug her boots into the car seat and launched headfirst through the gap, sensed freedom, rejoiced in her plan coming off, but then she got caught on something. The steering wheel. It dug into her side and she screamed.

Just as she remembered to be quiet, a hand grabbed her foot.

Juniper kicked, felt her boot make contact, then her foot coming free. She thrashed and pulled, slithering through the hole left by the windshield and sliding over the car hood. She hit the canteen floor with a cry and instinctively curled up around her wounded abdomen, prayed for porcupine spikes to burst from her back to protect her. She heard Knock-Knock Nancy scrambling around in the car, maybe retrieving the ax.

Fucking. Move.

Groaning, Juniper clambered to her feet, stumbled over the debris on the floor and limp-ran for the canteen doors. She noticed that the trunk of the car was open and glimpsed a body inside. A man in a suit.

The driver?

She didn't have time to check, focusing on getting away.

The doors swung open at her touch, and she hobbled down the corridor, hearing noise from the canteen, but no footsteps behind her. Not yet.

At the clubhouse foyer, she fought a wave of wooziness, tried to steady herself. She realized she hadn't expected to live this long.

She'd felt the same way a few months after she got the cancer diagnosis.

A part of her had expected to be dead within weeks, but her body had kept going regardless. Some primal part of her took control. There were no guarantees, no certainty that she'd live to see another week or month, but that primal part of her was still there. Keeping her going, despite the odds.

She felt that part of herself now. It carried her to Bebe's office, where the door was still locked. She rattled the handle, tried to speak, but her throat was still painful.

"*Buck!*" she wheezed, trying to call for him, but her voice was little more than a pained sigh. He couldn't help her anyway, tied up behind a locked door.

Juniper staggered for the panoramic window, clutching her stomach, keeping her insides where they should be. Through the glass, she saw shapes by the lake. It looked like Willow, Bebe, Misty, and Dani.

Juniper beat the glass with her fist.

"*Willow!*" she tried to shout, but her voice wouldn't sound. Her throat felt swollen.

She heard a noise behind her. The scrape of metal dragging over hardwood.

Over her shoulder, she saw Nancy approaching. Her shoulders were hunched, head hanging low, mouth agape. She dragged the ax behind her, pacing slowly, a predator that knows its prey is cornered.

Something about her was different—she had removed her mask. Too far to see from here in the dark. Or maybe Juniper's grip was slipping.

"*Stay the fuck back,*" she tried to say, vocal cords silently screaming.

Nancy raised the ax, and Juniper banged on the window again, trying to draw the attention of the women by the lake. And despite the fear, despite the exhaustion, despite the pain radiating through her body, Juniper almost laughed. Because she'd been reduced to the role of Victim Banging at Window after all.

There are no small parts, only small actors.

Only now she understood the part. If she had the strength, she would run for the steps that lead down to the picnic area. If she hadn't lost two pints of blood, she'd throw herself at Nancy again. If her side weren't shredded and leaking. If she hadn't just been in an automobile accident. If she weren't too goddamn old for this shit.

She banged the window again, and all four women looked up. They saw her.

They saw her.

And Juniper smiled.

"Do your worst," she told Nancy, and this time her voice pushed out, filling the foyer. "Bring it the fuck on."

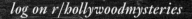

WHATEVER HAPPENED TO JUNIPER BROWN?

Posted by u/freddystolemyheart

  I'm curious. She was such a huge figure in the 80s and 90s, but suddenly she hasn't made a movie in a decade, and nobody seems to know where she went. Did she pull a Bridget Fonda and quietly quit the biz? What's the deal?

250 COMMENTS

XenaFiles Didn't she have a fallout with some producer?

Fisherman1997 Sam Jackson totally has her locked in his basement.

BrendaDidIt I heard she became a junkie or some shit. Actual fall from grace.

Candyham Isn't she in a movie next summer? I swear I heard somebody say she's making a big franchise comeback, like JLC in H20/Halloween 2018.

SheRahhhh She got canceled. Like everybody else in Hollywood.

XXXII

The banging sound disturbs the eerie still of the night.

As we reach the end of the boardwalk and walk with the lake on our right, the sound carries through the air. A flat thumping, nearby but far enough to make an echo.

"What is that?" Misty asks, shivering.

My gaze goes to the clubhouse, which is as dark as the rest of camp. The power is out there, too. The panoramic window reflects the moonlight, and the shimmer makes it difficult to see inside, but I make out a shape on the other side of the glass. A person slumped on the floor, beating the pane with their fist. It looks like—

"*Juniper!*" I shout.

A shape looms over her. I glimpse hair as white as milk, and my chest shudders as I see an ax glinting in the dark.

I spring into motion, racing toward the clubhouse, fumbling a knife from my bag as I cross the picnic area and burst inside. Taking the steps two at a time, I burst into the foyer, then skid to a stop when I see Juniper. She leans against the panoramic window, looks half-dead, holding her side, red between her fingers. She sees me and her mouth twists into a smile.

"About time," she wheezes.

The figure that towers over her is dressed in a long black gown, white hair tumbling over wide shoulders. They have an ax. It trembles in the air, preparing to swing, and even though I'm just an ex–sitcom star who weighs 165 pounds soaking wet, I charge.

My mind is in a frenzy, knife ready in my hand. I throw myself onto the figure's back, raising the knife, but the figure bucks and grunts beneath me, attempting to throw me off.

I hold on tight, trying to bury the blade in their throat, but the figure whirls, and I'm hurled free.

I hit the floor so hard, the breath is knocked from me. My elbow jars against the hard wood and the knife clatters across the floor, disappearing under the sofa.

I look up to find the figure standing over me, feet braced wide, ax creaking in their grip, and terror pierces my heart.

White hair hangs in his face, but I glimpse wrinkled, weather-worn skin, high cheekbones, and thin, cruel lips. He's older, but it's him.

It's the preacher from the photograph.

The man who killed Nancy.

"Red," he says, his voice a rasp; a blade dragged over flint. Dark eyes glitter like obsidian. "Good to see you, Red."

I'm frozen in fear.

See you soon, Red, the text had said, and now there's a man saying it to my face. Standing over me. The ax looks heavy in his hands, a threat that wants to be fulfilled.

How does the preacher know about the text?

"Nathaniel?" I say.

"Get away from her!"

A familiar male voice fills the foyer, and Kurt emerges from the game room. He moves fast, jaw set with determination as he crosses the floor, charging at the man with the white hair.

There's no contest.

The preacher can't get the ax up in time, but his fists aren't quite so slow. He barely breaks a sweat as he slams a fist into Kurt's face, knocking Kurt off his feet.

"Kurt!" I yell, grimacing as he goes down hard. He lands on his back, looks dazed as he blinks up at the man looming over him.

"Willow!" Dani yells, and I see her at the top of the stairs with Bebe and Misty.

There's an explosion so loud, it makes me jump where I lie. Orange light flares in the foyer, and I realize Bebe fired the gun. The preacher jerks, stepping back. I can't tell where he's hit.

Bebe strides toward him, firing twice, three times, but the preacher is a moving target, stepping sideways and ducking. There's enough distance between them that Bebe's aim suffers. One of the bullets sparks against the head of the ax; another hits the bookcase.

Bebe stops five feet from the preacher, and her gun clicks. Empty.

They stand staring at each other. Bebe's face is taut with emotion, eyes like storms.

"Hello, Father," she says, and I see now that the black dress is a priest's robe, tattered and worn.

He breathes hard, face to face with his daughter—his middle child—and their hair is the same silver-white.

I'm still reeling from the fact that the preacher is here. He's returned to the camp, after decades away.

Father and daughter stand just feet apart, and I can't breathe. Can't tell what either is thinking.

For a moment, I think the preacher might back down. There must be some humanity in him. Maybe he regrets what he did to Nancy. Maybe he returned after all these years to atone. Make peace.

Or maybe he really has gone mad with grief. Maybe he's reliving the night he killed Nancy, driven by some awful, unshakable impulse to re-create his daughter's death again. And again. And again.

I watch the cruel lips pucker, his face creasing with revulsion, and the ax swings, quick and lethal.

Bebe is too slow getting out of the way.

The blade goes into her neck. Her head rolls off her shoulders and blood sprays up, hitting the foyer ceiling. Her body slumps to the floor and her head bounces across the wood, stopping at Misty's feet.

Misty screams.

I'm rigid with horror.

Bebe's body lies just a few feet from me, resting in an expanding pool of blood.

She's dead.

Bebe's *dead.*

"I will repay," the preacher growls, and he's looking at Misty and Dani by the stairs. "In due time their foot will slip."

"Fuck," Dani says as the preacher starts walking toward them.

I scrabble to my feet at the exact same moment that Kurt recovers. He hunches by me, shaking off the daze.

"Who is that?" he asks, his gaze resting on the preacher.

I ignore the question, shouting "Dani!" and shooting my knife across the floor to her. She catches it just in time, raising the blade as the preacher reaches her. She lunges, aiming for his chest, but Nathaniel Carver grabs hold of the hand with the knife, stopping it midair. He twists. Even from across the room, I hear the brittle crack of bones.

Dani screams, a sound that causes my heart to explode.

"No no no," Misty whimpers, backing away, transfixed by the man in black.

"Rise up, Judge of the Earth," the preacher intones. "Pay back to the proud what they—"

"*Get the fuck off me!*" Dani screams, and her voice activates something in me.

I surge up from the floor, charging the preacher again, and he must hear me coming, because he knocks Dani to the side, sending her tumbling down the stairs.

He swings at me, and I duck just in time, feeling the ax whirr past the top of my head.

Kurt is right behind me. He throws himself at the preacher, and the man growls, easily shoving him off. Kurt crashes into the wall, then lands on the floor. The impact knocks a water cooler from a table. It smashes on impact, gushing water and cucumber slices over the floorboards. Kurt's out cold.

The preacher reaches down and picks up something from the floor.

Bebe's head.

He puts it in a black bag that's fastened across his body, almost indistinguishable from his robe.

"Do something!" I yell at Misty, who's still cowering by the wall. The preacher is already on me again. He swings the ax, and I leap back, tripping, going down, the ax missing me by an inch.

Misty darts past us, running to Juniper. I finally wrench the skewer from the bag. My last weapon.

I look at the man looming over me, and time seems to freeze. I see the priest who came to the house in the weeks before Brandon went to camp. A soft, moon-faced man with round spectacles and red cheeks. So unassuming, you'd never suspect he could judge another human being, let alone a scared seventeen-year-old.

I remember Father Reilly going into the living room with Grams and Bran. I only heard soft murmuring as I listened at the door, and when the priest left thirty minutes later, Bran went up to his room and fell apart.

I lay on his bed with his head in my lap, stroking his hair and telling him it would all be okay.

Lying to him, over and over again.

The preacher, Willow says in my mind. *Stop the goddamn preacher!*

I grit my teeth and leap up from the clubhouse floor, aiming the skewer at the preacher's throat.

But then I feel coldness at my abdomen. It rises into my rib cage, and I look down to see—

Blood. My shirt is covered in blood.

And a knife is buried in my side.

The one I threw to Dani.

The preacher must have retrieved it from the floor, and his face is so close to mine, I see the true depth of the black in his eyes.

"Red, Red, Red," he says. "Give me your head."

I stagger away from him, gripping the knife handle, knowing I shouldn't pull it out. The number one rule every horror film ever broke was the fact that you should *never* remove a knife. Nevertheless, my body is desperate to be free of it.

I feel woozy, the floor slanting beneath my feet, and I'm backing into the middle of the foyer with nowhere to hide. Moonlight slashes through the panoramic window, and it's beautiful. Horrifying and beautiful. Kurt lies unconscious by the shattered water cooler.

"Hey, kid," Juniper's voice rasps, and I realize she's right beside me, clutching her own side. We're stabbed in the same place. Gotta love a killer who's consistent.

"Help her," Juniper tells Misty, and Misty takes my arm, attempts to pull me across the foyer, toward the game room. Juniper stands firm, knife in hand—the knife that went under the sofa. She's put herself between us and the preacher.

"You better pray you kill me," Juniper tells the preacher through gritted teeth, her voice hoarse.

"Juniper, no," I say, but then the preacher is on her. He swings and Juniper ducks, thrusting the knife at his gut but missing, instead impaling his leg.

The preacher doesn't scream. Doesn't yell. He backhands Juniper, knocking her to the floor, and then he rushes at me and Misty, his face a mask of silent fury. The knife doesn't slow him a beat. I stumble backward with Misty, my abdomen so cold it's like it's been doused in ice water. I look back at Juniper, who's lying on the floor.

"It's not a mask," she murmurs, her voice barely audible. "Not a mask."

"We're gonna be okay," Misty whispers. "We're gonna be okay."

The preacher swings, and something hot sprays the side of my face. I taste metal.

Misty's grip on me loosens and I hear the thud of her body hitting the floor, then something else falling. Bouncing.

No. *No!*

I can't look. I keep my eyes on the preacher. I'd rather look at a killer than what he did to Misty.

The preacher wrenches the knife from his leg and tosses it, spattering the floor with more blood.

"He will punish those who do not know God," the preacher's voice rumbles as he picks up another object from the floor—an object with wild brown curls and black-lined eyes—and stuffs it into his bag.

"Not today, Satan," Juniper says. She's right behind him, clearly in pain, but she's still Juniper Brown. The baddest badass there is. She seizes the preacher's hair and drags him away. They crash against the panoramic window. It creaks but holds.

"Juniper!" I cry, bent over, holding the knife that's still buried in my gut, willing my body to move, but every breath is agony.

Juniper shoves the preacher off her, and as he tries to recover his balance, her gaze meets mine. I see warmth and determination and acceptance.

"Be smart, kid," she wheezes. "Be smart, and ru—"

She's cut off by the ax.

In horror, I watch it go through Juniper's neck and strike the window.

The glass shudders and cracks. The window comes down with a sound like thunder.

Paralyzed by shock and terror, I watch Juniper's headless body slip. Her hands flail, catch hold of the preacher, and as she falls back through the window, she takes the preacher with her. They sail through the air, vanishing from sight.

I drag in an agonized breath, and I scream.

When the end comes,
you'll know it,
because I'll be there.
I'll be front row center—and
I'll be smiling.

—Maggie (played by Juniper Brown)

XXXIII

The scream tears out of me like a demon. I taste blood. It feels like the vessels in my throat are bursting open, and I can't believe what just happened. Juniper. Bebe. Misty.

Dead.

They're all dead.

My stomach foams. My body feels numb. Every part of me is cold, apart from my side, where the blade pulsates heat, causing me to sweat from every pore.

My mind is full of static.

I don't know what to do. What to say. How to think a single thought that doesn't break apart and re-form a thousand times over trying to make sense of the blood and agony and death.

"Willow, oh my God," Kurt says, sounding breathless as he appears at my side. His face is pale behind the blood spatter, and his eyes are huge, focused on the knife in my gut.

"I'm okay," I say.

"You're stabbed," he says. "You're—"

He reaches for the knife. His hands stop centimeters from the handle, trembling in the air. Panicked.

I take his arm, pulling him toward me.

"Kurt, look at me," I say. "I'm not going anywhere. I'm right here. Okay?" He stares at me. Softer, I say, "Okay?"

Finally, he nods. Licks his lips. His breathing calms. I'm not somebody else he needs to mourn. Not yet, anyway.

A hammering sound makes us both jump, and we turn to look at the office door.

"Let me the fuck outta here, man!" a voice yells from inside.

Buck.

He's still in Bebe's office.

Somehow, I remember Bebe has the key. I limp to her body and take the key chain from her pocket, keeping my gaze unfocused so I don't have to take in the details of her lifeless body. I go to the office door and search through the keys, my hands shaking, slippery with blood. Finally, I get the right one, and the moment I slot and twist, the door opens from the inside.

Buck looks frantic. He must have heard the whole thing. Behind him, the chair he was cuffed to has been destroyed, and the handcuffs dangle from his wrist. He stares at me, then Kurt, then the foyer, his mouth open.

"What the fuck . . ."

"They're dead," I whisper.

"What . . . who . . . ?"

"The preacher," I say. "Bebe's father."

I see again that cruel mouth. Those dark, pitiless eyes. The deep rumble of his voice, thick with judgment and discontent.

And suddenly it all makes a horrible kind of sense.

We really are being punished. Canceled all over again—this time for good. But not by Bebe, or some unquiet phantom. By a flesh-and-blood human being who has killed before and will probably kill again.

"That was Bebe's father?" Kurt asks, voice hoarse.

Buck doesn't seem to know what to do with that information. He's missed a lot.

"Were you stabbed?" he asks, and I nod, suddenly feeling exhausted.

"Let me look," Kurt says, but I push him back.

"Dani . . . stairs . . ." I murmur, and that's all I can manage. Kurt puts an arm under my shoulder and together we struggle to the stairs. A part of me almost doesn't want to see, fears Dani could be down there with a twisted neck.

But then I see her getting to her feet at the bottom of the stairwell, and a sob chokes from me.

I half trip, half fall down the stairs, Buck and Kurt anchoring me on either side, and when we reach the bottom, I throw myself at Dani, kissing her once, twice, relief almost overwhelming me.

"Careful," she says. I see that her wrist is bruised dark purple from where the preacher bent it.

"Is it broken?" I ask.

"Feels like it. Oh my God, your side . . ."

I can't think about the knife. I can only think about—

"Juniper," I murmur, and even though my vision is edged in black, I find the strength to push outside.

Not Juniper, Willow whispers. *Not Juniper Brown.*

The ground is covered in glass shards, and there's only one body. No sign of the preacher.

The glass crunches under my sneakers as I stagger to Juniper, and when I drop to her side, I don't care that the ground cuts into my knees, stings like teeth. I've reached maximum capacity for pain. Tears fill my vision and I wipe at them, choking. Part of me hoped I imagined it, but she's right there by a picnic bench.

Juniper lies on her side. One hand faces up, elegant fingers unmistakably hers, the other hand still pressed to her stomach, as if trying to stanch the flow of blood from a grisly wound.

I touch her hand, still warm. Her multicolored jacket is soaked through with blood, and I'm crying. Lost. I see Juniper. *Juniper Brown.* Broken and gone. The injustice of it smolders like a howl in my chest, and I want to scream again, but I can't draw enough air into my lungs. It catches on the way in.

I should have done more.

I should have attacked the preacher one more time, sent him barreling through the window.

Not Juniper.

I hear heavy breathing. Kurt. He's panicking, but he taps his sternum, the way I showed him, calming the anxiety. Still, his gaze lingers on Juniper, and I wonder if he's thinking the same thing I am. Where does all that energy go? The energy of a life. Juniper had so much of it. She was big and loud and funny. She vibrated with energy. What happens to all of that, now that she's gone? Does it fade? Is it released back into the atmosphere? Or is it still trapped in her body, like a memory?

"Where's the rest of her?" Dani asks.

I stare at the space where Juniper's head should be, and I feel the screws of my sanity loosening.

"He took it."

"He took her head?" Kurt says.

In my mind, I see again the ax going into her neck, the look of calm in her eyes as she looked at me.

If Juniper couldn't survive the preacher, what hope do we have?

"He killed his daughter Nancy years ago," Dani says, "that's what Bebe said. Looks like he's back for more."

"He killed Knock-Knock Nancy?" Buck asks.

"And Bebe ... and Misty ..." Kurt murmurs, and he keeps tapping his chest. Keeps trying to stanch the horror.

We all saw what happened to Bebe and Misty. We're covered in their blood.

I struggle to focus. Darkness further clouds my vision. Am I breathing? I can't tell. My body feels separate from me, as if another Willow has taken over. I don't know if it's Sitcom Willow or Willow 2.0, or something else. Something new.

Silver winks in the moonlight, bringing me back into my body. I look at Juniper's other hand, seeing that she's holding something that shimmers. Reaching down, I untangle a silver cross on a chain from her fingers and lift it up, making it twirl in the air.

"I didn't know Juniper was religious," Dani says.

"She wasn't."

Fresh tears fill my eyes and my throat stings.

We're alone out here. Completely and utterly alone.

Bebe called the cops, but who knows how long it'll take for them to reach us, if they even *can* reach us after the storm. We could start walking the road out of here, but what if the preacher's watching the road? What if he's waiting for us out there right now?

THE ROAD IS MINE, the note said.

Juniper would know what to do.

She'd have a plan. Some kick-ass strategy to get us to safety. Away from the preacher and this nightmare of a camp.

I wish we could wake up, Willow says. *You could say "Thank Timothée Chalamet it was only a dream" and then we'd jump in the lake and—*

"Willow," Dani says, "we have to remove the knife."

I'm confused for a moment, and then I remember the blade in my gut. I'd almost thought the constant pain was just grief.

"We have to patch you up," Dani says.

I guess she's right, but I struggle to care. I'm lost in the forest darkness. She helps me to my feet, and I pocket the necklace from Juniper, allowing Dani to lead me back toward the clubhouse.

In Bebe's office, Dani eases me onto the desk, because Buck destroyed the chair while freeing himself. He stands in the door, keeping watch over the blood-soaked foyer, while Kurt searches through the cupboards. I stare at the floor, seeing nothing. I'm vaguely aware of Kurt handing a first-aid kit to Dani, who comes over to the desk and opens the box, rooting around inside.

My mind is still with Juniper. I don't think it'll ever leave her.

"I'm pretty sure you need surgery," Dani says, making a gasping sound. I think that she's binding her own wrist, but I can't respond.

"How handy are you with a needle?" Kurt asks.

"I think we'll have to settle for packing the wound and bandaging you up," Dani says, and their voices are a comfort, but they feel distant, speaking in another space just out of my reach.

Something rattles. A bottle?

"Oh shit," Dani says. "Fentanyl. They were in the first-aid box. The label says 'Juniper.' I guess Bebe was keeping them for her?"

Through the fog that has cloaked my brain, I process the fact that Juniper was the one taking fentanyl.

Because she had cancer.

I remember asking if she'd be okay. Telling her that the world needed Juniper Brown.

Gee, kid, you'll make me blush.

The fog thickens, surrounds me.

"Here, take one," Dani says. "It should help with the pain."

She tips a pill into my palm. I look at it, thinking it looks like one of the teeth in the tree house. I'd toss it if Dani didn't guide it to my mouth. I toss it back, swallow. It catches on the way down, but I swallow a couple more times and it's gone.

Thanks, Juniper.

I can't lift my head.

"What's wrong with her?" Kurt says.

"She's been stabbed," Dani says, and I laugh, which causes the knife to scrape my insides. I groan. The pain almost feels good. It reminds me I'm alive, even though the office feels hazy and out of focus. Dani is moving around, leaving vapor trails behind her, and I can't keep up.

"Okay, I'm going to remove the knife," Dani says. "As soon as I have, I need you to press down with this gauze to stop the blood. Press hard. Do you hear me?"

I nod, which makes the room swirl, colors bleeding together, forming a painting that starts to look like the mural in Bebe's house. Jesus's cool blue eyes laser into me.

The Lord is a God who avenges . . .

"This is going to hurt," Dani says. "A lot."

"Do it," I say.

Kurt's hand encloses mine, squeezing tight.

"Okay," Dani says. "On three. One, two—"

She pulls, classic fake-out, saying "sorry sorry sorry" as the blade comes out of me. My vision swims and as heat flushes through me, I look up into my brother's face. Brandon is beside me, holding my hand.

"*Pain is just an itch that's being a little bitch,*" he says, quoting Juniper's alligator movie.

"Press harder," Dani says, taking my other hand and digging it firmly into my side. I cry out, feel like I might vomit up an organ, but I manage to keep it down.

"You're doing great," Kurt says, "really great."

I remember it's Kurt's hand I'm holding. Not Brandon's. For a second, I forgot he was dead. The realization hits me in the same place I'm currently bleeding from. Raw and bright and hopeless.

"Let me," Kurt says, and he holds the gauze to my side, pressing firmly.

"Let's focus on this," Dani says, and she starts wrapping the bandage around my abdomen, like I've just won the most fucked-up version of Miss World.

I want to lie down.

"What are we going to do?" Kurt asks.

"I say we hide," Buck says.

Is Tye hiding? Willow says. *He's been gone for hours now.*

"I say we hit the road," Dani says. "We take all the weapons we can find, and we hit the road. Just start walking."

"Fucking A," Buck says.

"But the bodies," Kurt says. "The warning . . . He's watching the road. And we could get lost—it isn't all paved or so clearly traceable, out here . . ."

"Better to be out there, moving closer to the cops, than trapped in here," Dani says.

I reach into my pocket, feeling the necklace that we found on Juniper, and it's like I have a piece of her with me. I fumble with it, struggling to unclasp it. My fingers feel thick and slow.

"Here," Dani says. She takes the necklace, and her hands graze my throat as she fastens the chain, her wounded wrist shaking. The cross rests against my collarbone. It feels heavy. It feels like armor.

I swear I feel the pill, too, fizzing in my stomach.

The cramping pain has lessened. Become less paralyzing. My mind is clearer.

I just watched three people I cared about die. I just hope the rest of us can make it through the night.

"Okay," I say. "We take the road."

I did it. I finally did it.

You've done the right thing. You've done right by me.

When can I see you? I need to see you.

Soon.

XXXIV

The bodies are still there, lying on the steps that lead down to the road. Apollo and Chef Jeff, their limbs stiff, bent, and awkward. And they're starting to smell, filling the air with an overripe perfume that burns my nostrils.

Silently, we maneuver around them. I nearly slip on the blood-soaked wood, but Kurt helps me, and even though his arm around my midriff makes my wounded stomach spasm, I'll take it.

Dani fronts the group, brandishing one of the knives from the foyer. We collected the knives that were scattered during the preacher's attack, and the others are in my bag now, ready to be used. They've already tasted blood, and they want more.

The road rolls out between the trees, a tongue of darkness that leads into a hungry, gaping throat. I remember thinking the road felt endless during the drive here. How will it feel now that we're on foot?

It's so quiet, all I hear is our breathing. Tight, short, wary. We're all struggling to keep it together.

"Okay, let's go," Dani whispers.

We move in the dark.

Lanterns would give us away, and the light wouldn't be reassuring; it would only make it harder to see anything lurking in the shadows.

You're doing the right thing, Willow says. *It's long past bail time.*

It doesn't feel right, though. It feels like I'm doing exactly what I did at the start of all of this.

Running away.

Hiding.

Disappearing.

I think about what we're leaving behind. All those dead people.

And Tye. Sadie.

She's lost two sisters now, and we're just leaving her.

Abandoning her to the preacher.

I just have to hope that the cops reach us soon. Hopefully they'll meet us on the road, then take over. Raid the camp, rescue Sadie and Tye, and finally bring this awful night to an end.

"Do you hear that?" Kurt whispers.

We stop moving. I hold my breath.

Knocking.

The sound echoes between the trees.

My skin crawls.

"It's him," I say.

"Oh shit," Buck whimpers.

The knocking continues, and it's accompanied by a rasping voice calling out.

"One knock, two knock, three knock, four, Caleb's about to feel real sore . . ."

"Fuck this, man," Buck says, and he breaks into a run.

"Buck, stop!" I whisper-shout, but he's already twenty paces away, disappearing down the road, into the dark.

"Shit," Dani whispers.

"What do we do?" Kurt asks.

"Move," I say, and we start moving as quickly as we can, chasing after Buck. I know I'm slowing us down. I grit my teeth and run as fast as I can, but my legs are slowed by pain.

A scream punches a hole in the night.

Buck.

We stop again. Listen.

Silence falls.

Then a shape appears in the middle of the road, from the direction Buck ran in.

The preacher's hair glimmers silver. Cold and otherworldly.

He brandishes an ax cross-body, panting, and then—

—he charges.

"Willow, run!" Kurt says. He pushes me into Dani's arms and positions himself between us and the preacher.

"Kurt, no," I say, clinging to Dani's shirt.

"Get her out of here!" Kurt yells at Dani.

"This way," she says, dragging me toward the trees. I catch a final look at Kurt—brave, crazy, musical Kurt—before we enter the forest. We lumber between tree trunks, the ground uneven, putting obstacles in our way.

"We can't leave him," I say.

Another scream tears through the night.

It's not Kurt, though. The voice is too deep.

"Tye," I murmur.

I can't tell which direction the scream came from. The road? The camp? The night has become a confused jumble. Am I hallucinating? Hearing things that aren't real?

Tye screams again, and Dani's breath hitches.

"They're getting massacred out there," she says. She leans me against a tree. "Stay here. I'll be back. Just don't move."

"This is no time to be a hero—" I begin, but she kisses me, cutting me off. Then her hands leave my body, I hear her running, and she's gone.

"Dani?" I turn on the spot, wooziness causing me to stumble. The forest tilts. The trees spin as I trip.

I'm on the ground.

I hear a scrabbling sound. A scuffle.

"*Dani?*" I shout, and shouting hurts, too.

An object sails through the air. It moves in an arc, hitting a tree trunk and landing on the forest floor. It rolls to a stop at my feet, and even in the dark, I recognize the tangle of brown hair.

It's Buck's head.

His mouth is fixed open in a scream, his eyes rolled back so that only the whites show.

I stare at it in horror, right when Dani's voice punctures the night. "Willow? Where'd you go?"

She sounds far away now. I can't tell where her voice is coming from.

"Where are you?" I call, and my voice comes out hoarse, pain-sick. I dig my fingernails into the dirt, push myself onto all fours. Then I use a tree to haul myself up.

It's so dark, I can't tell where I am. I can't see the road.

Silence has settled once more.

I start limping in the direction Dani yelled, certain she's still at the road.

Please let her be okay.

Please.

I don't reach the road, so I keep going, sure that any moment I'm going to stumble across it, find Dani, Kurt and Tye.

But the forest just keeps going. How far did we run off the road?

I quicken my pace. I'm moving too slowly, that's all. I have to speed up. Bite down the pain and find the way out of here.

Just keep swimming, Willow says.

After what feels like forever, there's still no road.

No way out.

My breathing is ragged. I feel my consciousness slipping, whether from panic, pain, or exhaustion, I don't know.

All I see is trees.

And then I hear a knocking sound. Three knocks, slow and solid, somewhere behind me.

I keep running, fumbling my way through the dark, away from the knocking.

My heart's beating so hard, I'm forced to stop. I lean against a tree trunk, battling for air.

And that's when I feel the lines gouged in the bark.

I turn to face the tree, digging my nails into the rough surface, and a sick kind of elation throbs in my chest, because it's something familiar.

It's an *N* carved into the trunk.

As I run my fingers over the letter, though, I realize it's different from the one I found two days ago behind Buck's cabin. It's older. The bark has grown around it, like a scab.

Unless I'm imagining it?

I want so desperately to be back at the camp.

Dani and Kurt could be there, safe with the cops.

I stumble in what I hope is the direction of the cabins. I'm certain I can see a wooden structure ahead, solid between the trees. As my vision clears, though, I see that what I've moved toward isn't a cabin. It's too small.

It's something else.

I blink at the dark shape that rises from the ground, trying to bring it into focus.

It's a squat structure that crouches in the night, as if preparing to extend long, branchlike arms and drag me into a smothering embrace.

My heart stutters. I'm nowhere near camp.

I've wandered too far into the woods.

And I'm pretty sure I've found the freaky place Buck mentioned earlier. The place where he found Kat's body.

It's the preacher's home, Willow says.

ear rakes my spine. The preacher's house is so gruesome that it takes me a moment to realize it's a shack. It grows out of the forest floor, like something the woods birthed. Organic and malformed. A lumpen structure made out of interwoven branches and vines that weave together to form eight-foot walls. Objects stick out of the construction. Antlers and bones, animal skulls, and teeth hanging on string.

No, not string. Hair. Glimmering silver hair.

Any doubt in my mind about who built this place is stamped out.

This is his house, Willow whispers.

"I know," I say.

I stand looking at it, and I can't help the goose bumps that prickle my arms. I feel faint, the trees spinning around me, reaching out with their branches. And I swear the skulls decorating the shack see me, just like the eyes gouged into the trunk near the tree house.

An eye for an eye.

It's almost like the shack has been waiting for me.

I start to back away, but then I see what looks like a figure standing beside the structure.

They don't move.

They're so still, they could be a mannequin.

I step sideways, trying to see better, even though my brain is screaming at me to flee.

It's a statue. And not just one. I count seven of them, lining the left wall of the shack.

Seven wicker statues.

They're life-size, and each is posed differently. One presses wicker palms together at their heart in prayer, another holds their arms out in welcome. Each has a pair of wings that fan out behind them, and each is topped with a head.

A real human head.

My skin cools as I look up at Juniper.

Apollo.

Kat.

Chef Jeff.

Bebe.

Misty.

I don't recognize the final head, but the dead eyes of my camp-mates look down at me, and I realize what they are.

Angels, Willow says, and her voice is so loud in my mind, it's all I can hear.

He's turned them all into angels.

"That sick fuck," I choke.

As I stare in horror, I hear a noise inside the shack.

A low moan.

My shoulders tense and I don't move, unsure if it's the preacher.

The moan sounds again, somebody in pain. Someone's inside.

You should run, Willow urges.

But I don't run.

It could be Kurt or Dani. I can't leave them.

Maybe some of Juniper's energy went into me when it left her body. At least a little of it, because even though I'm afraid, I'm not paralyzed.

I know I should be. I should be terrified out of my mind—alone, my friends most likely dead, my insides half hanging out of me. And maybe on some level I am, but mostly I feel a cool kind of clarity. It feels like my whole life has been crashing toward this moment. The moment I stop and turn and face the thing in the dark.

Own your space on this Earth, Juniper said on the way to the tree house. *Own it shamelessly, without regret, and no fucker has any power over you.*

Juniper knew what she was talking about, Willow says.

I squeeze the cross necklace in my fist, feeling protected. Not by God or Jesus or some force beyond human understanding. By Juniper. By whatever strength she has inspired in me my whole life.

I enter the shack.

It smells like damp and earth and rot. The scent lodges in my throat, and I only just manage to suppress a cough.

Candlelight flickers around the makeshift walls, lighting up a rickety wooden table that is laid with a red and gold cloth, plus an assortment of rusted cups and plates. An altar.

I hear the moan again, coming from the other side of the altar.

I could still run, before the preacher gets back.

But I'm not a victim. I refuse to be one of those characters in a horror movie who take it lying down.

Wondering whose injured voice is calling out, I realize the camp has answered a question I didn't even know I was asking. It's shown me the reason I keep going back to horror movies, the reason they've sustained me for so long. It's because horror isn't about fear—it's about love. It's about seeing people at their absolute worst and still caring. Still fighting.

My hand trembles as I reach into my bag, removing a knife. I grasp it tight, moving around the altar.

First, I see sneakers, then blood red fabric. I don't understand what

I'm seeing, adrenaline spiking my system until I swear I'm looking at Santa Claus slumped on the ground.

And then I realize it's a costume.

It's Tye.

He's been gagged. A rope is tied around his head, caught between his teeth, and his wrists and ankles are bound. One eye is closed tight, puffy and bruised, and there's a purplish-yellow discoloration along his jaw.

Has he been here ever since Misty watched him run to the boathouse? Willow asks. *How'd he end up here?*

"I don't know," I say.

Tye stares at me with his one open eye and there's terror in it. He grunts, seems to be trying to say my name, and suddenly this was all worth it. The forest. The pain. It was worth it if I can save just one more life.

I don't like this, Willow says, but I ignore her.

I go to Tye.

"Hey," I say, and I hear the pain in my own voice. My whole body is lit up with discomfort and exhaustion. "Hey, it's okay, I'm here now."

He keeps trying to speak. I consider the knife in my hand, and then I set it on the floor, close enough for me to reach if I need it. I remember Tye's wild grin when he played with the knife around his fingers, and I know I have to be careful. I can't afford to make any more mistakes.

Don't get killed, Willow says. *Just don't get killed.*

Tye sits rigidly as I attempt to untie the rope that's gagging him. The knot is tight. I can't get a good grip on it. Tye snorts air through his nostrils and keeps making noises that I can't decipher. Trying to speak.

His gaze moves past me, and I stop wrestling with the rope.

I'm sure I heard a noise outside.

What if the preacher has returned?

What if he has Dani and Kurt bound and gagged, Willow says, *just like Tye?*

I listen but there's nothing. And I still can't untie the gag.

Tye's chest heaves. Panic. Fear. I have to get us out of here before he hyperventilates so much he passes out. There's no way I can drag him back to the clubhouse. Just supporting my own body weight is tearing me apart.

I move down to his feet, struggling with the rope, my wounded abdomen thumping its own agonized heartbeat. The rope loosens, and Tye kicks his feet free. Now he can move, at least.

Careful, Willow says.

"Come on," I tell Tye. "Let's get you out of here."

I retrieve the knife, and Tye manages to get up from the floor. We lean against each other as we stumble through the chapel and back outside into the night.

I sense the unnatural quiet of the forest a moment before the preacher emerges from the dark.

He stands a few paces away from us, and he looks twice the size he did in the foyer. A giant with white hair that glimmers in the moon-light, his face stretched into a pointed grin.

The sight almost snaps the final threads holding together my mind.

"Red," he says.

Why does he keep calling you that? Willow says.

It's just like the text.

Does he have a phone? Willow asks, and I almost laugh, because it sounds nuts for him to have something so modern out here in the woods. But it also sounds weirdly legit.

What if the preacher messaged me before check-in? What if it was all part of his game? We found a whole trunk full of phones in the tree house. He could easily have taken one for himself. And he could have gotten hold of my phone number from Bebe's files—the same files that told him exactly how everybody at camp had supposedly transgressed.

Psycho killers always have cell phones, Willow says.

"They do," I say, and I can't tell if I'm speaking out loud. It's so difficult to tell now where Willow starts and I end. Willow 2.0 seems like forever ago, and Sitcom Willow has been gone for weeks.

Maybe I'm a new version of Willow. The Willow who's finally made the transition from sitcom to horror, like all those CW actors who showed up in glossy horror remakes in the 2000s.

I shake my head, try to focus.

The preacher stands assessing us, seeming to savor the fear we must be radiating, his grip tightening around the handle of his rusted ax.

Fight or flight, Willow says. *Which is it?*

My own grip tenses around the knife.

I think of Juniper.

"Fight me," I say.

XXXVI

R un," I tell Tye. He looks terrified, snot glistening below his nostrils, chewing on the gag, wrists bound.

"*Run!*" I yell at him, and he gives me a final desperate stare before he springs into motion. He flees into the forest, faster than I thought possible, given how roughed up he is.

The preacher remains, glowering at me.

Shit, Willow says.

Maybe I say it, too.

"Why did you come back here?" I ask.

The preacher doesn't speak, but I see the disgust in his curled lip, and I can figure it out for myself.

It's his home. And Bebe let a bunch of sinners in.

You can never go home again, Juniper said during stone circle, but the preacher did. He came back, and I'm guessing he didn't like what he found. He's thin, but he's strong, too. All muscle and resentment. Fueled by his own sick, pathological hatred for anybody who's different.

"Red, Red, Red, I want your head," he says, and I'm done being taunted.

"You aren't chopping any more heads tonight," I say.

He smiles again, and I grip the knife tightly in my fist, blade pointed down, ready.

I don't give the preacher time to come at me.

I charge.

The tactic works as I'd hoped. He's surprised. By the time he recovers, I'm just a foot away from him. He raises the ax too late. I throw
myself at him, and he loses his grip on the weapon. The ax drops to
the forest floor.

I aim for the preacher's throat with the blade, but at the last moment, his hand goes up, and my knife penetrates his palm. It sticks
there.

He grunts. Doesn't scream.

My jaw shudders under his fist. He's struck me with his other hand.

I stagger backward, only just remaining standing. My ears ring
and, for a second, the darkness is complete. I can't see.

For one blissful moment, I feel nothing.

I'm nerveless.

Bodiless.

I'm free.

Not time for the credits yet, Willow says.

I shake my head, and my vision returns.

The preacher tears the knife from his palm and tosses it aside.

The ax is on the ground between us. Before I can lunge for it, the
preacher is on me. I feel hands on either side of my face, pressure
against my skull, and then my feet leave the ground.

The preacher lifts me by my head, snarling, spitting, staring with
eyes as pitch-dark as the night sky.

"Their doom," he rasps. "Their doom rushes upon them."

Hot liquid burns one side of my face, and I realize it's his blood.
His wounded palm is pressed to my cheek.

"Get off me," I grunt, and I tear at him with my hands, but he's too
strong.

I hear creaking bone.

I feel my skull bending under his grip.

And then another figure with white-silver hair streaks out of the forest and rushes at the preacher. I almost can't believe what I'm see-ing. There are two of them?

The second figure stabs the preacher in the back with a knife.

The preacher's eyes go wide.

He releases me.

I fall for what feels like eternity.

The wound in my side seems to split open to release a torrent of lava. I open my mouth to scream, but no sound comes out. The pain catches on my vocal cords, and through the agony, I hear the preacher fall.

He lands beside me, facedown.

Blood glistens at his back, and it's in his hair, too, turning it pink. The knife is lodged in his spine. I can't tell if he's dead. His eyes are open. Staring. Not seeing.

Lying on the forest floor, I feel the cold of the earth seeping into my body. Claiming me. Encouraging me to let go. And I'm so tired, it would be easy to let the forest have me. To finally surrender to Camp Castaway.

But I look up at the second figure.

There's another preacher? Willow asks. The figure darts back a few paces, and then it turns. It raises a hand and tosses something onto the ground.

Long, silver hair, which tangles amid the underbrush.

I've been on set enough to realize it's a wig. Discarded on the for-est floor.

A few paces away, the figure tosses a fleshy object with a couple of holes cut into it.

A mask.

Then they shrug off a bundle of off-white fabric.

A robe.

Growing unease cramps my insides, and I raise my tired-as-hell corpse off the ground.

The figure starts pacing back and forth with their head bowed.

One of their hands is raised, and it flutters before them. It takes me a moment to grasp just why the movement is so familiar.

It's because it's somebody tapping their chest.

Tapping it lightly, to calm panic, just like I showed him.

It's Kurt.

XXXVII

K urt?" I say.

He stops pacing, looks at me in surprise, as if he didn't expect to see me out here in the middle of the woods. Then his face crumples.

"I couldn't let him hurt you," he says.

"What are you doing? Why were you dressed like the preacher?"

Kurt shakes his head, seeming to signal that he doesn't know. He shifts to one side, which is how I see the body slumped at the foot of the shack—the body Kurt must've brought back from the woods.

It's Tye.

His hands are still bound with rope, and he's still gagged, the rope trapped between his teeth. I can't tell if he's breathing. His face is even more of a mess than it was when I found him behind the altar.

My mind attempts to haul itself together. I think about the discarded wig. The mask. The robe.

"Kurt, what happened?" I ask.

"He tried to hurt me, but I stopped him."

"Tye? Tye hurt you?"

Kurt nods, but he's not blinking. His eyes are wide and staring.

My heart is a block of cement in my chest. My brain is waterlogged in my aching skull.

As I look at Kurt, an alarm starts screaming in my ears.

The preacher's dead, but Kurt is acting like a stranger. Like somebody else has taken control of his body.

What's he holding? Willow asks.

I look at his hands. One hand is pressed to his sternum, while the other holds a small black object. It's been so long since I saw somebody using one, it takes me a second to realize what it is.

Kurt has a phone.

"Where did you get that?" I ask.

He eyes me. "I found it."

"Found it where?"

He doesn't respond. He looks wary, his lips pressed together, knuckles white around the cell phone.

"Do you have service? Can we call for help?"

Kurt makes a guttural sound, and I realize he's crying. Fat tears trail over his cheeks, and his mouth turns down, wet lips quivering.

"Please don't hate me," he says. "Please. I just wanted to make everything right."

My pulse picks up.

It sounds like a confession.

What would he be confessing? Willow asks.

We saw the preacher in the clubhouse. We saw him murder Juniper, Bebe, and Misty. We saw him attack Kurt.

But now I find Kurt with a phone and a creepy costume?

My hand brushes my bag, and it feels empty.

My knife is gone, stuck in the preacher. I don't want to make any sudden movements.

"Kurt, you need to start talking," I say. "Now."

"Do you think people get what they deserve?" he asks. He's not crying anymore. There's a detached calm in his eyes. "If a man kills another man, who gets to decide his fate?"

The dark has turned his skin waxy, and his eyes are black as ink.

"Kurt," I say, "what did you do?"

Kurt's brow lowers and he smiles, but the smile is painful-looking, like he's chewing raw onion. I feel like I'm being turned inside out, every nerve and muscle exposed. Not just because of the wound but because of the expression on Kurt's face. So alien to the person I know.

His gaze drills into me, and I see something in his eyes that chills me to the marrow. Triumph—and despair.

He wipes his nose, looks down at the phone in his hand.

"She went away," he says, almost to himself. "But I got her back. It's okay now."

"Who went away?"

"Courtney," he says, and I feel ill.

His sister.

He's talking about his sister, who died in the car accident. The one that he said was his fault.

"Did you know she had the most beautiful voice?" Kurt says, and this time his smile is warm. Loving. He tilts his head, as if he can hear her. "She sang in the school chorus. Her version of 'Titanium' blew Sia out of the water. I could listen to it over and over. And I did, until Bebe took it away from me."

He reaches into his pocket and pulls out an object. It's the broken iPod. Charred and in pieces, but unmistakably an iPod. The one that Bebe destroyed on my first night at Camp Castaway.

"It was yours?" I ask.

Kurt runs a finger over the broken pieces. "Apollo saw me with it the day he left. He must have told Bebe. But they didn't understand that this wasn't like handing over your phone at check-in. I needed it. For her voice. This was the last bit of Courtney I had left, and Bebe took it away from me."

His tone is light, fragile, and I feel like I'm seeing the part of him that I saw in the shower block two days ago, only it's more troubled than I ever imagined.

And I get it, because I have a memento of Bran in my own pocket. A physical thing I struggle to live without.

"You had a recording of her?" I ask. "On your iPod?"

"Messages, songs. Bebe ruined everything. But then Court found me again, and she told me what I had to do."

My gut twinges at his words.

Court found me again.

I try to keep my voice level, but I feel so woozy, it's difficult to focus.

"Kurt," I say, "your sister's dead."

"No, she's not. She's right here." He holds up the phone, and his face is drawn tight. "It feels so good to tell you. I've wanted to tell you for days, but she told me not to."

I swallow, my throat dry as dust.

"What did she say?" I ask.

"She told me there were bad people at camp. She told me where to find proof of what they'd done. And she told me how they had to pay."

No.

His words refuse to make sense.

His sister's dead.

Bad people. Make them pay. Sounds like the preacher, Willow says.

He always wanted a son, Bebe said, and a shudder travels through me.

"Kurt, where did you get the phone?"

He chews his lip.

"I found it in my cabin right before you checked into camp. And when I powered it on, Court messaged me. She told me where the dress-up boxes were. She told me everything I had to do, in order to see her again."

Jesus. This can't be happening.

"Kurt," I say, "that wasn't your sister."

Kurt wrinkles his nose. "You wouldn't get it. All you have is a photo. I have the real thing."

The way he speaks, something clicks in my mind.

"You took the photo," I murmur. "You took the photo of Brandon."

He smiles that warped, alien smile, confirming it.

"You put it in Misty's cabin," I say. "To cover your tracks."

"And to make you hate her even more," he says with a shrug.

Christ.

He's played me this whole time.

"They had it coming," he says, and suddenly I want to hit him.

I want to bury a knife in him the way I did the preacher.

She had it coming, everybody said when I was canceled. *That bitch had it coming.*

But it's Kurt.

Sweet, musical Kurt.

I think about him vanishing at the roadside, then Buck's head rolling across the forest floor.

"Where's Dani?" I ask, voice raw.

"She got away from me," Kurt says, and I think I believe him.

"What about Buck? Did you kill Buck?"

"And Apollo," Kurt says. "Kat. Chef Jeff. I'd have killed Juniper, too, but she was slippery. Damn near killed us by crashing the car into the canteen. Luckily, the preacher stepped in and finished the job."

My failing brain realizes it took two of them to take down Juniper Brown.

The hairs on my neck bristle.

Between them, Kurt and the preacher have killed seven people at Camp Castaway.

Kurt must have smashed the emergency cell, stolen our personal phones. Made sure it was impossible for us to call for help.

"You got into the safe and the lockers," I say.

Kurt shrugs. "Those things are easy when you can look people up online. The combination was Nancy's birthday."

I want to scream. Or cry. Or fall apart.

He killed our campmates, all because he thought his sister told him to.

The preacher goddamn catfished him, Willow says.

"What the hell is wrong with you?" I murmur.

Kurt opens the phone and it lights up, picking out his cheekbones and the whites of his eyes, casting him in a spectral glow.

"I'm not like you," he says. "I didn't come to camp because I got canceled. I came to make things right. I had to make him pay."

A jag of ice cuts through me.

"You had to make who pay?" I ask.

Kurt's lips draw back, another smile that sends a shiver across my neck. He nods at the motionless figure slumped by the shack.

"Tye," I say. "Why?"

"Because he killed my sister."

XXXVIII

My mind feels like it's taken a machete blade right down the middle.

Tye killed Courtney?

Camp Castaway groundskeeper Tye? Tye who's worked for Bebe since the camp reopened five years ago?

I had assumed Kurt was behind the wheel the day his sister died.

It was my fault, he'd said.

But now he says *Tye* killed her.

I can't keep anything straight in my head.

When Kurt speaks, his voice trembles with emotion.

"They were dating. Courtney had been in Chicago for a month when she met Tye. He was new in town, and she was smitten. She'd text me saying how great things were working out, how much she loved college life. How she met this guy who was amazing and wild and hilarious."

Kurt's mouth twists. "One night, they went out in her car, and they hit a woman. She died. They didn't stop at the scene, but the cops got her license plate from surveillance cameras. She was arrested right after that. She said Tye was driving. Tye told the police Court was behind the wheel. It was her car, but there was no way to prove it either way. They both escaped jail, but after that, Court became the chick who killed somebody her first month of college. Nobody would go near her."

I blink, try to process what he's telling me.

"But you said it was your—" I begin, only for Kurt to cut me off. His eyes are glazed, like he's watching the past, a movie only he can see.

"Nobody believed that she wasn't driving," he says. "Not even me."

He's pale as stone, his breathing shallow, guilt and grief in his face.

I notice the preacher's ax resting near his motionless body. It's too far away for me to grab. If I tried, Kurt would beat me to it. Jesus, why didn't I pick up the ax when the preacher dropped it?

Just chill, Willow says. *Listen to the kid. Wait for your moment.*

"I was sixteen," Kurt says. "What did I know? I was a stupid teenager who hated that my sister left for college. I just wanted her to come home. Our parents sucked, but that didn't matter when she was there. After the accident, Court moved back, but she was different. He'd ruined her."

Kurt stares at Tye, lips wet, eyes pinned wide.

"I should've known she was telling the truth. Court was always careful on the road. There's no way she'd run someone down."

Kurt looks at Tye, in the same tense, unblinking way he's looked at him the entire time he's been at camp.

I remember Tye's wild laugh when he played Bishop on the picnic bench until Kurt forced him to stop. There's a recklessness to him that unsettled me, because it made me wonder what else he might have done to attain that weird, breathless high. Where he drew the line—if there even was a line.

As I look at Tye now, beaten and bloody, I feel a surge of loathing.

Like so many of the campers, he must have come out here to hide. To start over, after the accident.

But he didn't post offensive comments online or troll other users on social media.

He killed somebody.

He actually killed another human being.

And he let somebody else take the fall.

"A month after Courtney moved back home," Kurt says, "I found her in her room. There were pills . . . she wasn't moving . . . She . . ."

He stops, can't go on. He raises his hand, starts tapping his chest, and the sight unnerves me more than anything he's said, because I showed him how to do that. I showed him how to center himself.

And what if that's what enabled him to kill?

What if managing the panic helped him keep it together enough to hunt down and murder our campmates?

Yeah, I really need that ax.

"Kurt, I'm sorry—" I say, but he talks over me again, so un-Kurt-like, his face screwed up, slick with perspiration.

"Stop."

I fall silent, torn between sympathy and revulsion.

I can see what the loss has done to him.

Kurt taps his chest, and his gaze keeps returning to Tye, motionless against the tree. It's clear he wants to tear him apart with his bare hands. Finish what he started. I can't tell if Tye's even still alive.

I remember all the times I noticed Kurt staring at Tye. Blushing. Stuttering.

I'd thought he was infatuated. Crushing on the handsome groundskeeper.

I couldn't have been more wrong.

I wonder if Kurt got a sick thrill from the sense of anticipation.

Kurt considers me, and he's calmer now. His voice detached.

"Nobody pays for their sins nowadays. Criminals pin it on the other guy, celebrities have lawyers, killers buy their freedom . . . and the public has a *real* short memory."

His cheeks dimple. "But Knock-Knock Nancy had the right idea.

Revenge. When I turned up here, I wanted to make Tye pay for what he did, but then Court showed me this wasn't a camp of well-meaning victims. They were just like Tye. Getting away with their crimes. Identity theft. Attacking innocents. Fentanyl addiction."

"Juniper had cancer!" I cry. "The fentanyl was medication."

Plus, Knock-Knock Nancy never killed anybody, Willow says, which is true.

The legend was made up. But Kurt believed it. And he used it.

Looking at Kurt reminds me that I'd thought he was like Brandon. I'd thought I could help him in the way that I couldn't help Bran. Kurt told me I made things better for him, and the idea makes me ill. All this time I've been trying to look out for him, and he's been killing our friends.

You can stop him, Willow says. *It's on you now, love.*

I don't know if I have the strength.

The ax is still so far away, and it's Kurt. I don't know if I can hurt Kurt.

"Would Courtney want this?" I ask.

Kurt's teeth flash. "Don't say her name."

Tye moans, and I'm stunned that he's still alive.

Kurt turns toward him. It's surely a matter of time before he grabs the ax himself.

There has to be something I can distract him with. Something he wants.

I realize I know exactly what he wants—his sister.

He wants the person he lost when she died. The kind, smart companion who understood him.

He wants someone like Willow.

Yeah, I know Willow.

She's right here.

I played her for three years, before she was taken away from me.

Looks like I have to play her one last time.

"Kurt," I say, speaking in Willow's sitcom octave. Higher than my regular voice. Unthreatening and naïve. "Kurt, I understand. You did what you had to do. I get it."

He frowns, looks confused.

"This place is so messed up," I say. "Like, you see right through it. You see through the bullshit and the lies. I love that about you. I love that you see the truth."

Kurt's expression lifts. "Really?"

I nod, and Sitcom Willow is so comfortable to wear, it's like putting on a pair of jeans that have molded perfectly to my form. I keep my gaze on him. I don't look at the ax. Don't give away my plan.

"Totally," I say. "My life's been upside-down for so long. It's like something's been missing, but you've helped me. You've mended that part of me that's had a hole in it for the longest time."

It's a line from the show, but Kurt doesn't appear to recognize it. Misty would get it.

Kurt's shoulders relax at my words. A little of the darkness leaves his expression. He smiles.

"We're tired. It's been a long day," I say. "Let's make like a Tom and *cruise* the hell out of here."

The smile vanishes. "No. We have to finish it. That's the only way this works. Everybody has to die."

"Please, Kurt, I don't want anything to happen to you. I need you. And I'm hurt."

Concern enters his gaze. He moves toward me, and I stiffen, expecting his hands to go for my throat. Instead, he reaches out to touch my hair. The feel of his fingers makes me shudder. Fingers that have killed.

I grab hold of Sitcom Willow, surround myself with her. My armor. The costume that kept me alive in L.A. for so long and is keeping me alive now.

"You get why I did it," Kurt says. "We understand loss. We've been through hell but we're going to be okay. Tye will take the blame for what happened here. That's why he has to die last. He's finally going to take the fall, and you'll be a hero. We're going to go on. Together."

Despite the horror of what he's saying, I force my mouth into a smile.

"Yes," I say. "We're going to be okay. If we leave now—"

"*No!*" Kurt yanks my hair, and my neck twists painfully. He gasps and cradles my head, presses his mouth to my scalp.

"I'm sorry. I didn't mean to hurt you. It's just that I need you. I realized it when we were in the shower block that day. I need you, Willow."

He tilts my head so that I'm looking at him, and then his mouth covers mine. I try to push him away, but the kiss is hungry. It's like he wants to consume me. I try to bite him, but he seems to take that as encouragement.

Finally, he lets me go. He's grinning, panting, flushed with excitement.

"See? We're meant for each other," he says.

What now? Willow says, and I don't know. I don't know.

One thought rings through my mind like the gong Bebe strikes at the end of every affirmation ceremony.

The ax.

I need that fucking ax.

You're an actor, right? Willow says. *So act.*

But this isn't a sitcom, this is goddamn horror . . . and I know how horror movies end.

I force myself to smile back at Kurt, and then I let my expression drop as I look past him at the preacher's body on the ground.

"Oh God, he's not dead," I say, a classic horror fake-out. Kurt's own face falls. He turns to check on the preacher, and I launch myself at him. It takes everything I have, but it's enough. I collide with Kurt, knocking him off his feet, and as he crashes to the ground, I land on top of the preacher's still-warm corpse.

I don't have time to grimace at the feel of him.

I summon my final reserves of strength and seize the ax.

Somehow, I'm upright, brandishing the ax in front of me, just as Kurt gets to his feet.

He stands staring at me, looking puzzled. Doesn't understand what happened, the poor lamb.

"Willow?" he murmurs.

At the sound of that name, my shoulders drop. I allow the resentment and anger to burn in my gaze. I discard Willow, throwing her out of my body like an exorcism.

"Sorry, Kurt," I say, "Willow's dead. You're stuck with me now."

Kurt blinks, confused for a second. Then his face pinches into a snarl, and he lunges for me.

I swing.

The flat side of the blade strikes his temple with a dull *whump*, exactly as I intended.

Kurt goes down, a dead weight, limbs flailing. He lies in the dirt, his chest softly rising and falling.

Out cold.

The silence that follows is a blessing.

"Sleep well, you poor, poor psychopath," I tell Kurt.

I keep hold of the ax, pressing my wounded side with my other hand as I look around the forest.

It's over.

You did it, Willow says in my mind, but her voice is different.

It's not Willow speaking.

I realize it never has been.

The easy, breezy voice in my ear . . . it's Brandon.

It's *his* voice that urged me to embrace Camp Castaway.

To take a risk on Dani.

To finally be myself. At last.

You did it, Brandon says, and he doesn't just mean stopping the killer. He means everything that he would have encouraged me to do if he'd been alive.

Tears sting my eyes, because suddenly it's so clear, I can't believe I never realized it.

All those years I played Willow, I wasn't really playing her. I was playing a version of Brandon. The source of light and laughter in my life.

By playing Willow, I was keeping Brandon alive. That's why my life fell so spectacularly apart after tweetageddon. Not because of the tweet, or my ruined reputation, or the never-ending tide of hate . . . but because I'd lost Willow.

I'd lost Brandon all over again.

Willow gave me so much, and she's kept me alive for so long.

But now I have to say goodbye for good.

Not just to her, but to Brandon, too.

I've seen what happens when you don't.

I stare at Kurt's unconscious form, and tears streak my face as I whisper, "Bye, Brandon."

Just like that, my mind calms.

Willow's gone, and so is my brother.

A shape lurches from behind a tree.

I reel backward, attempting to raise the ax, but then a female voice yells, "It's me!"

I'd recognize that voice anywhere.

"Dani," I choke as she emerges from the dark, looking ashen and beat up but flashing that rock-star grin that lights a hundred sparks in my belly.

All strength leaves my body as she wraps her arms around me.

"You're okay," I say.

"I am now," she says. "I've been looking for you forever."

"I know what you mean."

"Where's Kurt?" she asks.

I nod at the unconscious body on the ground.

"It was him," I say, still hardly able to believe it. "Kurt and the preacher. They're the ones who killed Kat and Juniper and everybody."

"Kurt?" Dani sounds shocked. Then she closes her mouth and shakes her head. "You know what, I'm actually not surprised. I always thought there was something off about him."

"You did?"

"Never trust the adorable ones."

A groan sounds to our left.

By the shack, Tye's legs scrape the ground, and my heart jumps at the sight. He might make it.

"What the hell happened here?" Dani asks, eyeing Tye, then the preacher's body and Kurt's unconscious form.

"I'll tell you about it later," I say. "But there's one more thing I have to do."

THE FINAL CHAPTER

Dani coughs into her hand, looking around in horror at the angels posed beside the preacher's shack.

"What the fuck?" she says.

"Yeah, I know."

"The preacher did this?"

I nod. "I guess he thought he was saving their souls or some shit."

Dani backs away, looking overwhelmed and ill.

"I say we torch this place," she says. "Burn it to the ground."

"We're not leaving them here," I say, meaning the heads. "They're our friends. We have to help them."

"I think they're beyond help."

"We have to get them down. They deserve to be returned to their loved ones. Not strung up as some sick effigy or burned to ash."

Dani's face is gray, but she nods.

"Here," I say, and I duck inside, moving as quickly as I can. I tear the cloth from the altar, scattering the religious paraphernalia across the dirt floor, and rejoin Dani. "Tie it to make a sack."

Dani takes the cloth from me, wincing as she tries to use her broken wrist, but she doesn't complain. I look up at the angels, the thought of touching them making my stomach turn. I swallow, remind myself that these aren't grisly trophies, they're our friends.

I stand on tiptoe and reach trembling hands toward Juniper. Her skin is cold, and I shake off a tremor. It feels overly intimate, touching her like this, but I know I'm doing the right thing.

"It's okay," I tell Juniper as I lift her off the wicker angel. "It's going to be okay. We're here."

I turn to see that Dani has completed making the sack. I set Juniper's head inside.

I do the same for Kat and Chef Jeff. There's Apollo, too, and Bebe and Misty. So many dead. Fresh anger boils through me.

Only one head remains. One that is far older. It's little more than a skull with leathery sinew holding it together. The hair is long and as white as snow, and the sight of it sends a pang through my chest when I realize who it is.

"Nancy," I murmur.

"Shit," Dani says, staring up at her.

"Hi, Nancy," I say, thinking about what Bebe said about their older sister being their protector. The one who kept their father at bay— until she couldn't do it anymore.

"You're going to be okay now," I tell Nancy. "We're going to look after you."

Gently, I take her down and set her in the bag.

Dani's face shines with perspiration, but she's also looking at me with a strange smile on her lips.

"If only the world could see you now," she says.

"The world doesn't need to see this."

"*Now* do we torch the place?" she asks.

"No. We leave it. Nobody will believe us otherwise."

Dani bites her lip and hoists the sack over her shoulder. It's too heavy for me to carry in my present condition. She turns to start walking away from the shack, and I follow, finding that the light is changing. The sky above the tree line is on fire.

The sun is rising.

Morning has arrived.

It looks like we survived the end of the world.

Tye is standing now, half hunched over by a tree, looking exactly how I feel.

I force myself to meet his gaze.

Tye whose actions brought Kurt to Camp Castaway.

Tye who lied about Courtney.

Tye who has to live with his guilt for as long as his lungs keep taking in air.

"Hey," he says to me. "Thanks. For what you did. For saving me."

His right eye is still sealed shut and he's been beaten to a pulp. I know he's suffered, too.

"Let's get back to the clubhouse," I say, because I can't think of anything else.

Tye nods and starts limping ahead of us. Beyond him, I see Sadie dancing between the trees. Sadness seizes me. She's lost her whole family. She's the last one standing. I wonder what her life will look like from now on and make a silent pledge to ensure that she's treated right. By the authorities. By the world. It's what Bebe and Nancy would have wanted.

Dani stands looking up at the brightening sky.

"Ready for morning affirmations?" she asks.

"Sure," I say. "I affirm that all summer camps are cursed and should be left to be reclaimed by nature. Also, you are cute even when you look like a beat-up zombie clown."

"Thanks." Dani thinks for a second, face serious. Then she says, "I affirm that I'm not held hostage by my shortcomings, they don't define me, and I'm willing and able to grow from them."

My eyes mist. It's what Juniper said during her affirmation two days ago. Dammit, how does Dani always know the exact right thing to say?

"Hey, I finally found enough material for a book," Dani adds . . . and just like that, she's ruined it. At my unimpressed stare, she grins. "Kidding."

I turn my gaze up at the sky, and my mind is still. There's no Willow. No Brandon.

Just me. And Dani. And—

Kurt.

He's tied to a tree. We used the rope that bound Tye, making sure to fasten the knots as tightly as we could. Kurt's not going anywhere. At least, not until the cops show up.

"You can't leave me here," he says, and he sounds like the Kurt I thought I knew. Vulnerable and wounded. His voice tugs at my heart, but I'm not the person I was three days ago.

I take Dani's hand and start walking away.

"You can't be fucking serious," Kurt yells. "You need me! You're nothing without me! Your life is fucking over!"

I say nothing.

His words are meaningless.

Funny, I guess I've learned how to block out that sort of noise.

As we walk, I shoot a final glance over my shoulder at the preacher, lying dead a few feet away from Kurt.

They tried so hard to punish us for our imperfections.

But they failed.

Because no matter how loud or determined or insidious they were, they were still just a couple of men trying to reshape the world in their own fucked-up image, and it'll take more than a couple of men to bring me down.

It'll take more than a crowd.

The whole human race could turn against me, and I'll only ever go down fighting.

It's what Bran would want.

It's what I want.

Holding Dani's hand, I look at Kurt, and the preacher, and I take a breath, filling my lungs with the air of a new day.

There's only one thing I have left to say—not just to Kurt and the preacher, but to the world.

"Better luck next time."

REBECCA: *Welcome to* The Truth, *the podcast in which we set the record straight—*

NORA: *—or more accurately queer—*

REBECCA: *—about everything from Hollywood hearsay to the real story behind that cancellation everybody keeps talking about. I'm Rebecca, but you probably know me best as Willow McKenzie from the Netflix sitcom* We Love Willow. *And I'm joined by . . .*

NORA: *Nora, formerly the Gossip Goblin. But I'm totally reformed.*

REBECCA: *Look, we know this show sounds like* Mythbusters, You're Wrong About, *and a dozen other awesome and popular podcasts. But this is where we're different: we've been part of a bullshit legend. We've been on the wrong side of cancel culture.*

NORA: *Yeah, we know how this shit works.*

REBECCA: *And we survived. So if you're looking for barefaced authenticity, you've come to the right place.*

NORA: *Shall we get into it?*

REBECCA: *We shall. We're starting where our journey started, focusing on an individual who was horrifically canceled decades ago. We've found out a ton of stuff about this person since everything that happened at Camp Castaway last year, and the more we learn, the more fascinating she becomes. So let's not waste any more time.*

NORA: *Yeah, let's do this.*

REBECCA: *Welcome to case file number one: the legend of Knock-Knock Nancy.*

ACKNOWLEDGMENTS

First and foremost, thank you, dear reader, for going on this venture into the woods with me. There's a high chance you love slasher movies as much as I do, and I hope this book gave you a thrill and a chill, plus a few chuckles along the way.

At Putnam, thank you to my editors, Mark Tavani and Aranya Jain. Mark, thanks for your boundless encouragement and patience in the early stages of writing. Aranya, you came armed with a knife-bag full of ideas and suggestions that transformed this into *Heads Will Roll* 2.0. Thanks for having Willow/Rebecca's back (and mine, too). Thank you Vi-An Nguyen for another fantastic cover, and thank you to Sally Kim, Ashley Hewlett, Shina Patel, and Brennin Cummings for everything you do for books. Thanks also to my copyeditor, Amy Schneider, for polishing this to a shine. And thank you to Laura Corless and Lorie Pagnozzi for the woods-y book design.

Every author says they have the best agent in the biz, but I really do have the best agent in the biz. Thank you, Kristina Pérez, for always being on hand with guidance and a giggle about some movie or other. (Is that my stapler?)

Thank you to my beta readers Troy Gardner and Kat Ellis for taking a (gentle) machete to an early draft of this book. So many friends, family members, and writers support me in ways they may not be aware of, but I am so grateful for you all.

Penny, you're the Jason to my Pamela. Never change. And Thom, you always manage to keep my head screwed on. Thank you.